FROZEN BEAUTY

Lexa Hillyer

FROZEN BEAUTY

HARPER TEEN

An Imprint of HarperCollinsPublishers

Library of Congress Cataloging-in-Publication Data
Names: Hillyer, Lexa, author.
Title: Frozen beauty / Lexa Hillyer.
Description: First edition. | New York, NY : HarperTeen, [2020] | Summary:
"When the body of 17-year-old Kit Malloy is found out by the woods frozen to
death and half-undressed in the back of the boy-next-door's truck, her sisters Tessa
and Lilly are left to pick up the pieces, search for answers, and ultimately find their
own voices." Provided by publisher.
Identifiers: LCCN 2019009516 | ISBN 9780062330406 (hardcover)
Subjects: | CYAC: Secrets Fiction. | Sisters Fiction. | Murder Fiction. | Mystery
and detective stories.
Classification: LCC PZ7.H5648 Fro 2020 | DDC [Fic] dc23 LC record available at
https://lccn.loc.gov/2019009516

Typography by Molly Fehr
20 21 22 23 24   PC/LSCH   10 9 8 7 6 5 4 3 2 1
❖
First Edition

To my two sisters, and my brother, too,
who has, after all, had to put up with all three of us

Prologue

NOW

FEBRUARY 4

SECRETS, SECRETS. EVERYONE HAD THEM. Everyone kept them from Lilly, kept her out.

This is what comes of curiosity, the wind whispered hard and cold in her ear, swishing up into her skull. She shuddered. Snow soaked her boots.

As the youngest of three, this was the story of her life: this winter coldness, this left-out-ness, this butt-out-and-don't-complain-or-you'll-sound-like-a-whiny-baby-ness.

But here they were now: two glowing yellow headlights through the swirl of falling snow, through the blur of fading streetlights, through the dark of Route 28. Twin golden keys to the fucking *treasure.*

And she had to have it, she thought, her hands shaking—had to know the secret. Between Kit and Tessa, Lilly was always excluded from the things that really mattered. But this time, she *would* know, would force her way in. The warmth of the golden orbs called to her with some kind of dark, irrepressible magic, and there was so little magic in this world. Lilly only wanted her share.

It was a Saturday night. Lilly and Mel had been having their customary Saturday night sleepover at Mel's house, which sat just on the edge of Devil's Lake, the weeds and trees in her backyard giving way to the protected woods. Lilly had started to believe that their friendship was back on track. But when she'd awakened after midnight to find Mel gone, and the bedroom window cracked open, letting in a tiny but steady stream of frigid air, she'd had to assume the obvious: Mel had snuck out.

And if she had snuck out, it could only be for one reason: to meet up with Dusty, her on-again-off-again something. After all, Mel had been texting furiously all night, even during the rom–com sex scenes.

In a mix of disappointment and curiosity, Lilly had pushed open the bedroom door and crept down the quiet hall, past the den where all of Mel's dad's hunting rifles hung proudly in a row, polished and gleaming black even in the dark. Mel wasn't in the house.

So, naturally, Lilly had slithered through the front door, into the slowly filling pocket of snow by the side of the house, then went in search of her friend—and answers. Maybe Dusty's car would be parked around the corner of the cul-de-sac.

But what she'd found was a whole other kind of secret. Not more than the length of a football field down the main road sat a truck, its engine still going. Only yards from the edge of Mel's property, if you cut through the woods.

And it wasn't just any truck. The red truck. *Boyd's* red truck. It was parked at the side of the road near the preserve, a hulking metal animal heaving its breath into the cold . . . and of course, her curiosity had snagged like a loose-knit sweater on a chain-link fence.

She felt that pull, that need to understand.

She reasoned: what if Boyd needed help, needed *her*?

A flash of doubt flooded Lilly's brain for a minute. What if Mel had gotten back already and wondered where Lilly had gone?

No—Mel was with Dusty, she was sure of that much. Mel had chosen her loyalties.

Now: a male voice drifting out over the wind. The sound of a car door slamming. She was almost there, and the heat of discovery drove her on.

But it was so cold. So cold and so dark. The sparse street-lights did little to help, spinning patches of air into gold-hued snow blurs. She had to hurry.

Lilly scrunched her winter hat down lower. Still squinting, she made out a figure—no, two figures—floating from the shoulder of the road, toward the looming darkness of the woods that backed up to Devil's Lake from Route 28.

Mel and Dusty?

Mel and *Boyd*?

Voices took clearer shape in the air as she got closer, though the words themselves wove and dodged and blew away. Holding her breath, hidden by the hounding snowfall and the heavy dark, she came all the way up to the driver's side—the side facing the road—without the figures noticing. She peered through the window. The keys were still in the ignition, a faint silver clump dangling in shadow.

Shivering, she rounded the back of the truck, careful to stay hidden from view behind the glow of the taillights.

A guy and a girl, arguing.

Her heart hammered. She had to strain to see them in the bad light and the fierce snowfall, but she recognized Boyd by his height and his hunting hat. And the girl with him wasn't Mel at all. . . .

She was unmistakable. She wore no hat, and her golden hair shone even in the darkness.

It was *Kit*.

Lilly took a step back. Was she being crazy right now? You didn't just traipse along the road late at night by yourself, in the middle of a storm. She should head back. What was she thinking?

But then again, she could almost hear Tessa's voice in her head: weren't Boyd and Kit—the ever-trusted boy next door and the older sister everyone in school worshipped—up to something crazy, too? Tessa was always talking about likelihoods and hypotheses. Lilly wasn't exactly a star at science, but you didn't have to be a neurosurgeon to solve *this* equation: if you were those two and you were driving around in Boyd's truck together on a Saturday night, *in secret*—you didn't pull over in a storm, either. Not unless something was wrong. Not unless *something was going on*.

Secrets. Secrets.

Lilly watched from behind the truck as Boyd put his hand on Kit's arm, and she shook, possibly crying.

Was he grabbing her now? Had she let him?

Slowly he pulled open her coat.

Lilly shuddered hard. Kit said something, but Lilly caught only snatches of her words: *please* and *you're making a mistake* and *I don't believe you*.

The racing of Lilly's heart became a loud ringing through her ears and head. What was happening? Kit's voice, dancing on the wind, seemed to ebb and peak and break.

Lilly trusted Boyd; of course, she did. Hell, she *loved* Boyd. But she also knew how angry he got sometimes. Once he'd shoved Tessa so hard she'd fallen into the gravel on the playground and torn open her shin. Then again, that had been right after Tessa kneed him in the balls. They were ten then, and nothing like that had happened since.

But still. Lilly remembered. Lilly always remembered.

She stood on the verge of calling to them when Kit got quiet, moving closer to Boyd. Then she was touching his face.

And he was leaning down, and they were kissing—mist rising from where their faces met.

Hot breath in the cold night.

Oh.

So they weren't fighting.

A flash of mortification.

Everyone was coupling off, hooking up, lying to Lilly about it.

Secrets, secrets.

She backed up toward the road, the thrill of voyeurism bursting suddenly into hot shame. A car rushed past her and honked.

She gasped, startled, realizing how easy it would have been to get hit.

Sweat tickled the back of her neck even in the freezing cold. Had the honk drawn Kit's attention? The last thing she wanted was for Kit to think she'd been spying—which was, of course, exactly the truth. The last thing she needed was to give anyone more ammo for treating her like a fucking *kid*, one more reason to say *butt out* or *I told you so*.

Quickly, without looking back, she raced through the trees, taking the shortcut into Mel's backyard. She couldn't have been gone very long, but still. A person could die out here, on a night like this.

Icy pellets of snow blew into her eyes and Lilly could hardly see at all now—but that didn't stop her from replaying the moment she had just witnessed over and over again: Boyd's plaid hunting hat as he leaned down toward Kit's face, and their lips met, and they kissed.

And above them, in the winter air all around them, the echo of Kit's voice, saying *please*.

Later, long after she'd curled back onto her side of the trundle bed in Mel's room—after she'd awakened the next morning to her friend lying beside her, softly snoring—Lilly would recall that word, *please*, and know for certain that it had been Kit's final plea for her life. That if only she had stayed, or shouted, or called for help, maybe things would have gone differently.

Maybe her sister would still be alive.

PART ONE

Chapter One

BEFORE

AN OLD SAYING: ALL GOOD things come in threes.

Or was it that all *bad* things came in threes?

Pushing his too-long hair out of his face, Boyd drove the lawn mower across his dad's quarter-acre of grass. The early September sun cut jagged lines of shadow through the scattered cottonwoods.

Some of the places he'd seen over by Detroit, where distant cousins lived, boasted that cookie-cutter perfection you dreamed of when you thought of a small town, all even squares and matching houses in a row like straight little teeth—one big suburban grinning mouth—but out here in Devil's Lake, the yards ran amok, mangy and undefined, lapping over one another and swarming in constant land disputes and neighborly grudges. Always a roamer buck hunting or firing pellets at squirrels on someone else's property.

That's why he'd convinced his dad to go in on a used John Deere—the kind of mower you got up on and rode like a tractor—and now he actually enjoyed this chore, this chance to work outside and hover above things for a little while, carving out a space that belonged to him.

Evening was coming on, though, and the sunlight left its weight on his shoulders somehow, like it felt tired and had to rest from a long summer of burning itself up. He could smell fall's approach, too: the early hint of decay, of mud hardening, preparing itself.

Boyd probably should've prepared, too, he thought. It was junior year, starting tomorrow. The year of all the tests that supposedly determined your future, slapped a number on you and sorted you like cattle. Some ended up in college. Some ended up working seasonal land jobs. Some ended up leaving town with no good plan at all except to get away.

He should've been thinking about graduating, about what would come next—about whether what came next would take him far, far away from Devil's Lake.

Or at least about final papers. Maybe he'd write one up on Chizhevsky, something that would make Tessa smile when she read it. She read nearly all his homework, either her or Kit, to catch all the spelling nicks. Never Lilly; her schoolwork was a mess, like his.

As usual, Boyd couldn't stay concentrated too long on

school, though. All he could think about right now—on this warm almost-evening that had his skin prickling with a pleasant layer of sweat—were the three girls next door. They'd lived there most of his life—moved into the area with their mom after their dad died in combat off in some location Boyd only learned about later and still couldn't pronounce.

He'd been about six at the time. He'd never seen anything like this tribe of women.

All good things come in threes.

His mom had once taught him about the constellations—or at any rate he had a memory that she had told him about the stars, even though he probably shouldn't trust that memory, because she died when he was two and who remembers anything from then? Anyway, he liked to imagine the Malloy sisters that way: three bright points in his sky, their bedroom lights coming on every night, then flickering out a little while later, and with each, he felt connected, rooted to something.

Everything else might be completely fucked—an unending string of garbage news on the television, angry politics, countless hours of half-inspired homework and his dad getting uptight all the time, about jobs going sparse and bank accounts shriveling into shells and bottles running out too soon, or their aging dachshund, Jimmy, shitting on the living-room carpet again.

But the Malloys shimmered through it all—livelier than stars, really. More like lightning bugs you caught in a jar—the three of them living in the house next door, so close to his, moving about in the routine of their lives, crying out to one another like fighting cats in the night, cursing under their breath or, sometimes, singing, loud and off-key. Whispering. Scheming and assessing, the way sisters do. Building a world in which your part was only ever passing by, on the periphery.

He had been close to the inside most of his life—over the years they'd made him their pirate overlord and beast prince, their evil doctor, their pony, their priest. They'd teased him and tagged him and angled to have him take their side over the others, though he never could for long. He had even brushed and braided their hair. This was long ago, and at the time, that fine silkiness in his hands had given him an otherworldly shiver— Kit's golden, Tessa's pale, and Lilly's firelike. It made him kind of mortified to think about it now.

Mortified, but still proud. Because they were his, after all, even if he couldn't explain how or why. They were Narnia, or Terabithia, straight out of one of those old magical books they loved to read out loud: living dream, accessible through some trapdoor in the universe that just happened to be right here where he could reach it—a door that opened into a constantly unknown and yet intimately familiar landscape of balding dolls and hairballs, catfights and tears and egg-salad sandwiches with the crusts cut off and only-green grapes, the kind whose skins were always splitting, overfull of juice. A world of rules and vows and secrets and allegiances and competitions and handshakes and the intoxicating scent of—

"Hey!"

Boyd yanked his headphones off his ears to catch his father calling him in. Probably needed him to run an errand. Boyd could guess what kind. He'd been to the bottom of more than one bottle since dawn. Sometimes there were just bad days.

The sun was drooping now, darker red at the center, then bleeding out like a shot animal.

He leaned forward to shut off the engine and got jolted forward as the machine let out a whining grunt. Probably ran over a stray rock or an old shoe. Weird shit ended up out here, who knew how—dragged by wild animals, coyotes maybe, or local kids from his school with nothing better to do (not always a huge difference between the two). Definitely not by Jimmy, though—the dog was too old to drag his own tail most days.

Boyd hopped down off the mower and examined what had gotten jammed in its teeth. In the failing light, he squinted at the shiny piece of crushed plastic for a second, finally identifying the stuck object as an old Barbie, its hair chopped at a crude diagonal, its too-big eyes squished onto either side of a flattened head, one arm bent backward and the other snapped off entirely.

Odd. He used to see these things over at the Malloy house all the time, but they'd outgrown Barbies long ago. The doll had super-shiny golden hair, reminding him of Kit.

A big smudge of dirt darkened its squashed face, and out of some deranged instinct, Boyd thought to swipe it clean with his thumb. This broken detritus of girlhood. This piece-of-shit bit of plastic once shaped to look aspirational and sleek, with its red satiny outfit, all torn up. It seemed, now that he thought about it, kind of slutty and cheap. Kind of sad.

He shoved it into his pocket, kept it like a piece of crucial evidence, this birthing of the backyard muck, a relic, a reminder of the Malloy sisters' unchanging ever-presence. It would make an okay chew toy for Jimmy, at any rate, he thought as he headed inside to see what his dad wanted now, trying not to wonder too much about how it had ended up out here, on his lawn, in the first place.

It was a mystery, or an omen, and Boyd disliked both, about as much as he disliked bloody hangnails and all of Devil's Lake. He'd never been particularly good at guessing the truth, or what terrible thing was coming next.

WAITING
BY KATHERINE MALLOY

Devil's Lake is only half what its name indicates—
more like a pond, more mossy than sheer,

hidden in the preserve past Route 28,
covered in slick green slime all year . . .

except when it freezes over in winter.

But it isn't frozen yet, not when my story starts,
the tale of my own thawing: ribs like the tinder
of an unseen fire, burning not just in our hearts
but without and around—consuming the forest,

coating the trees with smoke black as ink,
making ash of all that was August.

The lake winks, like it knows I'm on the brink,

like it can see this invisible spark:
I'm waiting for you. You'll be here by dark.

Chapter Two

NOW

FEBRUARY 7

THEY'D BEEN SHOVELING DIRT OVER the coffin for what felt like hours.

The priest said they couldn't have an open casket, or maybe it'd been the coroner. Her body was too . . . blue. Her lips, her fingertips.

Tessa never saw it—her, *Kit*—that way, only heard the facts listed in a bland sequence, each one contained and separate: a dot unconnected to any other dots.

The torn clothing and lacy bra.

The truck, abandoned at the edge of the nature preserve out on 28.

Lilly's frantic confessions, her babbling, all adding up to

what the woman in the fitted suit called "a formal accusation," "a potential testimony."

And, of course, Boyd's name, on repeat, in hushed tones, in voices of shock and anger.

It was only the first week of February, and last week had seen some of the coldest nights in years. But winter out here had a funny way of shifting underfoot, and this weekend the ground had started to thaw and the snow to melt—like it remembered its past as disconnected, unwhole, just a collection of molecules that had stuck together for a while and were now content to part.

And so the service, taking advantage of this brief reprieve from the frigid temps, would be held outside, where Kit would have wanted it. She wasn't outdoorsy per se, but she always talked about the beauty of nature, wrote poetry about it. Still, they should have thought it through first. Tessa had never realized before how these things are planned in such a rush. All the details—the flowers, the chairs, the music—coordinated in a sickening daze within hours of the worst moment of your life.

They should have realized it would be way too cold for this. Tessa couldn't feel her body, couldn't feel much of anything.

Maybe that was for the best.

The fog, winding its thick, lazy way along the mud and frost, nearly muted the minister's voice, calling her name. *Tessa. Tessa.*

It was time.

Her hand plunged into her pocket . . . but the speech

she'd written—about what a perfect older sister Kit had always been—was nowhere to be found. She dug her hand deeper, feeling a small hole in the satin lining of her navy peacoat, the width of a couple of fingers, big enough, she realized with a sudden jolt of panic, for a note that'd been wadded up over and over again in her sweaty palms to have fallen through.

A string of alarmed curses flew through her brain and she froze, unable to come forward. She'd never been a good writer anyway—that had always been Kit's job. And she never wore this stupid peacoat—it smelled like the musty walls of the hall closet. She'd forgotten how beaten-up it was, full of tears and holes—mostly on the inside, where no one could see.

Okay, stay calm.

But after fishing around in the other pocket, it became clear: the note was definitely gone.

"Tessa." Her name rang out again, and she shivered, feeling everyone's gaze turn her way. Now would be a great time to perfect her disappearing skills.

Yet another area where Kit had her beat: this time, she'd pulled off the kind of disappearing act where you never, ever come back.

Tessa swallowed the lump in her throat. She should probably be crying now, but her eyes remained a stinging dry and her chest tight, trapped under a thick layer of ice. All she could think was how weird this felt, everyone staring at her.

Most of the time, people overlooked her—and she was fine with that. In between her two sisters, she was the least remarkable. People who didn't know the Malloy sisters often saw them as variations on the same theme. After all, they were each born only a little over a year apart and shared an uncanny resemblance in the eyes and cheeks. But the differences out-shone the similarities when you looked closer.

Lilly: the unpredictable one, the selfish one, the baby of the family—all brawl and tears and flash and fire—hated discord and caused nearly all of it. Kit, to the contrary, was—*had been*—the good girl, the oldest, the one to whom everyone turned in a time of crisis. Kit was butter melting into toast. She was light through a high stained-glass window or a cat curled on a lap. Everything comforting. When they were kids, their dance teacher called what Kit had "grace." But it didn't just appear when she danced. It lived in the way Kit moved through the world—with *ease*, like she had some sort of privileged arrangement with gravity.

Then there was Tessa, known for tripping on her own feet, a clumsy shadow in Kit's wake. Not a shadow, actually, but a negative, all bleached out and odd to look at. She had Kit's blond hair, but paler, and Kit's big eyes, but wider spaced, one blue and one green, more alien than pretty. Even down to the cells, Tessa was a kind of genetic mash-up. She had this thing called chimerism—which meant that some of Kit's DNA had slimed off on her when she was still developing in their mom's womb, left over from Kit's stay in there. She was *mostly* Tessa, sure—that's what the doctors had told her when they discovered the condition, more common than most people think.

But she had real hints of Kit within her, too—strands woven through, making Tessa not really, wholly Tessa, but a mess of her and not-her.

Right now, she wished she was anyone but herself.

She pulled her traitorous peacoat tighter around herself and stepped in front of the first row of plastic chairs, turning to look at the crowd gathered in the graveyard behind the church— her mother's tear-streaked face, Lilly wrenching her threadbare beanie down around her ears.

You can still take it back, Tessa wanted to shout at her.

Lilly's best friend, Mel, sat beside her, shaking in the cold and looking pale as the snow. Tessa glanced around for Patrick Donovan—she would have expected him to be here, but then again, she didn't know him that well. He was Lilly's problem. And he wasn't here.

Next to Mel came several of Kit's teachers—her Spanish teacher, Ms. Luiz; her English teacher, Mr. Green, and some pretty woman who must be his girlfriend. A few neighbors.

Incredibly: Innis Taylor, Boyd's dad. Red-eyed and openly weeping.

And the notable, gaping absence beside him: an empty spot where his son should have been. Would have been, if he weren't, right now, sitting in the county jail, awaiting trial for Kit's murder.

He did it, Lilly had told the cops, the special investigator, their parents, through the spinning, sickening blur of the last two days. *I saw it. I saw them.*

And even if her younger sister hadn't seen a thing—Boyd's fingerprints everywhere told the story for her.

Boyd. Her Boyd.

No—not her Boyd.

Staring at the empty chair, Tessa knew she couldn't go through with this. That saying a bunch of fake words about Kit now would be the worst lie she ever told.

Or it would be the worst truth.

So she did what any sane human would do, or even any half-sane half human, like her.

She ran the fuck out of there.

Chapter Three

BEFORE

9/6

Dear Diary,

Ah, the first day of school. Nothing's quite like it. That's why I'm finally writing in you. Kit's the real writer in the family, but it seems like a waste because nothing interesting ever happens to her. Or to any of us.

This year is going to be different, though.

Hopefully.

Everyone's awake, and it sounds like the house is going to come down in all the commotion outside my door. Tessa has spent all morning moaning about how she lost one of her shoes or something (how do you lose just one, by the way?), while sucking on a giant mug of black coffee (which, ew). Kit keeps racing up and down the stairs, putting in her earrings while *sorting through notebooks while also carrying on a full conversation with Mom about her after-school plans—some dizzying combo of volunteering, tutoring, and babysitting.*

Diary, I don't care about any of that.

Diary, I have locked my door, and I plan to lock you, too, which is why I can first tell you this:

I'm naked right now. (!!!!)

Not to be vain (~~vein?~~), but I've been staring at myself in the mirror, feeling ready, finally. I mean, not ready for school, obviously. (!!!) But ready-ready. As in, ready for things to start happening.

I'm a sophomore now. My face is still too big for the rest of me, and the gap between my teeth has not disappeared, despite what Mom keeps saying. As for my boobs, they are bigger than plums but smaller, I think, than oranges. My hips are rounded at the sides but sharp in front. The carpet, newly trimmed, matches the drapes. (Ugh, I really hate that phrase, it's so gross!!! And why are our bodies supposed to be compared to stuffy old living rooms? Anyway, I finally decided last night that if I'm going to be stuck with fire crotch my whole life— and everyone being able to guess at it—then it may as well be a neat and tidy fire down there!!)

I wonder whether anyone can see me through the window blinds right now.

Okay, not anyone. (Boyd.)

Here are the reasons BND (Boy Next Door) is fated to be my boyfriend:

1. He once rescued me from an angry pit bull.

2. He protects me from my sisters during snowball fights.

3. He lets me go first in board games.

4. I've just always imagined that he would be my first! Do I need more reason than that?

Hold on, Diary, I'll be right back. . . .

Yeah no, his blinds are down.

Whatever. Hold on, again. I need to get dressed. . . .

Okay, I'm back. Sorry that took so long. I spent all my school-clothes money (and part of Tessa's leftover budget since what does she need it for when she literally only wears those ratty jeans with tank tops every day?), but it still took me forty-five minutes to decide what to wear. Here goes: a floral jumper from Lupine and a blazer that used to be Mom's, with the sleeves rolled up. It's a mix of retro and easy!

I just heard the screen door slam.

And now Boyd is outside honking his truck. He seriously almost made me mess up my eyeliner.

Another honk.

Deep breath.

It's Go Time.

Lilly slammed her diary shut and shoved it under her mattress. "For fuck's sake, I'm coming!" she called out.

"Let's have less cursing, sweetie," her mom said as Lilly burst out of her room with her bag in one hand and took the strawberry Pop-Tart wrapped in two layers of napkin her mother held out to her with the other.

"Sure, Mom." What the fuck had she even said?

She jogged down the driveway and hopped up into the cab of the truck. Even though Kit had scooted over as far as she could, Lilly still had to shove her way in so she could fit her entire butt *and* shoulder bag in the car. "This is getting cozy," she said to everybody.

"You're welcome to walk," Tessa replied, taking a sip from a giant to-go mug. The scent of her coffee filled the cabin and probably ruined the smell of Lilly's hair forever. Tessa was squeezed on the bench seat right up next to Boyd, who sat, obviously, behind the wheel. Next came Kit, and Lilly on the end.

"You're welcome to not be a bitch," Lilly told her, shuffling her bag down near her feet so she could finish her breakfast.

Tessa grinned from the corner of her mouth. "Touché." She sighed dramatically, resting her head on Boyd's shoulder while he pulled out of the driveway. "Another year. Another opportunity to revel in the glory of DLHS."

Boyd laughed. "We're halfway through, Tess. There's a light at the end of the tunnel."

Kit put one arm around each of them, and Lilly got a whiff of her perfume—something with jasmine. "What's everyone most excited about?"

Boyd shrugged. "Seeing Mrs. Barrington."

They all laughed. Mrs. Barrington was one of the lunch ladies, and she had eyes only for Boyd.

"Learning geometry," Lilly said. "Just kidding. Probably wearing all of my new clothes."

"Advanced English," Kit said.

Lilly had to snort, despite what Kit said about snorting (that it is not classy).

Tessa sighed. "Well, I'm most looking forward to it all being over in two hundred and eighty-eight days."

"Tess." Kit rolled her eyes.

"Okay, then, I'm most looking forward to winter break."

Classic Tessa. Boyd laughed.

"It's going to be a good one. I can feel it," Kit announced to no one.

Tessa sniffed—which was apparently classier than snorting. "Easy for you to say. You've aced all your classes. All you have to do is coast this year."

"Yeah," Boyd put in. "Didn't you get like only one B?"

"It was a B-plus," Lilly said, finishing her Pop-Tart.

Kit turned to her. "How do you know?"

"Because I looked at your report card." Lilly rolled down the window for some air, trying to not ruin the first day of school by showing up wrinkled and sweaty.

Kit pulled her arms back to her sides. "Lilly, no one gave you permission to do that!"

"Since when do I need permission? We're flesh and blood, right?" It was hard to explain, but Lilly kind of liked it when Kit yelled at her. Like something she'd done mattered. Besides, it was not fair that Tessa always seemed to know things about

Kit instinctively, without even having to ask. It was their whole chimerism thing, which Lilly had honestly never totally gotten. Tessa shared some of Kit's DNA from birth, and the result was that Tessa had a built-in excuse to act like a moody brat whenever she felt like it, and to claim she "understood" Kit better than anyone. It went beyond biology to more eerie stuff. Like, even though they had different personalities, sometimes they'd say the same thought out loud at the same time. And occasionally when Tessa woke from a nightmare, she'd find Kit was having the same one—or so they claimed.

"Kit, we all know your grades," Boyd said. He lifted a hand off the wheel to run it through his floppy hair, causing Tessa's head to bob away from his shoulder and sending a domino effect of shuffling throughout the cabin of the car. "Pretty sure the whole school knows. It's kind of like a thing."

Lilly grinned, giving herself an internal high five like she did whenever Boyd took her side.

Kit leaned forward to look at him. "A thing?"

Lilly could practically hear Tessa's eyes rolling. "Yeah," Tessa clarified. "An everyone-knows-Katherine-Malloy-is-King-Midas-and-everything-she-touches-turns-to-gold thing."

"That's absurd," Kit said as the truck turned into the parking lot and Boyd swung them into one of the few remaining spots. "And let's hope it's not true. Didn't Midas die alone and unloved?"

"Whatever," Tessa replied.

Lilly had no answer—she was barely listening by then.

Kit shrugged. "Well, lucky for you guys, I saved all of my notes and study guides."

"Yeah, lucky us!" Lilly said, already halfway out of the truck. She didn't care that much about grades, and knew she had a full year before testing for colleges would even matter. She hoped to focus on other types of scoring in the meantime.

And as much as she would have liked to linger and quiz Boyd about the status of his blinds this morning, it wasn't going to happen with both of her sisters around, like always.

She spotted Melissa and Darcy sitting on the front steps and headed their way, slowing down when Mel noticed her and Dar waved.

Eager was pathetic.

She was working on being less eager.

As she got closer, she noticed Dar had gotten thinner since she'd left to spend all of August at her dad's house; an overlarge black sweater drowned her frame. Mel looked exactly the same as always—in fact, she appeared to be wearing a favorite outfit from freshman year, consisting of tight red jeans, a striped button-down, and a silk scarf Lilly had given her last Christmas. But her smile looked more like a smirk.

Lilly bent for a three-way hug, then dropped her bag and took her spot, a step lower than the other two. Mel passed her a half-finished diet Dr Pepper. It was their tradition to share one before school every single day of the year. It had started sometime in eighth grade and just stuck.

Lilly took a big slurp, then passed the can to Dar. "So what did I miss?"

Dar blew her blond bangs out of her face. "We were just talking about the Donovan kid."

"Kid?" Lilly knew of the Donovans—the elderly couple who lived on the little cul-de-sac right off 28, at the edge of the preserve. They were on Kit's volunteer circuit and pretty close to Mel's house as well. Liam Donovan was losing his mind, Kit said. And the wife—Lilly couldn't remember her name—had apparently gone half blind. Lilly had heard nothing about a kid, though.

"Dude, get with it!" Mel said, grabbing the soda from Dar, taking a huge sip, then burping. "He's in our *grade*."

"How can the Donovans have a kid in our grade? They're like four hundred years old." Lilly rolled her eyes. Mel was always dramatic.

"Not their actual offspring," Dar explained. "Nephew or grandson or whatever. His family tree's not the point."

"Right," Mel added. "The point is, he's supposed to be *hot*. And also a criminal of some sort."

Lilly leaned back as Mel handed her the soda can again. Across the parking lot, Olivia Khan stepped out of her mom's old Camry in tall espadrilles, her shiny black hair and bright red lipstick accenting her pale brown skin. According to online rumors, Olivia had lost her virginity over the summer, to Jay Kolbry, her new boyfriend, who was known to be a dealer. This was long after Olivia dated Boyd (which was back when

Lilly and Olivia were both in eighth grade and Boyd and Tessa were in ninth). Still, Lilly experienced a pang of envy as Olivia walked toward the building, a sly grin on her face.

She turned back to her friends. "Where did you guys hear all this?"

Mel shrugged. "My mom." Mel's mother, Joanna Knox, reported for *Devil's Daily*, the local paper that, as far as Lilly could tell, mostly ended up being used to cover the floors in Boyd's house to form an impromptu shit pad when his dog couldn't be let out for long stretches. Lilly had never read it, come to think of it. Anyway, the line between journalism and gossip was fairly nonexistent in the Knox household. "I would have texted you guys as soon as I heard, but I was grounded from my phone all day yesterday."

Lilly smiled, shaking her head. "For what, taking the Lord's name in vain again?"

"Anyway, his name is Patrick and Mel wants one of us to date him," Dar filled in, exchanging a quick look with Lilly. It was the save-me look. "I already told her I'm not into law-breakers."

So far their group had been, while not exactly peripheral, not prime-cafeteria-table status-worthy either, and it had become clear sometime during freshman year that the pathway to high school dominance was paved with *pairs*. So last April, Mel had called a meeting between the three of them and determined that they were going to do things differently from then on—they were all going to get boyfriends.

Lilly had resisted at first, until Mel finally got her to confess that she was still clinging to her childhood crush on Boyd (which Mel kindly termed "borderline idolization"). But Mel had said that the *what* (getting a boyfriend) outweighed the *who*. Eventually Lilly had seen the merits of her argument: maybe experience was the important thing, and true love would follow.

And so Lilly had made out with Rohan Reddy at Allison Riley's May Day party, and Mel hooked up with Wesley Abraham at the Abrahams' graduation party for Wes's older brother Connor in June. Neither had stuck, though. And as for Dar, she'd hovered in the background, easy not to notice in the end-of-year swirl of parties and drama and goodbyes.

But then, while Mel's family went away for the Fourth of July weekend, Dar told Lilly to follow her up into the old tree house in her backyard. Lilly would never forget the moment they both sat down cross-legged, facing each other, the old tree creaking slightly as its branches swayed, and Dar cleared her throat, then blurted out that she thought she was gay. And that she didn't want Mel to find out. "You know what her family's like," she'd said to Lilly, a determined look on her face, the same expression she always wore when about to call gin in a hand of rummy.

It was true. Lilly loved Mel like another sister, but the Knoxes were Jesus lovers, gun owners, and big talkers: not the most promising triumvirate of qualities if you happened to be a newly burgeoning high school lesbian.

And so Lilly had promised.

She savored having a secret in her possession—the trust Dar had bestowed on her. She wasn't used to being the guardian of secrets, but the exposer of them, and this new responsibility had brought her a kind of sorrowful joy. Joy because in some small way she could help her friend. Sorrow because, well, things were complicated, and it had to suck to feel like hiding was your best option.

Of course, it hadn't been all *that* difficult, when keeping Dar's secret meant more guys for her. Still, she couldn't help but hope the various covert kisses and clandestine grope sessions she'd had in the past few months were building to something *real*. Something meaningful.

Boyd's face flashed in her mind.

Mel rolled her eyes, almost as though she was reading Lilly's thoughts. "It's obvious that Lilly is as hung up on BND as ever, so I call Patrick."

As though that hadn't been her plan all along.

"But," Mel added. "Lilly's going to ask him out for me."

"I am?" Lilly crumpled the can as the bell rang.

Dar cocked her head. "What is this, eighth grade all over again?"

Mel pushed Dar's shoulder. Dar suddenly seemed so thin and fragile that even a playful nudge could topple her. "Lilly will do it because that's what *friends* do," Mel said pointedly.

Dar adjusted her huge sweater and stood up. "Whatever you say, Mel."

Lilly stood too. "Fine, I'll ask him for you. On the condition that he turns out to be as hot as you say, and depending on the nature of his past crimes. Oh, and also on the condition that you stop referring to you-know-who as BND. He's going to figure it out!" How many things could it stand for *other* than Boy Next Door?

"That's fair," said Dar, at the same time Mel said, "Picky picky."

Then Mel smiled—her signature huge grin. She threw her arms around Dar and Lilly. "Thanks, babes. I'm so happy to be with my girls again."

Dar laughed. "We love you too, but stop suffocating me."

Lilly fist bumped them both and headed to class, bouncing in her Converse. It was a new year, full of new opportunity. And while at home she might be the baby in a lineup of three sisters vying for Boyd's attention, at high school, she was just *her*—a girl with a plan.

Chapter Four

NOW

FEBRUARY 7

ICY GRASS CRACKLED UNDERNEATH HER boots as Tessa veered off Woodrow Avenue, then cut through the big parking lot behind the diner, and out onto County Route 28, which wound its way out of town limits. After the gas station ran a stretch of shoulder and, beyond it, the woods. She hopped the rail and made her way to the trailhead.

These woods are lovely, dark and deep—something Kit used to say.

She ran harder, into the mottled shade of the winter trees, trying to burn away all thoughts of Kit. But the mind works a lot like osmosis, it turned out, always seeking equilibrium—the more tears she held in, the more memories flooded out instead:

She and Boyd, lying side by side on their stomachs in Tessa's bedroom, propped up on their elbows, the AP Bio textbook splayed open between them on the floor. Just last week—Wednesday—when Kit was still alive.

Mrs. Jenkins gave quizzes on Thursday mornings, and Tessa always prepped with Boyd. Bio was their mutually favorite subject. Ever since Tessa had learned about her chimerism, she'd gotten interested in genetics, which had been like a gateway into all sorts of weird scientific fascinations. The latest was marine biology. Most people don't realize how many weird-ass creatures live beneath the ocean—there are estimated to be about a million species and we only know of a fraction of them. It's like a wealth of colorful, floating secrets down there.

Anyway. An empty Fritos bag lay strewn on the carpet along with the flashcards she'd made—their studying had already devolved into a random debate about photosynthesis. She couldn't even remember what side of the argument she'd been on or what point she'd been trying to make.

The point had only been this: let's keep doing this. Let's not ever end this.

Let's stay here, in this moment, forever, talking about the magic of plants and phytoplankton sopping up the sun and turning it into the essence of green; of fresh starts, always there, waiting in our cells for a little light.

Kit had just come home from babysitting for the Nestors, and she popped her head into Tessa's room to say she was using the shower. She hadn't made eye contact with Boyd, but Tessa didn't wonder too much about it in the moment. She'd been far too distracted by the static electricity in the air, as though Boyd was a big balloon she'd rubbed her head against—it felt like every tiny hair on her arms was standing on end, for some reason. Things had been like that lately around Boyd, which made no sense since nothing had outwardly changed—they still had all the same inside jokes and banter and bizarre obsessions with biological anomalies and board games.

"I have a non-bio-related question," Boyd said after Kit left the room.

They could hear the sound of the shower turning on in the bathroom across the hall, its quiet scream through the old pipes. The Malloys' house was built in the 1940s, one of the few that survived the fire of '82, making it one of the oldest homes on their road. And thus, by the transitive property, also one of the most run-down. But Tessa was used to its creaks and moans— sometimes they provided just the right soundtrack to whatever mood she was in—and the sound of hot water rattling and hissing seemed inseparable, in that particular moment, from the rattling of her pulse and the steam building at the back of her neck.

"Shoot," she said, turning toward Boyd.

He was so big—Tessa was hardly two-thirds his size, her head barely coming up to his chin when they were standing, but right now, he was propped on his side, reclining, and still, his eyes came several inches higher than hers. He looked down and cleared his throat like a lecturer about to make a speech. It made her feel suddenly formal, like she should sit up and take notes.

She wondered if he was going to bring up the homecoming dance. It had been a few months ago, but they hadn't really talked about it since.

What he said surprised her. "Remember when I went out with Olivia Khan?"

She squinted at him. "Yeah?"

He'd dated Olivia for all of two weeks, in eighth grade. Olivia Khan was one of the prettiest girls in the middle school and high school combined. That hadn't changed over the last two years, either, though now she was dating Jay Kolbry, who none of them knew that well. Jay had a reputation for dealing. He was one of the popular jocks, always smiling, a natural fit for Olivia, probably.

She thought Boyd might elaborate, but he just lay there, his face hovering less than ten inches away from hers, his lips slightly apart. She could feel herself blushing, but she honestly couldn't tell if she was embarrassed for herself or for Boyd.

He licked his lips and swallowed. She'd known him since they were kids, and yet watching him do that sent a shiver down her spine. She felt like she needed to move her legs but forced herself to stay still, waiting for him to finish his thought.

And then, he was leaning toward her, tucking a strand of her hair behind her ear. His face looked bigger up close, his own hair flopping to the side. He hesitated, leaving his hand behind her neck, and Tessa drew in a sharp breath before doing a crazy thing:

She leaned up toward him.

And then, they were kissing.

Tessa rolled onto her back on the carpet—her arms suddenly too shaky to hold her up. He hovered over her, then leaned down and kissed her again. His lips were wet and soft.

Heat raced through her body. Her brain felt numb. She and Boyd . . . they were kissing. Full-on, lying-on-the-floor kissing. It made no sense.

For whole moments, she was just Tessa—no trace of Kit or chimerism or the nothingness she feared hovered just outside of who you were, waiting to prove you were just like it: that you were nothing, too.

Lips, breath, fingers trailing along collarbone. Something like a caught-back laugh, half hilarious, half delirious.

And then, they heard the sound of the shower turning off across the hall . . . and Boyd was sitting, then standing, closing the AP Bio book and tucking it under his arm. "I gotta go," he said, and left before Tessa could respond. He didn't explain why he'd brought up Olivia. He didn't explain why he'd kissed her. He was just . . . gone.

Tessa had flopped back onto her carpeted floor, staring at the speckled ceiling. Her whole body tingled—every spot where Boyd's body had touched hers. Her lips felt swollen. Her head felt stuffed with cotton. Her stomach tightened like it did when she was at the very top of a roller coaster—a tangle of excitement and dread. For some reason, she started giggling uncontrollably, rolling onto her side, until her eyes were full of tears.

"What's so funny?" Lilly asked, opening her door.

Tessa grinned into the carpet, catching her breath. "Nothing."

"Oh." Lilly paused for a second, clearly suspecting a secret. "Well, Mom says it's dinner."

She hovered in the doorway, waiting.

Tessa nodded, at a loss for words. Everything was changing too fast, the earth was spinning off orbit, and it felt like her whole life would never be the same again.

She hadn't known then that her life really *wouldn't* be the same after that night.

That early Sunday morning, only three days later, Kit's body would be found, bruised and frozen, in the back of Boyd's truck.

Now, her boots skidded across the shore of Devil's Lake and onto its surface—frozen over since last week. She slipped, landing hard on her knee and wrists. She panted, out of breath, exhausted and yet eerily not. She could hardly feel her body. How far had she just run?

Out here, all thoughts of Boyd—his lips and his hands in her hair—flew away into the cold. All thoughts of what Lilly had said when she'd pointed the finger at Boyd: that he and Kit had apparently been seeing each other in secret, right under all their noses, for months. That he'd been kissing *Kit* that night, had threatened her too. That they'd been fighting out on the side of the road, late, just hours before her body was found.

Not far from this very spot.

Tessa looked around. In the summer, this place was lush and green, but now the skeletal trees surrounding the lake pricked at the sky, a giant crown of thorns. Veinlike reeds laced the ice, which was murky and marbled with frost—and, in some places, beginning to thaw. She wondered, briefly, what it would be like if the lake simply cracked and gave beneath her, sucked her under. Her chest hurt. The back of her throat burned.

When she looked down again, her own freakish, discolored eyes—one green, one blue—stared back up at her between her bare palms, her face and body distorted just slightly: a shorter, more petite version of Kit.

She gasped.

Or *was* it Kit gazing back at her through the ice?

Now Tessa's pale hair grew longer in reflection, more golden, one blue eye cooling into green. She could feel herself disappearing as she looked into her sister's face. She could sense Kit's presence, thought maybe Kit really was lying there, just beneath a thin layer of ice, waiting for it to melt and free her.

He hurt me, Kit said with her mind, inside Tessa's mind.

Or maybe it was the part of Kit that lived on in Tessa, that remaining DNA trapped in her own cells, haunting her from within her own head.

Or maybe she'd simply snapped from the shock and chaos of what had happened, her final tethers to reality fraying, and she'd drifted off into pure hallucination.

Real or not real, a chill raced through her, causing her arms to shake.

He hurt me, ice-Kit said again.

42

And then, *He lied*.

Tessa felt sick, dizzy. She stumbled back to her feet. Her phone buzzed. A text from Lilly.

Where'd you go? We need you.

She went to turn her phone off but another text followed.

Please don't hate me. It's not my fault. I'm so sorry.

She sighed, shaking her head. Leave it to Lilly to make any of this about *her*.

She was about to type a response when a sound rang out, the blast of a rifle from far off. Her phone leaped out of her hand, crashing to the forest floor, its pale white-blue light ricocheting off branches and roots, illuminating a glint of silver in the dirt.

Another rifle shot, and a burst of wood thrushes taking to the sky.

She hated hunters. Lilly's best friend Mel's family, the Knoxes, were big into game hunting. Her dad had something like a thirty-gun collection.

Tessa bent to pick up her phone. Saw again the gleaming sliver of metal in the dirt, and bent down to pick it up, not caring as icy mud got under her fingernails.

It was a ring.

A mix of dread and curiosity moved through her as she stared at it.

Not silver, probably. Something more expensive, like white gold or platinum. In the setting gleamed a teardrop-shaped sapphire surrounded by tiny diamonds.

Tessa knew instantly what it was: an engagement ring.

VERIZON SERVICE RECORD
FEBRUARY 7, 2:34 PM

Tessa Malloy's iPhone: [gasp] I—Boyd?

County Jail: Are you there? I didn't think anyone would answer.

Tessa Malloy's iPhone: [pause] Yeah, it's me. I'm here.

County Jail: [muffled sound, possibly a cough or sob] Sorry, I just. For a second I wasn't sure who answered. I've been trying all morning and they only give you so many calls here.

Tessa Malloy's iPhone: It was today. The funeral.

County Jail: [silence] Jesus. I'm sorry. I should have realized.

Tessa Malloy's iPhone: [muffled sound]

County Jail: Are you still there?

Tessa Malloy's iPhone: Yeah. I just . . . I don't know what to say. This is . . . hard.

County Jail: [crying now] I know. I miss her so bad.

Tessa Malloy's iPhone: [voice cracking] Yeah. [pause] You know, the funny thing is, I keep thinking, Kit would know what to do now. Right? Like, she would know the right thing to say. But I'm just useless here. I'm just so numb. I can't even think, Boyd. I can't do anything.

County Jail: [pause] Yes, you can. [pause] You can help me.

Tessa Malloy's iPhone: [swallows] How?

County Jail: I shouldn't be in here. It's terrible here. Just gray walls and this feeling of guilt and suspicion and—I could really go crazy in here. The kinds of questions I've been asked. The kinds of things they think I've done . . . [voice cracks again]

Tessa Malloy's iPhone: [breathing]

County Jail: Are you still there?

Tessa Malloy's iPhone: Yeah. I'm just . . . I'm trying to think.

County Jail: This whole thing is just so wild, what they're saying. Like, manslaughter. Voluntary, involuntary—all these terms I didn't even know about before.

You have to help me. I don't know how it got to this. Everyone's just assuming this horrible stuff about me, and no one even cares what I have to say.

Tessa Malloy's iPhone: What do you have to say?

County Jail: I mean, that I didn't do it, obviously! That this is nuts! [sound like something hitting a wall, possibly the palm of a hand]

Tessa Malloy's iPhone: [silence]

County Jail: [pause] You know I didn't do it, right? You believe me, right? You know this is all just insane and unfair and . . . [pause] [whispered] You know me.

Tessa Malloy's iPhone: [silence]

County Jail: Hey . . . are you—

Tessa Malloy's iPhone: Yes, I'm still here. And I . . . yes, yeah. Of course. [shaky sigh] I believe you. At least, I think I do. I want to. I'm just . . . scared.

County Jail: [shaky sigh] It's okay. I don't blame any of you. I mean, I'm mad, it hurts, but it's okay. Like you said, I get it—everyone's just scared. Or maybe, maybe—

Tessa Malloy's iPhone: Maybe what?

County Jail: I don't know, I just have had a lot of time by myself here, a lot of time to think over the past couple of days, and I'm wondering, like, what if someone wanted me to take the fall?

Tessa Malloy's iPhone: Like who?

County Jail: Like whoever really killed her.

Tessa Malloy's iPhone: [silence]

County Jail: So . . .

Tessa Malloy's iPhone: Where would I even start?

County Jail: I overheard something when I was at the station. You won't want to hear this, but . . . apparently Patrick Donovan has gone missing. Since that night.

Tessa Malloy's iPhone: Wait, what?

County Jail: Yeah, apparently one of the Donovans called in to say their great-nephew hadn't come home Friday night. I'm not saying this means anything, I'm just saying . . . it's worth following up on, don't you think?

Tessa Malloy's iPhone: [pause] I—I don't know. But what about your fingerprints?

County Jail: What do you mean?

Tessa Malloy's iPhone: They were everywhere. At the, the scene.

County Jail: [sigh] Oh, come on, really? It was my truck. How could my fingerprints not have been everywhere? I drive it every day. I—I can't believe I even have to explain myself. Not to you. Not to any of you.

Tessa Malloy's iPhone: So are you saying you weren't there at all that night? Out on 28? What about—

County Jail: Kit had a copy of the keys. I made her a copy for Christmas. Those were the ones in the ignition—no one's saying it, but they have to be. Mine are at home on my nightstand, where I always leave them. If someone would just come to their senses and look, they would see my keys are at home and they were never in the truck with her, because she went out alone. She took the truck without asking me. I didn't even know.

Tessa Malloy's iPhone: You didn't notice it was gone all night?

County Jail: Did you?

Tessa Malloy's iPhone: [pause] I didn't know she had your keys. Are there any other things I should know about you two?

County Jail: Don't do this.

Tessa Malloy's iPhone: Don't do what?

County Jail: Don't start doubting me. Listen to me. Listen to what I'm saying. Listen to sense. I have always cared so much about all of you. I have only ever done right by you. I don't deserve this. I can take being blamed by cops who don't know me, who just want the easy story. I hate it, but I can take it. But I can't stand being doubted by you. I'll really lose it, if I think that you . . . [crying]

Tessa Malloy's iPhone: What do you want me to do?

County Jail: [sniffing] The person who did this, [whispered] the person who killed your sister. You need to find him. [pause] I would do it. I would try. But I'm stuck in here and you're out there.

Tessa Malloy's iPhone: [silence]

County Jail: They're saying this will go to trial. They want me to plead guilty so it will make my sentence less bad or something. Which is crazy. Why should I admit to something I would never do? Listen, I don't know how soon this is all going to go down. We're waiting on a court date. Okay?

Tessa Malloy's iPhone: Okay, what?

County Jail: So you have to hurry. [pause] But—but I want you to be careful, okay? Can you promise me you'll be really careful? [crying]

Tessa Malloy's iPhone: Boyd. Boyd.

County Jail: [sniffing again] Yeah.

Tessa Malloy's iPhone: Okay.

County Jail: Okay?

Tessa Malloy's iPhone: I'll help you.

Chapter Five

BEFORE

9/13

Dear Diary,

September is a lie.

It's supposed to be fall, you're stuck in class all the time, but out here the leaves are blazing green and the sun is just mocking us with this tanning weather. It's lunch period and we're lying on the grass right now. Dar is saying, I don't know, something hilarious about what happened in gym today. Mel literally just snorted out her chocolate milk (how unclassy) and some got on your pages. I'm sorry for that. My friends are heathens.

While they're talking I've been observing the boy across the quad. Patrick. Aka THE CRIMINAL. He's sitting alone under a tree with one ankle over the other, wearing head-phones and tapping his pencil against an open textbook like a drum. All around him, the Frisbee kids are in a heated game.

I've heard at some schools the people who play Frisbee are the cool ones? Yeah, no, that's not a thing here at Devil's Lake. Here they're the geeks who aren't actually smart enough to be in the real geek clubs such as Roman Coins.

Here are some things to know about our school:

Studio Band is hot. Orchestra is not.

Art class is hot. Art Club is not.

Winter musical is sorta for losers but the student-directed spring play always has people waiting in lines that wrap all the way down B hall and into C (mostly bc of the epic student theater cast parties).

I'm not going to lie. It's nice to be a sophomore and know this stuff.

Patrick probably feels lost without all this information.

Not that I feel sorry for him or anything. He is the criminal, after all.

Also, much as I hate to admit it anywhere but here in the privacy of your gold-and-pink-lined pages, Diary . . . he is also just as hot as Mel (and her mom, gross) have said. Like, when he pointed out in fourth-period geometry yesterday (our only shared class) that the volume of a cylinder is contingent not just on its width but also its length, Mrs. Gluckman literally broke the piece of chalk she was holding against the chalkboard, okay?

Just trust me.

His hotness is kind of weirdly exaggerated by the fact that he saves his voice for only these occasional comments. This is a good indicator that he is a complete asshole, but fuck it.

I made a promise to Mel. And, Diary, you should know that people do NOT break promises with Mel.

Besides, I already tried to tell her he seems like bad news and she was like wah, you're not even giving him a chaaaance. He's probably just shyyyy. He doesn't knoooow anyone here.

Now she's bugging me to make our move before "someone else nabs him first." I swear, to her dating is the exact equivalent of bargain shopping on Black Friday. Pure mania, and you don't even really know what you're bringing home until you open your bags later and go WTF did I just do?

But Mel . . . she's like an undertow, okay? She asks you to help her with something—running for class pres or asking out a boy—and you say yes. You get sucked into her rhythm, into doing things her way or else toppling over and landing flat on your face. And sometimes Tessa will say that Mel is making me her gofer or whatever, but that's easy for Tessa to say because she doesn't really HAVE friends (other than a few weirdos).

(And Boyd.)

(I think he's mostly friends with her out of pity, and the fact that they are the same year.)

Anyway. I know deep down Mel's just terrified of rejection. She's really pretty and everything, even though she says her nose is too crooked, but it just goes to show that even people who look great on the outside are sometimes hot messes on the *inside. And lately, it has seemed worse, like even though she puts on a great show, she's fragile and could shatter. I don't know when that happened, or why. All I know is, I'm her buffer.*

Also, whatever. I don't have anything better to do.

This is not going to be easy, though. I mean, we're a full week into sophomore year and I've seen this guy speak maybe three or four times so far (including the geometry cylinder thing).

Also? He's been sitting alone every day during lunch. People are actually afraid of him, haha!

But he doesn't really look like a criminal to me. He has the scruffy jeans and messy hair (again, hot) but up close (in math class—he sits behind me), I could see he has these freckles that make him seem like just a kid.

To try to warm things up earlier today, I turned around and offered to lend him a pencil, since Mrs. Gluckman was all "Why aren't you people taking notes?" He gave me this half grin and held up his own. It's seriously like he has mastered the Zen Art of Avoiding Speaking Altogether. I swiveled back around and wrote him a note during Gluck's mind-numbing lecture. "Do you have a girlfriend—yes/no." While she was handing quizzes back (I got a B!!!!), I dropped it on his desk.

BUT HE NEVER ANSWERED IT.

And I swear I could feel his eyes boring into the back of my neck for the rest of class and okay, the note was very immature, but it's still MORE immature not to respond at all, isn't it? Like, he could have just said yes even if it wasn't true and I would have gotten the hint. But noooo.

RUDE.

The guy is a jerk. It's unequivocal. Or equivocal. I forget which means which. Dear Diary, do not ever let Kit read you, she will scream at the bad grammar and it will be the first and last scream from her pure, untouched being, a scream of torment and despair. Children will weep and flowers will wilt.

What was I talking about? Oh yeah, math class. Well, anyway, who cares what Patrick thinks of me? I'm not doing this for me, I'm doing it for Mel, so I may as well get it over with. . . .

"So what's our move?" Mel asked, poking Lilly in the rib with a plastic fork.

"Ow." She sat up and closed her diary, tucking it into her backpack where it was safe. "I'm still working on it. But really, you're going to regret this. Best-case scenario, he says yes—and then you're actually stuck going out with him!"

Dar played with her bangs. "Do you think he really went to juvie?"

Mel shook her head. "That's a rumor. He got expelled over a fistfight last year, that's all I know for sure."

"Oh," Dar said. "*Just* a fistfight."

Lilly laughed and Mel folded her arms, fake pouting. "Fine. You guys can laugh all you want." But behind the pout, Lilly could sense something else—a flicker of something *real*.

Sadness? Loneliness? Doubt?

"Oh, Mel." Dar sighed, breaking the spell, and Mel shoved her in the shoulder.

Lilly took a deep breath, stood up, and began walking over to Patrick. As much as she didn't want to interact with him, it was better than disappointing Mel. Ever since last year and their "vow," the girl had dated five boys without ever asking a single one of them out. It was kind of like how she lined up all her lip gloss along her sink at home, from darkest to light. It looked like a makeup museum. You had to be super careful, because if you knocked one over, you'd knock over all of them.

As Lilly made her way through the crowded field, she was aware of Tessa sitting at one of the picnic tables near the cafeteria door, blowing a spitball at Boyd. Almost everyone ate lunch in the quad until the last possible moment. Sometimes even when it snowed last winter, Lilly would find Tess eating her lunch outside at the picnic table, bundled in a parka that made her hair go staticky.

She didn't see Kit anywhere, but that was not surprising. She was usually tutoring or on a planning committee or catching up on homework in the library—a missed opportunity, from Lilly's point of view. Kit could easily be DLHS royalty—center quad status, homecoming queen material, and everything else that came with being pretty, smart, and liked by literally everyone. But Kit acted like those things didn't matter.

It was high school: what else *did* matter?

As Lilly came closer to Tessa's table, she caught Boyd's eye. She smiled but kept walking, hoping he got a good look at the cut-out in her T-shirt, exposing her back, which stopped just above the line of her shorts. She'd cut it herself over the summer.

Passing by, she felt something wet smack against the small of her bare back. She yelped and turned.

Tessa was grinning as she threw a straw under the table. Too late, though. Lilly saw.

She scraped the slobbery blob from her skin and marched over to Tessa and Boyd and the weirdo table. "Tess, what the hell?"

Tessa laughed. "Oh, relax, we were just playing around."

Lilly's face went hot at the word *we*. Like Boyd was automatically on Tessa's side. The side making fun of her. Treating her like a kid they could just pick on when they wanted to. She took a deep breath. "Tessa, why don't you just grow up and find a hobby or something?"

"Why would I, when I'm having *so* much fun bugging you, sis?" Tessa was smirking like it was the permanent shape of her face, which maybe it was.

But then Boyd wrapped his big arm around Lilly's waist. "Chill, little Lill. I will personally make sure that no further saliva-covered items touch your delicate skin."

A giant shiver raced through Lilly's body. This was the thing with Boyd: he was always so casual with all of them. Throwing his arm around them like a protective brother. Wrestling in the yard. Teasing them. How could they ever tell if it was more than that?

And what was that he'd just said about saliva and skin?

"Fine." She turned to face him, blocking out Tessa on purpose. "If you *promise*." She leaned toward him, wondering if he could see her cleavage and if that was gross and eager of her to think.

"I promise." He reached up and mussed her hair. Great. Just like that she was the baby all over again. But before she could figure out what to say next, she caught Mel's eye across the quad. She still had a job to do.

"Gotta go."

"You're always in high demand," said Tessa, but not as a compliment. She tore a piece of celery in half and crunched on one end of it. For such a tiny girl, she had all the grace of a horse.

"Actually, I'm about to ask that guy out," Lilly said, seeing an opportunity. She tilted her head in the direction of Patrick, who was no longer leaning against his tree but was, in fact, in the process of shoving his book into his bag.

"Ooooh, good luck," Tessa called to her back, which was still faintly damp in one spot, as though she'd been marked.

Lilly had to run to catch up with Patrick just as he was rounding the far end of the quad, toward the parking lot. She grabbed on to his shoulder. "Hey."

He turned, a surprised look on his face, which, combined

with the freckles, struck Lilly as young looking. His eyes were bright blue. Ugh.

"Sorry." She dropped her arm.

His expression remained unreadable.

"I just, um, wanted to catch you."

His eyes darted across her face like he was trying to connect the dots and figure out what her problem was. It made her blush, which was annoying.

"I mean," she stammered on, losing her rhythm, "you never replied to my note. From math."

He licked the corner of his lips and she wasn't sure if he was preparing to say something, so she paused. He shifted his weight, still studying her like she was a bug on the wall and he wasn't sure whether he should squash her or set her free.

"Anyway," she went on, unable to stand the silence, or the awkwardness blooming from her chest to her face, "I was asking for a friend. Melissa. The one with the dark hair who I was sitting with earlier? She wants to know if you'll go out with her. I told her I'd ask you, so."

Was Boyd watching? She hoped so.

Patrick cracked a smile at last. Relief flooded her. But it was replaced almost instantaneously with a flurry of other sensations, not entirely unpleasant but still destabilizing, as though she'd just touched an electric fence.

He still didn't say anything.

"So?" she prodded, starting to get annoyed.

"So what?" His voice wasn't deep and low like some guys'

voices, but it had a bit of gravel to it. Maybe this was his strategy—making people so desperate to hear his voice that when he finally spoke, even just two words, you savored them like two SweeTarts (Lilly's favorite) dissolving slowly on your tongue while you wait for a movie to start.

"So what's your answer?" she said more slowly. She was beginning to feel sidetracked.

"Oh." He bit his lip and shifted his backpack. "No."

She stared at him, trying to read his expression, still half a smile lingering there like he'd meant to remove it but got distracted halfway through. "No, you don't have a girlfriend, or no, you don't want to go out with Mel?"

"Both."

He turned and walked over to where a motorcycle was propped near a sign in the student parking area. She watched, brow furrowed and jaw hanging slightly open, as he put on a helmet, hopped onto the back of the bike and revved the engine, then drove off the school lot.

It was only after he rounded the corner and the bell rang loudly, signaling the start of sixth period, that she closed her mouth and turned to walk back to class, realizing that it was still the middle of the day and Patrick was apparently cutting the rest of school, just like that.

It wasn't, obviously, proof that he was a *criminal*, but it was enough for her to know she didn't want anything to do with him, and his maddeningly cute grin and his rudeness and his . . . *no*.

Chapter Six

BEFORE

HIS FAVORITE FLIP KNIFE. Boxers. Deodorant. A handful of T-shirts.

People were, inherently, assholes. This was what Patrick Donovan was thinking as he slammed his belongings into the ripping army duffel his uncle Mike had given him, sometime before going on a thirteen-day bender that ended with his jaundiced body found plastered to the floor, half behind the old plaid couch in his work shed. Liver failure.

People just blatantly sucked. They were self-serving, always, even when it seemed like they were doing a nice thing. "Patrick, why don't you get a break from all this drama?" his mom had said before shipping him off. "It isn't healthy," she'd said.

Right, but sending her son away to the home of obscure relatives (because her first husband had split, her parents were dead, now her brother was dead too, and she didn't even speak to either of her sisters) was *totally* healthy. Even Uncle Liam (great-uncle, technically) and Aunt Diane had dished out plenty of BS about wanting to "reconnect." Sure, if by reconnect they'd meant take on a free house servant.

He was sick of it. It wasn't that mowing the lawn or cleaning out the garage or doing minor car repairs was so horrible in and of itself, it was just the fakery behind it all that pissed him off. It was fine if no one wanted him, but the pretending killed him. And anyway, he was just along for the ride. He hadn't asked to be taken in. And he'd be fine when he was gone.

It had to be better when you were on your own. No one to disappoint. No one to disappoint *you.*

Rain fell quietly on the attic roof—*tick-tick, tick-tick, tick-tick.* Outside, the leaves, just starting to fall, would be matted down into the grass. Someone would have to rake them after the storm, into sodden, heavy piles, to be bagged and set on the street. It was the first bad weather they'd had in Devil's Lake since he'd moved here in August.

He sighed, picking up the Cubs hat his dad had given him way, way forever ago. He stared at the faded C. He wasn't sure whether wearing it would fly in these parts or if he'd get the shit kicked out of him by a bunch of jacked-up Tigers bros.

He scanned the attic room to see if there was anything he'd forgotten—not that he had much stuff to begin with. It was a mistake to even come here. He should've taken off on his own before it ever came to this—moving to a new town, trying to start over at a new school, meeting a whole new set of people with their own histories and expectations and assumptions. In the city there were always a million people everywhere and a million things going on, constant lights and honking horns and angry landlords and *distractions*. But out here in Devil's Lake, it was dead silent at night, and he hated it. Hated how alone it made him feel, all that quiet. All that haunted, swaying grass on the side of the roads—made him want to flick a lighter to it and set the whole town aflame.

For some reason, this made him think of the Malloy girl.

It was true, he didn't have to be such a dick to her. She was a redhead, he'd noticed, just like his last girlfriend, Sari, pronounced like "sorry," which she hadn't been when she'd taken off, too. He didn't really know anything about this redhead other than what he'd overheard in gym the other day—some douche lacrosse player saying he wanted to bang all three Malloy sisters and one of his bonehead friends saying he didn't even have a chance with one. Apparently, the redhead had a couple of older sisters who were just as hot as her. Patrick actually knew that the oldest one came by on her volunteer route, leaving groceries. Supposedly she was super smart, advanced classes and all that. He hadn't interacted with her, though. He'd been standing in the shower when she drove up the last time, savoring the hot water, which there always seemed to be a shortage of back at his mom's apartment, so he didn't even see the supposed beauty in the flesh.

Patrick had pretty much tuned the jocks out after that one conversation, sticking to the corner of the weight-training room where he could focus on push-ups and sit-ups and other workouts that didn't involve fancy machines covered in other people's B.O.

It wasn't that he didn't want to talk about—or think about—girls. He liked them and the things he had occasionally been given the opportunity to do with them behind closed doors and in the back seats of cars, but he wasn't into the whole culture of conquest bragging. It just reminded him of the crap boyfriends his mom used to bring around, and generally grossed him out.

And maybe he'd been rude earlier, to the Malloy girl, but he had to keep her at bay. She had no idea what she was walking into with him. And her asking him out . . . for a friend? He cracked a small smile. Then he shook his head. That had to be self-serving too, in some way. He wondered what she really wanted from him, who she'd been trying to impress, or make jealous.

Anyway, it didn't matter. He wouldn't be around long enough to find out.

He tossed in the cap and started zipping the bag closed. The piece-of-shit zipper got jammed and he had to fuss with it, which was when he heard the creak on the attic steps, stopped what he was doing, and shoved the duffel bag beneath the bed. He stood up quickly, banging his head against a low rafter just as Diane entered the room.

He rubbed his head and plopped down on the bed. Already he felt bad, seeing his great-aunt, frail and bent over like that, winded just from climbing the stairs. She'd probably called up to him and he hadn't heard over the sound of the rain.

"How was school?" she asked, brushing wispy white hair away from her temple and carefully tucking it in to some invisible hairpin. The stray lock flopped down again as soon as she let go.

He shrugged.

"Well, I guess that's better than awful, isn't it," she said, more a statement than a question.

Either way, he didn't have a response. He hated the shame that sweltered him like a sweaty sheet in summertime whenever his great-aunt tried to converse with him. She'd never had any kids of her own. Why would she want to start dealing with a teenager now, especially one with "behavioral problems"? Which, by the way, was a highly hyperbolic term for having gotten into a total of one ill-advised fight. It wasn't like he'd gone out looking for it even.

"So," she said. "I'm making pierogi." She paused, then added, "It would be nice if you'd help with the potatoes."

She waited there until he followed her back down the stairs, the packed duffel sagging in the back of his mind like an unkept promise.

Later on, with the steam from boiling dumplings rising around their heads, carrying the warm smell of leek and starch, and Uncle Liam in a cheerful, semilucid mood, and the rain falling steadily outside, Patrick almost regretted his plans to leave here. He thought again of the sodden leaves filling up the yard. Who would clear them up when he was gone?

They were sitting around the dining room table and his great-uncle was talking about a paper he was working on for the university—something about cannibalistic ogres. He recalled his uncle used to teach a course or two on folklore and fairy tales, but he'd never really thought about how gruesome the stories could be.

"What do you think, Tom?" he asked suddenly.

Patrick did a double take, but Diane gave him a quick look he didn't quite get. "Sorry, what?"

"I could really use help organizing them, Tom. The notes are all over the place," Liam said.

Diane folded her napkin and got up to clear the dishes. "That's all right, dear. We'll discuss the paper tomorrow."

In the kitchen, she told Patrick not to mind. "He'll forget what he said."

"Who's Tom?"

"I have no idea," Diane replied. "Probably a former student." Her arm shook as she wiped down one of the plates.

"Let me do that," Patrick said, taking the plate and dish towel.

Diane beamed at him. "We're so happy to have you with us, Patrick. You've grown into such a good young man."

"It's no problem," he said, trying to avoid looking into her eyes.

"Don't let Liam's ramblings bother you," she went on. "He used to be quite successful, you know. His second book sold in six different countries."

Patrick nodded.

"He used to buy me presents—mostly jewelry, sometimes other artifacts, vases, that sort of thing—from every city he visited on tour," she added, a hazy look passing over her face. She laughed a little and shrugged. "Thousands of dollars' worth of mementos, probably. Ironic, a little bit, don't you think?"

Patrick didn't answer. He was thinking about the expensive objects she mentioned. The jewelry and vases. Thousands of dollars could get a person far. A lot farther than empty pockets. He squirted more soap than necessary into a glass and let it fill with water from the faucet, watching it foam over.

"Anyway," Diane continued, "he knows he's doing it. Sometimes. He'll realize it. Calls it dream chasing. I thought that was a nice way of putting it, don't you," she said—another statement question.

"Ogres who eat human flesh? Some dreams." Patrick shut off the faucet.

Diane looked at him funny, and it took him a moment to understand her surprise—it was more than he'd said the entire time he'd lived with them. He too felt surprised. He never thought of himself as a quiet person. Just seemed like lately he was the one who was caught in a series of bad dreams. No ogres, maybe. But other sorts of monsters.

"Not all the stories are bad. There are good fairies who grant wishes," Diane said, almost to herself, as though she didn't mean for him to hear.

But he had. And once again, his mind turned to the Malloy girl, with hair like pale fire.

Hooked

BY KATHERINE MALLOY

The fishermen's lines fly over the water,
making me think of hunger and desire

—each an intrinsic part of the other—
driving the fish to the end of the wire

on which its own death winks, silvery and hooked,
and on which somebody's survival may depend.

I lie on the shore, gazing at my notebook—
the lines of poems draw me toward their end:

full of sentiments that lack completion,
and holding hidden longing, long unmet—

while in the strong arms of the fishermen
I see your hands, that haven't touched me yet.

But who's been baited and who's the lure?
Who will give in first and ask for more?

Chapter Seven

NOW

FEBRUARY 7

HERE WERE TESSA'S LEADS. Okay, her one lead:

Patrick Donovan was reported missing. Had been gone since Friday night. At least, that was according to Boyd. She didn't know what to think of that fact. She hadn't really gotten to know Patrick in the months he'd lived in Devil's Lake.

It was suspicious, though, wasn't it?

It was something.

She stepped through the back door into her house, feeling the tiny weight of the engagement ring in her pocket. It was quiet—everyone would be coming home soon from the service, but somehow she'd gotten here first. Casseroles and fruit salads slouched on the counter in shrink-wrap, waiting for concerned visitors and distant family members to expose and devour them. The thought of it—all that potato salad and pity—sent a violent wave of nausea through her.

She ran up the stairs and barely made it to the hall bathroom before puking her guts out.

She kneeled on the floor for a few minutes, then got up and ran the faucet, hot. As the mirror fogged, she felt herself disappearing. She tried to conjure another memory of Kit, tried to make her be *here*.

What happened? she wanted to say. *Come back.*

Her hands shook. She decided to take a shower to clear her head, stripping off her clothes in a stiff puddle on the floor, but in the shower sat Kit's mango-scented conditioner like a little statue and she was driven by some insane compulsion to open it and then the smell poured over and through her and she found she was shaking even harder.

Tears didn't come, though.

It scared her, this lack of tears. She'd cried that first morning, or thought she had, but then it had all dried up—too fast. The sadness had evaporated and left her a husk.

She washed her hair and let the water run down her face until she learned how to breathe again.

She could hear the front door opening and closing. So they were home. More people would be arriving soon, too.

She looked at her hands, tried to concentrate. She was desperate to help Boyd. She knew it wasn't him—it couldn't have been him. He wouldn't hurt Kit. He'd spent his whole life protecting her, protecting all of them, like he said. She'd known that he was innocent from the first moment Lilly accused him of doing it, had been shocked and outraged and confused by Lilly's stricken, sincere conviction.

But Lilly wouldn't lie, either. Well, sure, maybe about whether she'd finished her homework or eaten the last cookie, but not about something like this. She adored Boyd just as much as Tessa and Kit did. Tessa believed that Lilly must have really seen him out there on the road. She wouldn't just make that up, and her story was way too specific to be false: she'd been staying over at Mel's house, had snuck out that night and seen the truck parked with its lights still on, had forged her way up the road on foot to see what was going on, had witnessed Boyd and Kit arguing, had decided it was none of her business and fled, telling no one, until it was too late.

Maybe it was Boyd who had lied—about being out on the road in the middle of the night with Kit—to cover his ass, to seem less suspicious. Maybe he *had* been out there with her, but then he'd left, and *then*, that was when the terrible thing had occurred. After Boyd abandoned Kit out there, in the storm, alone.

Her heart raced. But why would he do that?

And that didn't explain why his truck had been left there, too.

Also, his fingerprints had been everywhere.

And he had no alibi. Said he was home studying for a quiz when they both knew the quiz had been *Thursday* and this all happened on a Saturday.

But then, what about Patrick Donovan?

These contradictions toggled around in Tessa's head, growing louder than ever, as if someone had actually reached inside her brain and yanked up the volume.

The water had gone cold. She shut off the faucet, reached for a towel. Kit's bathrobe still hung on the back of the door. She grabbed that and, tenderly, slipped into it. It was so soft. It smelled so familiar, wrapped around her, like an embrace.

For a second, there it was: the grief, a little gremlin strangling her from the inside, screaming silently along her throat, making her head go hot.

She suddenly forgot everything.

What was she doing, standing here, dripping wet?

Oh yes, she'd just taken a shower.

What day was it?

Tuesday.

Why wasn't she at school?

Because today was Kit's funeral.

Kit's funeral.

She had run away instead of giving her stupid speech.

She had found a ring in the woods.

Boyd had called, begging for help.

She wanted to believe him, *had* to believe him—when she'd heard his voice on the phone minutes ago, the old Boyd, the Boyd she'd known her whole life, had come back to her in an instant, and all the doubts had blown away like dandelion seeds.

But then, in the silence of her thoughts afterward, in the

constellations of facts and details that had emerged, what was she supposed to believe . . . that it was all a wild coincidence? That he was maybe lying but only about some parts and not others?

Tessa was a logical person, and when all the evidence said one thing, you were supposed to believe it: the boy obsessed with all three of them. The boy who had the most access to them all. The boy whose truck her body had been found in. The boy whose father struggled with money and drinking, who had a chip on his shoulder, who nobody thought was going anywhere. The boy with no mother. The boy who'd never been loved right, never been taught right.

Then again.

Ever since freshman year, Tessa had planned to become a science major someday, and nearly all the great scientists she'd learned about in school had been widely disbelieved in their time. Sometimes, she knew, the truth was bizarre: that the earth was round and not flat, even though we *experience* it as flat. That *we* move around the sun, even though we can't feel ourselves moving. That space is full of black holes that are not really holes at all, because instead of being empty, they are the densest form of matter. Science teems with seeming contradictions, full of theories that go against all instinct. The ancient, animal part of our brains only wants to believe what is right in front of us, what's immediate, what we can touch. As a scientist, you have to learn to shut off the animal brain and listen to the abstract, the euphoric, the wildly imaginative only-human part, the part that dreamed up string theory and smartphones and wheels on suitcases and the idea that every person accused of a crime remains innocent *until proven* guilty.

You have to believe in what you can't see.

Her breathing came back again and she turned the knob, hurrying out into the hall and ducking into her bedroom before anyone could catch her and drag her downstairs into the mourning festivities, the condolences and wilting condiments and half hugs. She began shakily getting dressed—old sweats, a thick sweater, her wet hair in a knot over her head.

What—were you supposed to dress up to honor death? Didn't that seem backward, to show respect for something everyone agrees to hate?

She pulled the ring out of her jeans pocket and stared at it again. A modest sapphire cut into a little teardrop and surrounded by tiny diamonds. Definitely an engagement ring. Not the kind of thing someone just forgets about or tosses aside.

She slipped it onto her finger.

For the first time since early Saturday morning, she felt a tingle of her old, *real* self, waking up. She was no detective, but she was good at testing hypotheses. She would solve this.

She knew she couldn't save Kit. It was the absoluteness that felt the worst, like a coil around her throat, growing tauter and tauter, unable to ever release.

But she wouldn't focus on that part. Even looking that straight in the eye—accepting death—*no.* She wasn't ready to look grief in the face. It would be like giving up, like walking into a grave and opening her mouth as dirt fell in.

For now, there was one thing she *could* do, though.

She could save Boyd.

She might be the *only* person who could. She might be the only one who *would*.

Still, it took some conniving for Tessa to get to the police station that evening. She thought about asking her mom point-blank to drive her over, but her mom had already decided in her mind that Boyd was guilty. Her eyes were ringed in red and she was barely holding it together. She'd already overboiled the pasta into a starchy swamp and they'd mostly just stared at the leftovers from earlier, unable to stomach much food anyway. All the distant relatives had gone as swiftly as they'd come, and her mom looked like she was ready to pass out face-first on the couch.

Luckily, no one had given Tessa a hard time about running off earlier today. Maybe grief and shock gave you a pass from formalities.

Or maybe, Tessa thought, they had hardly even noticed. Like with Kit gone, Tessa had somehow become invisible too.

In the end, she had easily slipped out of the house that night, saying she needed air, and took the long walk over to the station.

When she pushed open the door, she was overcome with lightheadedness. She wasn't sure what she'd envisioned, having never been inside this place before. Maybe something like in a seventies crime drama: low ceilings and yellowed walls, fat, old cops drinking strong coffee and referring to case files stored in manila folders. But the station in Devil's Lake had recently been redone: it was spacious and clean, full of giant windows that looked out on a well-lit parking lot. Everyone seemed professional, friendly, and well dressed. The soft clack of keyboards filled the open space, a calming soundtrack.

Tessa didn't believe in the afterlife, but if she had, she might've thought purgatory would be like this: bright light. Order. Process.

"How can I help you?" The woman at the front desk was slender and pretty, with dark skin and even darker hair swept up smoothly on top of her head.

"I'm, um, I need to talk to someone," Tessa fumbled. "My um, my sister, was, she was, well—"

The receptionist squinted, then her eyes widened in recognition. "Oh, honey, I know exactly who you are. Wait here just a minute." Tessa stared at her lips, which didn't seem to move as she spoke. The woman hustled out of her chair, leaving it spinning, and returned shortly, followed by a tall, young-looking cop with a buzz cut and dimples.

Tessa recognized him—he'd been in their house at least twice since Sunday morning. Officer Raúl García. His smile was so nice and accommodating that for a moment she forgot why she was here.

García ushered her into his office and offered her some water. She held it but put it down without taking a sip. She had the craziest thought that if she swallowed the water, it would rush through her, dissolve her body into nothingness, carry her away like a river.

At birth, 78 percent of the human body is water.

"I wanted to know . . ." She cleared her throat. "To know the details. About my sister. About Katherine. About her . . ." Once again, the word *death* lodged behind her teeth, refusing to come out.

García sat back in his chair. "What do you want to know?"

"I heard someone—a boy, Patrick Donovan—ran away on the night of . . . the night of." *Say it.* "The night it happened. Shouldn't that make him a suspect?"

García sat back in his chair. He looked at her for a minute, and it felt like he was seeing through her to the other side of the room. Like his mind had gone somewhere else, and his eyes were as blank as the frozen lake.

"I'm just saying, have you looked into whether there's any connection—"

"Listen." García sighed. "Sometimes, a case solves itself. Sometimes it really is that easy. It's nearly always the boy-friend, sweetie. I wish I could tell you otherwise. But facts are facts."

Boyfriend.

"But Boyd and Kit weren't—they weren't dating. It wasn't like that. He's our friend. He's—"

He's mine, she wanted to say. They were lying on the carpet in her bedroom, talking about bio. Then they were kissing . . .

García gave a weird half smile. "Are you sure about that?" He began clicking on his keyboard. "Fingerprints tell their own story. I'm so sorry, but it's just the way it is."

I'm so sorry. The words landed softly over her, like snow. *Just the way it is.*

She swallowed. "So he just left all the evidence for everyone to find it? The truck, the keys. That makes no sense."

"Actually, it's commoner than you might think. Almost like they want to be found—or in the moment, anyway, they just want to be seen. A crime of passion is often like that. Someone felt betrayed, felt invisible, this one act is their big send-off to the world."

It didn't sound like Boyd at all.

Her throat hurt. "But what would his motive have been?"

"Jealousy, usually?" García said. "Besides, we found all kinds of suspicious items on him, in the home."

"Like what?"

García shrugged. "A mashed-up doll that looked like the victim. That sort of thing." He said it so casually, but the image lurched into Tessa's stomach, making her feel like she'd been kicked.

"Look. All I can tell you right now is there's a state-appointed lawyer, and I'm sure she'll be arguing for involuntary manslaughter. Autopsy says cause of death was the hypothermia and not the injury. So we may not be able to prove intent to murder."

She practically choked. The words sounded so scary—so real.

"Usually a lighter sentence for that sort of thing. We're not talking death row. Least as far as I'd guess. Have to see how it all pans out, of course—not for me to say."

She was having trouble thinking straight.

Now he was hitting a button on his keyboard. Several documents began to rhythmically spit out of the printer next to the desk. *Zzzzrt. Zzzzrt. Zzzzrt.*

Zzzzrt.

Zzzzrt.

Zzzzrt.

The sound started to remind her of the quiet thrum of a heart monitor in a hospital room. She felt dizzy. Tessa wondered briefly if she was still in bed, dreaming this. Or if she was out in the snow, with Kit, cold beyond comprehension.

Jealousy. Could Boyd have been jealous? Or had it been the other way around?

The last memory Tessa had of Boyd, before that night, was their study session, their kiss.

What did it mean? Had Kit found out? But how could things have gone so badly unless . . . unless what this cop was saying was true.

No. No.

He turned to her and sighed. "You never really know someone, do you?"

He put the papers in a stack on his desk, tucking them into the mouth of a folder. "This is the report and the photos. For the protection of your family and issues of confidentiality, I can't let you leave the building with these, but feel free to look through, and take your time." He paused. "It may be difficult to see some of that. But it's your right to, if you want to know."

Was it her right? Why was he being so nice?

He vanished, and there the file was, a blank face.

She opened it. She tried to look for something about a ring, but the words blurred before her.

She focused. The first page was just a scanned form with hand-scribbled answers in the blanks, like the cover page of a school test: name, age, date, address, various badge numbers and car numbers. She flipped to the next page. Details of the scene. The truck, with its headlights still on. Footprints in the snow—some large, some small.

The fingerprints. Just like she'd been told: all over the car, the steering wheel. Boyd's truck, his hat. García was right. The clues weren't subtle.

And then, found on the ground near one of the truck tires: a small bag of white pills. Prescription sedatives. Tessa stared at this detail for some time but couldn't make sense of it. No one in her family had any prescriptions. She wasn't sure about Boyd or his dad, Innis. But the detail was unsettling. Had Kit been drugged that night? Why hadn't anyone thought to mention this detail?

The heat of anger, and urgency, began to burn her ears.

She kept flipping pages.

What followed was a hospital report. *Evidence of minor head trauma in the form of bruising along the right temple toward the hairline and right ear. Minor scratch along the upper left arm, exposed.*

No foreign substances found in bloodstream.

She breathed out. So Kit hadn't taken—or been given—any drugs, it seemed. Perhaps that was why she hadn't heard about them before now. But how did it all add up? She flipped to another page.

Hypothermia evident in discoloration of lips and hands. Believed to be cause of death.

Minor swelling on lower abdomen, probably due to newness of the tattoo.

Tessa paused and reread the line over again. Her heart rate picked up again.

Nausea and horror rolled through her as she turned the page and began to examine the photos of the scene. In them, the tarp that sometimes covered the bed of Boyd's pickup was pulled back to reveal Kit's body, curled in the fetal position. She was wearing her favorite jeans—a pair of form-fitting dark-wash Levi's—and her tall black boots. She had no shirt on, just a lacy lavender bra with a tiny silver pendant on it. The bra was dimly recognizable, though Tessa couldn't pinpoint why—it didn't seem like the kind of thing Kit would own, but that was not the detail that was bothering Tessa.

There were more photos. Too many. So many she got the sense that it wasn't just Kit but a series of girls, all strangers, all dead.

Most, she couldn't look at.

She flipped through the photos to find one at an angle where she could see the abdomen. It was hard to see clearly, but sure enough, as she squinted closely, she could make out a blurry tattoo, a dark blot, a bit larger than a quarter, with two little points along the top, possibly ears, and one pointed to the side. An animal's face, maybe? Sort of like a dog.

Possibly a wolf.

She stared at the tiny, inky wolf. Willed it to shed some meaning she could understand.

Head trauma. Bruising. Hypothermia.

Tessa slipped out of the station without saying goodbye.

THE RIDE
BY KATHERINE MALLOY

It was after school; I was running home, rideless,
while rain fell hard—streaming through my hair—

sky black as a groom staring down the aisle, brideless,
when your car came through the intersection, where

the crosswalk seemed to gleam, like an arrow or
a sign. You opened a door; I got in to dry off

and slowly the space between us grew narrower.
At first I had the urge to leave—fly off

like a bird at the start of its long journey south.
But you made me want to stay—as we talked and drove,

I couldn't keep from bending toward your mouth,
feeling cold and wet and alive, while the heavy rain wove

its inevitable path down the window's side.
Like me, it fell blindly, without any guide.

Chapter Eight

BEFORE

~~~~~~~~~~~

10/8

Dear Diary,

Dar thinks she looks like a sad, boobless puppet. We're in Mel's room and she's trying on Mel's blue bandage dress, which is definitely at least a size too big. I'm sort of annoyed with both her and Mel. Dar, because she looks great in everything and she's just being extra sullen lately. Mel because she's been harassing me literally all during the homecoming game today about why I haven't made moves on Boyd yet. As if I have all these opportunities for privacy with him. Also, she's threatening to try to get Patrick to notice her by making out with someone else to make him jealous. It's like she's gotten sex-crazed lately, and I can't figure out what triggered it.

Gone is the Mel of seventh grade who had never been kissed, who thought a blow job had something to do with dead leaves in autumn.

Anyway, this is just annoying, backward logic and so typical of Mel. I know she's going to end up kissing Dusty, who is weird and kind of gross, even for a band guy, though admittedly since we don't really hang out with his crowd I don't really know him. It's just, like, he became Mel's go-to sometime last year, for when nothing else is working. Her fallback boy. The whole thing is such a giant whatever.

Anyway, the dance is tonight and I need to straighten my hair/possibly set fire to all of Mel's teddy bears. Be warned, I am armed and dangerous, and it's Mel's fault for letting me use her hair iron.

However, Diary: despite my best friends being brats and losers, I do love them. And I am super excited for the dance tonight because, uh, Boyd will be there (!!!!) and so maybe in addition to getting Mel off my back for once, I will also get his solo attention, which would be nice. Maybe he'll dance with me.

Oh my god, my sisters would lose their minds! YES!!!!!!!!

Anyway, I should go because I'm still not dressed, Dar is sending me death glares that I'm guessing are code for something but I don't know what, and also, Mel is insisting that she has a "plan." As we all know, when Mel has a plan . . .

GTG—more later!

❄

"No, seriously. I have a solution to all our problems," Mel announced as Lilly shoved her diary into her bag. She gestured for Dar and Lilly to gather around her bed, handing Dar the flask they'd been passing around. Then she lifted the mattress and drew out a small velvet change purse. She unclasped it and held it open so the girls could see. In it sat a small, squiggly stack of plastic squares—at first Lilly thought they were individually wrapped candies.

"Ew!" Dar squealed, backing up. "Really, Mel?"

Mel rolled her eyes. "Yes, *really*. We need to be prepared!"

That was when Lilly realized they were not candies, they were condoms.

"Don't you think that's a little premature?" Dar looked like she was about to spit out her last sip of Fireball.

Lilly looked between her two friends. "I thought the plan was to pair off, not . . ."

"What do you think pairing off *involves*? Let's face it, sex is on the horizon. It's probably going to happen for one of us, sooner than we even think. I'm just saying, if we're prepared in advance, then when the opportunity comes along, we'll be sure not to miss it."

A startled feeling settled over the bedroom, like when everyone's been gossiping before the bell rings and then the teacher enters the classroom and they all go silent at once. Sex hadn't been part of the promise. At least not explicitly.

Mel's eyes darted back and forth between Lilly and Dar. If Lilly's expression looked anything like Dar's, she was sure her cheeks were on fire. Dar passed her the flask. She took a sip, letting its sweet spiciness sting her throat, heating up her chest.

Mel put her hands on her hips. "I feel like you guys aren't taking our plan seriously."

A loud clamor in the hallway shattered their condom-induced trance just as Mel's bedroom door burst open. Her brother Jared practically flew through the doorway and landed sprawled on the carpet, laughing.

"Dude!" Mel shouted, hastily stuffing the coin purse under her pillow. "Can you guys stop shoving each other around for a single second? Ever heard of *knocking*?"

Her other brother, John, stood in the doorway. He and Jared were twins and both football players, which sometimes made Lilly's head swim. It was a lot of muscle and maleness at a time in one space. "You look kinda ho-ish in that," he said.

Mel pushed him backward into the hall. "It's brand-new, and it's from Lupine!" She tugged the hem of her dress down with one hand.

Jared got up off the floor. "Well, good luck leaving the house."

All three girls rolled their eyes as they succeeded in kicking the boys back out of the room.

"Just wear a cardigan over the cutouts in the back until we get there," Dar advised.

"You're so lucky you don't have to live with brutes," Mel said to both of them.

Dar shrugged. "Kinda sucks having no one my age around."

Mel threw her arm around Dar. "Boo-hoo. You have us! Right, Lil?"

"Right."

The three of them finished up the last touches on their outfits and grabbed their purses, then Mel carefully doled out one condom each. Lilly tucked hers surreptitiously into the inner pocket of her bag like it was a tracking device or an alarm that might start blaring at random, thinking that maybe Mel was right—they weren't kids anymore.

They managed to bypass the concerned questions of Mel's parents and then, together with her two best friends, Lilly headed out of the Knoxes' house, and into the brisk night.

While the former-abbey section of Devil's Lake High stood regal and gothic against the moonlight, partially enclosing the courtyard, the modern side of the building sat low and squat, half unfinished, surrounded on two sides by parking lots, crawling with tall weeds and a few hunched stoners. Lilly spotted Boyd's pickup as they approached.

She got in line behind Dar, waiting for Mr. Hasenkamp to let them through the front entrance one by one, and clutched her shoulder bag to her chest, praying silently that the condom would not come unloosed from its spot at the bottom of the inside zipper pocket. Behind him, Mr. Green, the Advanced English teacher, held a stack of flyers about appropriate dance behavior—no touching below the waist (yeah, right) and that sort of thing. He was unsuccessfully trying to get everyone to take a copy on their way in. He would learn eventually. He was one of a handful of the younger teachers on staff, along with yes-that's-really-her-name Miss Gay, and Mr. Ruckerford.

"Ugh, ugh, ugh," Mel was saying, shifting from foot to foot. "It's so freezing out here. Why won't they let us *in* already?"

Lilly kept scanning for signs of Boyd, who was usually easy to spot because of his height and his favorite weirdo hunting hat—red and black with floppy ears. He was probably inside already. She didn't exactly have a plan, other than to make sure he noticed her.

This line was taking forever, though. Ever since Katy Delillio had to get her stomach pumped after downing a bottle of Smirnoff at the prom two years ago, the school administration had gotten stricter about checking everybody's bags.

Still, they always found ways. Chuck Brody brought a few water balloons full of rum to the spring dance last year, and rumors had been flying that Adelia Naslow had plans to show up tonight with powdered alcohol she'd ordered online. Apparently you just mixed it with soda, and voilà.

Lilly could still taste the cinnamon burn of their shared whiskey on her tongue, felt it warming her stomach as they entered the building.

"There's your sister," Dar pointed out as soon as they were inside.

Lilly followed her gaze. The standard method of mood lighting for school dances involved putting on just a single fluorescent overhead at each end of the gym, leaving all the rest off.

As a result, everyone danced in the darkest part of the floor—
the center—while the chaperones hung around guarding the
overly lit banquet-style snack tables, where giant bowls of
Doritos were consumed slowly and steadily by grubby-handed
freshmen boys, as though the offensive-smelling chips would
somehow speed up their growth spurts.

Sure enough, across the room, Tessa was lounging on the
indoor risers, wearing ripped jeans and a black tank top, pale
hair piled into a messy bun on top of her head. She seemed to
think it created the illusion she was taller. Nearby were a couple
of junior boys—Greg Heiser, who Lilly recognized as one of
Boyd's friends from band, and some other guy, Nate something,
whose hair frizzed out like he'd stuck his fingers in an electric
socket.

Lilly was overcome with disappointment and annoyance.
First of all, why did Tessa always surround herself with freaks?
Her one job was to show up with Boyd and Kit. And more
importantly, where *was* Boyd?

She'd been imagining a more magical entrance. He'd turn
and see her in the short, silky green dress that showed off her
legs and accented her ginger hair—worn down, of course,
practically reaching her butt. He'd make his way through the
throngs of sweaty dancers and approach, raising his eyebrows,
telling her she looked nice—stammering a little, maybe, to
show that he really meant it, and that she made him nervous.

Instead, he was . . . nowhere.

Jenny Albot and Toma Ramirez showed up, though, talking

about the big game earlier today and how cute Mel's brothers looked on the field, and how hard the world history quiz had been and how amazing everyone looked in their dresses, except for Toma, who was wearing a pantsuit with a plunging V-neck and had therefore surpassed "amazing" and been promoted to "shocking."

Jenny told Lilly that Fred Perovoccio—junior class perv— was staring at her again and Lilly told Dar that yes, Mel's old dress *was* flattering on her and then Toma chimed in to say that Dar was too skinny and Dar rolled her eyes and Mel whisper-shouted something to Jenny that caused her to snarf her punch, which was unsurprising because Mel was always causing people to snarf liquids.

Jenny sidled up to Mel, on the other side of Lilly. "So, where's hottie Donovan?"

Lilly snorted. "I bet he won't even show up."

Mel glared at her before turning to Jenny. "I don't know; I haven't seen him yet."

"Well," Toma chimed in. "You did have to pick the hardest-to-get guy in our grade."

Jenny nodded. "He may not be worth it, Mel."

"*Thank* you!" Lilly shouted. "Finally, someone else sees the light. I've been trying to tell Mel he's a jerk for*ever*."

"He's not a jerk, Lilly. He's just, like . . . tortured. Which is, as you know, my type."

A great song came on and they all forgot about Patrick and instead started screaming and jumping in place with their arms in the air, the bass thumping along the floor and up through their legs, and Jenny's punch splashed on Toma's pantsuit but she shouted that it was okay because it was black, and they were spouting the lyrics now, and Mel was shaking her butt at Lilly and soon everyone was wiggling their butts, and now it was a crowd, and the boys were gathering, and everyone was laughing, and that last shot of Fireball had gone to her head, making Lilly feel just the right amount of warm and fuzzy and soft at the edges, and it was a *dance* finally, the actual act of it and not just the buildup or the letdown but the heart of the thing itself.

Rohan Reddy was behind her, then, wrapping his hands around her waist—not grinding or anything, more like steering her hips as though she were a shopping cart. Even though their kiss last year had been underwhelming, Lilly hadn't ruled him out completely. He was on student council, which meant he must be decently intelligent and well liked. He had really dark hair, light brown skin, and a sharp chin.

He was short, though. Possibly too short.

And he was not Boyd.

He came around to dance beside her, squeezing in between her and Dar.

"Why do you dance like that?" he shouted into her ear after a few minutes.

"Like what?" she asked, still dancing.

Rohan scrunched his eyebrows together. "A parallelogram."

"What?"

He moved closer. "A parallelogram!"

Embarrassed, Lilly pulled her arms in at her sides. Her heart hammered, from dancing, from being talked to by a boy, from wondering whether this was a flirtation or an insult. She remembered their kiss. Sloppy. But heated. Hesitant.

"How does a parallelogram dance?" she shouted.

Rohan paused for a moment, like he was thinking. Which was sort of funny, in the context of all these people dancing around him. "Like you," he answered.

For a second she *thought* he'd said he liked her.

She shrugged. Parallelogram hadn't been what she was going for, even though it was nice to be studied that closely. She looked over at Mel. Dustin Schantz was, sure enough, swaying next to her, doing some sort of goofy arm movement—not geometric at all, more like an octopus. Dusty wasn't cute by standard definitions, but he *was* hilarious, she had to admit.

She caught Mel's eyes, and they both burst out laughing again. Dar took each of their hands and pulled them away from Rohan and Dusty and now they were leaping up and down again, shimmying in a vaguely synchronized way, but for as much fun as Lilly was having, she felt empty inside.

She looked for Boyd's red hunting hat in the crowd—she could swear she had seen a flash of it earlier, but once again she couldn't find any sign of him.

"I gotta pee!" she shouted.

"Want us to come with?" Dar asked. The next song was slower. People were starting to mill about. The circle was breaking up.

"No, it's okay," Lilly said. "Be right back."

Tessa was still at the risers when Lilly made her way there—a larger group had gathered around the top three rows, including Adelia Naslow, who kept fiddling with her bra.

"What's the deal?" Lilly asked Tessa, who was lounging with her legs stretched along the wooden riser.

"Adelia's doling out Pal." She sat up, responding to Lilly's blank expression. "Palcohol. The powdered stuff. It's in little baggies in her bra."

"Is it any good?"

"Of course not, it's disgusting."

"So where's . . ." *Boyd?* "Kit? Didn't she come with you guys?"

Tessa shrugged. "She said she left her Spanish text in the language lab."

Lilly rolled her eyes. "She has to get it *now*?"

"You know Kit," Tessa responded as Greg Heiser flicked her bun and handed her a plastic cup. "Quit it!" She swatted him away but took a sip from the cup, wincing. Turning back to Lilly, she said, "Yup, it's gross. Wanna try?" She paused. "Just don't tell Mom."

Lilly huffed. "Really, Tess?"

"What?" She made an innocent face—eyebrows raised like "What did I say?"

Lilly sighed. "Forget it." As if she was going to tattle on them. There had been that one time, but it was *sixth grade*. And it was only because Tessa got so stoned with kids from her track

94

team that she came home and broke one of their mom's favorite wineglasses trying to get it out of the dishwasher. Their mom said it was fine and Lilly blurted out, "She was smoking the weeds!" Because, yes, she thought that was how you say it. She was *eleven*. Come on. Tessa hadn't even gotten grounded for that long.

In any case, she wasn't interested now in spending more time with Tessa and Team Freaks. "Did Boyd go after her?" Lilly asked, trying to sound subtle, not really curious.

Tessa shrugged. "How should I know? He said he needed air."

"Well I'm gonna go look for her." (*Him.*)

Tessa leaned forward. "Have you noticed it, too?"

"Noticed what?"

"Oh, never mind."

"No, what?"

Tessa shrugged again. "She's just been acting kind of . . . weird. Boyd's been acting funny too. Maybe there's something going around."

"Maybe." This conversation was wriggling through her mind, making her a little nauseous. It was a dance. She was here to flirt and be noticed and maybe something more. She thought again of the condom; she was so conscious of its presence in her bag that it might as well have singed a hole through the fabric.

But now, curiosity had wrapped its grip around her guts and she had to know where Boyd had gone. And where Kit had gone.

And, she thought with a small taste of dread, whether the answer to both questions was the same.

The halls were quiet as she passed rows of abandoned lockers, their silver locks glinting like knuckles in the dim glimmer of emergency lights along the ceiling. Around the bend from B hall into C, the faint thud of the dance music faded. She jiggled the handle to the language lab door. It was locked. Peering in, she could see that the room was dark and empty.

Lilly turned, starting to feel both frustrated and intrigued. She had always been drawn to mysteries—who really *did* eat the last of the strawberry ice cream? Where did the remote control go, and how did it possibly get *there*? Why were so-and-so and so-and-so whispering in the bathroom?

Now her oldest sister and Boyd had both disappeared. . . . Even if the answer was simply that they were raiding the upstairs vending machines, she had to know. However, just as she passed the art classroom and rounded back onto B hall, a suspicious clicking sound interrupted the quiet, and she turned just in time to see, only about twenty feet away, Patrick Donovan, carefully closing a locker door.

She could swear, even from here, that it was locker 172.

Dar's locker.

She froze just as he looked up, locking eyes with her in the darkened hallway. Even in the dim light, his eyes looked sharp and bright. He took a step toward her. The movement sent a jolt of energy through her legs, and suddenly she was turning and running the other way, down toward the stairwell that led to the library, the principal's office, and the exit onto the courtyard. She burst through the double doors into the night, now chilly, carrying a warning, a harshness, and the smell of something fragile, like dried leaves. She had to find her friends—and tell Dar.

"Hey."

She turned. Patrick had followed her out onto the courtyard. He was not as big as Boyd, or as broad shouldered, but he was still pretty tall. The night made him seem less boyish than before, more dangerous. His brow was furrowed.

"What do you want?" she said, keeping her voice steady.

He stared at her. "Nothing."

"Then you should probably not be sneaking into my friend's locker, which is exactly what you were just doing, isn't it?" A breeze lifted the edges of her dress and she shivered.

"No," Patrick answered.

"You're saying you were *not* just opening locker 172 when I came down the hall?"

"I'm saying I wasn't sneaking." He stuffed both hands into his pockets.

"I don't get it," Lilly said, heat rising to her face.

Patrick shifted his weight. "You don't need to."

She stared at him. The moon hit his cheekbones, making his face seem more angular, whiting out his freckles even from only three feet away. He was looking back at her intently, holding her gaze, as though daring her to question his motives further. He seemed so confident in his actions, she began to wonder if maybe she was hallucinating, or if it had become totally normal to break into people's lockers during the school dance.

"Listen." She let out a breath. "I really don't get what your deal is, but just leave me and my friends alone. Okay?"

Maddeningly, he didn't say anything.

She wanted to slap him or shake him or something. For saying she doesn't "need to know" what he was doing in the hall, when Dar was *her* friend and he hardly knew anyone at this school. For refusing to give her a straight answer, about anything, ever. For making her feel like the crazy one, when *he* was the one who had been skulking around in an abandoned hallway doing who knows what.

He stepped toward her again.

This time she didn't bolt.

"You look cold," he said, taking off his jacket and handing it to her.

She stared at it for a second, her arms wrapped around herself to keep warm. Finally she reached out and took it. "Um. Thank you." She put it on. It smelled like cedar, and the lining was warm where it had been against his skin.

They stood there for another minute, just looking at each other.

"I'm going back to the dance," she said at last. She started to back up—just a small step.

He walked forward and reached out for her. His hands were

big and wrapped all the way around the slender part of her wrist. "Don't."

She tried to swallow. "Don't what?" She could see their breath faintly clouding the air, mingling together in between them. She swallowed again. "I have to go," she said. It was practically a whisper.

And just like that, her wrist was cold, where he was no longer touching her. He watched as she turned, and she felt his gaze on her the whole way back to the parking lot, where she was forced to wait in line again to reenter the gym. Part of her hoped, or at least considered, that he might follow her.

She was so distracted by the whole event, she barely registered that Janey Mackenzie was throwing up by the dumpsters. She hardly heard when a new song came on, blasting through the open doors—one of her and Melissa and Dar's favorites. She almost couldn't recall what it was she'd been trying to figure out before—Kit and Boyd, where they'd gone. She was still curious, but the curiosity had dimmed, like a flame wavering, easily blown out. In its smoke hovered Patrick Donovan's face, mysteriously still, handsome and unreadable, stark against the cold October night.

Chapter Nine
BEFORE

DAMMIT. PATRICK WALKED IN A large circle through the courtyard, unable to bring himself to leave the school property. It was a Saturday night and he had nothing to do. Even though dances were a ridiculous, barbaric tradition meant to create a school-sanctioned context in which jerk football players could feel up their girlfriends in public and where girls could put on the kind of shiny, sparkly dresses you normally only saw on TV, and . . . well, he had to admit that he'd never *been* to a school dance, so he was probably basing all of these assumptions on those very TV shows.

But still.

Dammit. He'd let it happen again. He'd been so good, keeping a low profile, staying focused on his goal: save up, work hard, get out of town, start fresh. He had to have a clear plan. He needed funds, he needed wheels, he needed safe passage. Which meant staying focused, saving, scraping by. Not getting distracted by girls with absurdly green eyes and striking hair and unexpected streaks of righteousness.

Should he stay? Should he walk in and, like, ask her to dance? Was that even what people did?

He pivoted instead and looked up at the flagpole that stood at the center of the courtyard, the flag secured at its base for the evening. Its strings flapped ambivalently in the wind.

She wasn't supposed to see him. No one was. He should have explained himself. Now she'd want answers.

She could find out from her friend.

No, she should find out from him.

He resolved to tell her after all. He headed toward the parking lot, where large circles of yellow light pooled around the mostly empty spots, and music from the gymnasium echoed across the blacktop.

But when he saw the clump of classmates hovering outside the entrance, he chickened out.

He couldn't go home like this, though. He was too wound up. He kept thinking about her lips. Her teeth. Other parts of her too—okay, her boobs. Her exposed legs. But also her eyes. Her voice. Definitely her red-blond hair.

Dammit.

He paced, winding back across the courtyard and around the tall, gothic library, ominous in the night. Beyond that lay the football field, idyllic, a series of stars strung up overhead, twinkling. *Actually* twinkling.

There weren't stars in Chicago—not like these.

He kept walking.

He wound down along the clay running tracks, thinking he'd do a loop to cool off. It was brisk out, but his head felt hot.

He had walked about a third of the way around the track when he heard voices—soft but urgent. An argument.

The sound burbled up from beneath the bleachers, and his first instinct was to get out of there before whoever it was realized he was watching. It was probably some couple making out.

He was overwhelmed, suddenly, by the possibilities, by the sheer quantity of alternate realities layered over his own: couples kissing and fighting and breaking up and getting back together. How everyone was the center of their own world. How we were all the star of some story, and we'd never *really* know how anyone else's story ended, only our own. Which meant no one would ever really understand us either. A line came to him from a book he'd read for class last year: *I was within and without, simultaneously enchanted and repelled by the inexhaustible variety of life.* He'd cut it out and stuck it to his wall. Within and without.

The thought made him feel like he was disappearing.

"You don't know what you're talking about!" The girl's voice carried over the wind to where Patrick was standing.

The boy mumbled something in response.

There was a continued back and forth, muffled by the shush of leaves in the breeze.

"Maybe you aren't who I thought," the male voice said.

A form emerged from the shadows. Tall, broad. Patrick recognized him, even in the darkness. That guy—something Taylor. Boyd. Boyd Taylor. A year older than him. Nice enough seeming guy. Very in with the Malloy sisters.

He wondered who the girl was, the one still lurking in the darkness beneath the bleachers.

One of the Malloys? It couldn't be Lilly—he'd just seen her, and she had definitely headed the other way. But possibly one of the other two.

Boyd's form slowly moved aside as he walked, presumably, toward the dance.

Patrick heard the girl—sniffling, he thought now. Crying, maybe.

He should go to her, say something. But what would he say? It wasn't his place to get involved.

Through the bleachers, he noticed movement—blond hair, shockingly bright between the silver slats of seats.

She emerged, but he couldn't tell which one she was.

"Wait," she called out. "Wait for me."

Boyd stopped and turned in the distance.

Neither of them noticed Patrick, but they could have, if they were looking. Once again, he felt invisible. Within and without.

Boyd put his arm around the girl—the Malloy—and they walked back toward the well-lit school, leaving Patrick alone in the darkness of the vast football field.

❈

The wind stung his bare arms as he rode home. He parked the motorcycle and removed his helmet, then entered the house quietly, assuming Liam and Diane would be asleep. He was startled instead to find Liam wandering the downstairs hallway in his pajamas.

"Uncle Liam. Is everything okay?"

His great-uncle stared at him blankly, then shook his head, turning and ambling back to the bedroom.

Later, up in his attic room, lying there in just his boxers, with the covers strewn off the side of the bed, Patrick couldn't sleep. His body throbbed, on fire. He kept thinking again about Lilly. How she looked in that dress. It was only a physical thing, he told himself. Lust. Irrational and meaningless.

The mind was just a pathetic servant to the body. Maybe he'd read that somewhere too.

He rolled over. Picked his jeans up off the floor, reflexively reaching into the front right pocket for the item he'd been carrying around with him for days—the ring. The reminder that he *was* someone. That he would be. The ring was the start of his new life.

It was then that he remembered he'd put the ring in his jacket pocket, and he'd given his jacket to Lilly.

How could he have made such a stupid blunder? He felt bewitched, somehow, like she'd known about the ring, had cast a spell causing him to hand it over, which was of course impossible.

Dammit.

Outside the small window, the stars blinked innocently. He lay back, trying to ignore the clanging in his chest—an *inexhaustible* desire for something he couldn't name . . . or maybe he *could* name it, he just couldn't have it.

Homecoming

BY KATHERINE MALLOY

Sometimes what's in front of us seems so far:
the end zone evasive as a horizon line,

lightning bug—a distant planet—winking in a jar.
I saw you every day, yet you couldn't be mine.

And then it happened: at last I got my chance.
Arriving in a group, we splintered off alone,

to wander the crowd at the high school dance,
celebrating the football team coming home.

We went outside, and you invented some reason
to tell me the story of a girl gone wild,

who, in the poem by Kinnell called "Two Seasons,"
felt "weary of being mute and undefiled."

Pressed up against the bricks, it came: the kiss.
And what I lost then, I never thought I'd miss.

Chapter Ten

NOW

FEBRUARY 7

MOST FAIRY TALES ARE TOLD in threes.

Three parts: beginning, middle, and end.

Three suitors, three wishes, three nights. Three sisters.

A princess waiting to be awakened by a kiss before the end of three full moons.

Old Liam Donovan began to sketch, his dark pencil swishing across the page in a soothing motion. He liked the sound of it: one of the few things that kept his mind and hand steady.

Most people didn't know that the first tales of Sleeping Beauty, the original versions of the story, were violent and strange. He drew an ear.

A maiden, taken in her sleep, only to awaken after birthing

twins, who, desperate and hungry, sucked the poisonous flax from her fingertips and saved her life. A king tormented by her memory—the unconscious lover who haunted him still—muttering "Talia sun and moon" in his sleep.

Liam knew there was something important in all this, but he couldn't name it, couldn't quite organize the instinct into coherence. A television chattered on in another room, like a lost person, mumbling.

He drew. Who was he drawing? The young prince, the one who killed the king, not realizing the king was his true father? Or the girl, waking up alone and dazed, helpless, her fate forever changed by a night she couldn't remember?

He put down the pencil to stretch his hand. Peeled back the metallic lilac wrapping on a chocolate egg. Easter candy, though it was only February. The crocuses had not yet poked up through the soil.

He had a memory—they came to him this way now, fluidly, in the middle of thoughts, interrupting his daily activity, placeless, sometimes formless, distracting. They left him disoriented. An Easter egg hunt. Dublin. The woman with the lovely eyes and teacherly skirt clapping along as he and his university friends performed a skit . . . some old Irish drinking songs, too. The egg hunt had been a tradition at UCD. She was a Polish American girl, traveling on fellowship. She wore a crown of flowers.

"I'm Diane," she'd said.

"Diana, the huntress," he'd replied. The goddess who

became trapped in a tree. No. That was Daphne. Diana was Apollo's twin, not his lover. The virgin who ran after deer under a full moon.

The goddess of birth, who swore never to marry.

Diane had made him forget all about Sarah, his first heartbreak, and the proposal she had rejected.

The ring she'd given back to him—a pale sapphire, like her eyes had been.

He sketched.

There was something else. The princess in the woods. The forest of high brambles that surrounded her sleeping form. The king who couldn't forget her. Her long, beautiful hair.

Sarah. The first cut was always the deepest. *He* was the king who still couldn't forget, the king who muttered her name in his sleep: *Talia, sun and moon.* The king who wanted to save her. Had wanted to make things right.

But the real world was much like the world of early fairy tales—full of violence and strangeness, accidents and lost chances.

He shaded in the dark eyes.

It was late. He must go to bed. Or it was early, he wasn't sure, winter sunlight streaking through the curtain, but he was tired, in need of a nap. He stood up at his desk, lightheaded. It was possible he would fall. He wanted to cry for help, but to whom would he call out? And where would he be taken? Where was he, even now—what kingdom had he entered? He didn't belong here: a scattered old man with wrinkled hands.

A deposed king. Words and names—he used to know so many of them.

He looked at the notebook before him and didn't understand what he had drawn, or why.

The face of a wolf, shadowed and fierce, stared back at him.

PART
TWO

Chapter Eleven

NOW

FEBRUARY 8

THERE'S AN ACRE OR TWO of rangy meadow over by Meetchum's Farm on the outskirts of Devil's Lake, all overgrown with goldenrod. Careful: the occasional corpses of broken rakes and harrows, stained with rust, come underfoot. Locals call it Hammer Head Field, though as far as anyone knows, it never used to have a name, until the story of the girl.

There's rarely a breeze out there—in summers the weeds stretch up, airless, eerily still, like an old painting.

That's where she was found, eight years ago: the girl with the hammer wedged deep into her skull. A shattering. No one seems to remember the girl's name or exact age—she'd been eleven, or nineteen, on one periphery of teenhood or another. But everyone has heard of it. Of her.

There wasn't even any story to it—that's the strangest part, really. It's all punchline: her body had been found like that, in the middle of the field, and the local investigators never figured out who did it. No suspects, no motive. She might have been fleeing a pursuer who knocked her out mid-sprint, or maybe she was dragged there and then done in with purpose, like the bang of a gavel—X marks the spot.

Death had always seemed like that to Tessa: anonymous and abrupt, crude in its specificity. It happened in the open but was smothered in silence, stifling as a hot day in August. It came without any good reason.

Then it walked away and never turned back.

Some people believe there's a heaven. But if there *is* a heaven, Tessa never thought it'd be way up in the clouds or whatever—not if you knew anything at all about space, which is full of rock and fire, chemistry and constant motion . . . not a bunch of human souls floating around carrying their eternal peace like a scratch-off lotto ticket.

No. If there were a heaven, it'd exist in the mist that sat heavy right over Hammer Head Field in late fall, ghost white and damp and stuck revisiting the world we know, coveting the shape of things we once could touch, tracing those long ugly stocks of heather and stitch grass.

Think about it: no one wants to die, except to end great suffering, and even then, rarely. Most of us are never ready to let go. When Tessa's grandmother lay in her sickbed those last weeks of her life, that was what she'd told them, all anxious and childlike: "I'm not ready."

Tessa couldn't forget that look of surprise in her nan's eyes, as if it was all just a misunderstanding, like when someone grabs your order at the Starbucks counter by accident. "Excuse me, but that one was *mine!*"

Except instead of an iced latte, it's your life, your *being alive*. It was supposed to be yours.

But then, one day, it isn't.

Tessa bolted upright in bed. Her clock blinked 5:37. Outside, the dawn had just started to slice the sky from the earth, a silver scalpel line.

The dream still dogged her, dark and panting. It'd started out just her, Kit, and Lilly, as kids, playing in the yard, the sprinkler going, the grass slick and matted.

Then a movement out past the trees. A gray wolf. Low. Mangy. Lurking closer. The girls were screaming then, and Tessa was running. The yard gave way to the nature preserve by Devil's Lake. She turned back, reaching out to Kit, who had always been slower.

Only then Kit *was* the wolf, snarling.

The wolf lunged.

Tessa woke.

Now she felt sick, her sheets slack with sweat.

Kit was dead; Boyd's trial loomed at some indeterminate

point in the near future. And beyond that? A void.

She got up and slipped slow-motion into her jeans. If she thought too much about the future, she'd have to think about how small and meaningless she was, just a particle in the vastness of it all.

The crumpled T-shirt on her floor went over her head.

She'd have to remember how pointless our little lives are.

Hoodie, zipped.

How your life could wink out so suddenly, without anyone watching.

Some books, shoved into a backpack.

How once you were gone, it was all over.

Her phone dinged, the sound puncturing her numb thoughts.

Your sister didn't know when to leave things alone.

Tessa stared.

Unknown number.

Another text followed.

Don't make the same mistake.

A bolt of fear ran through her. *Don't make the same mistake?* It was a threat. Someone wanted to silence her. Someone knew . . . what? Knew she was helping Boyd. Knew more about what had happened that night out at the edge of the woods. Knew, maybe, what had *really* happened to Kit.

Maybe it was the person who had killed her.

Tessa's hands shook so hard she couldn't hold her phone. It slipped onto the lip of her bed, then fell into the tangle of dirty clothes on the floor. There was a ringing in her ears.

No, the phone was ringing, now. She couldn't dig it out

of the blankets. She was so freaked out and disoriented, all she could think was that it was going to wake up the whole house. Who would call at this hour? Was it the killer?

Then she had a worse thought: what if the person was watching her, even now?

She shot up and ran to the window, heaving, her breath tight in her chest. The phone was still ringing. Then there was a banging on her door. She gasped and turned around, just as the door burst open.

Lilly was standing in the doorway.

The phone had stopped ringing by now. Both sisters stared at each other, both breathless.

"You gonna answer that?" Lilly asked. Her voice sounded weak—far.

"Sorry, I just . . ." Tessa sank to the floor, pulling her knees up to her chin. "I had a crazy dream and then the phone was ringing and I was too scared to answer and I dropped the phone and . . . I'm just. I'm really freaking out lately."

In the early gray light, Lilly looked like she had tears in her eyes. "No, Tess, *I'm* the one who's freaking out." She came and sat down next to Tessa, both their backs against the wall beneath the window.

Tessa turned to her sister. She had dark circles under her eyes. Clearly, Lilly wasn't sleeping much either. "You okay?"

Lilly shook her head. "I just feel so alone right now. Ya know?"

"Yeah. I do. I really do. But . . . we still have each other. Right?"

Lilly let out a little sniffle and nodded.

Tessa rubbed her back. She wasn't used to being this nice to Lilly, but, she supposed, a lot changes when your sister dies.

"The funeral was intense," Lilly said softly. "It was surreal."

"Tell me about it," Tessa said.

Lilly laughed a little. "You weren't even *there*."

Tessa sighed. "True, I guess. I couldn't really take it."

"Well, *that's* no surprise."

"What's that supposed to mean?"

Lilly turned to face her. "Oh, come on, Tess. You're the one who likes to turn movies off just before the ending—even happy ones! You can't handle endings. You never could!"

Tessa nudged her with her shoulder. "Well, in this case, Lilly, I really don't think it *is* over yet."

Lilly went pale. "What—what do you mean?"

"I mean, there's more to what happened that night. Out in the woods. Don't you think?" She almost didn't trust her voice to go on, but she pushed through. "Come on, you can't *really* think Boyd did it, right?"

"I *saw* him," Lilly whispered.

"Are you *sure*, though?"

"It was snowing hard," Lilly said, her voice rough, "and it was late. But I could clearly see him. He was outside the truck. He was wearing his favorite hunting hat. They were arguing, and, and . . ."

"Maybe you did see him, then," Tessa replied, pulling herself up by the window ledge, then offering a hand to Lilly.

"But you didn't see what happened after that. You didn't see *everything.*"

"So what did I miss, then? What don't I know?"

How was she supposed to tell Lilly? That *Tessa* was the one who'd kissed him—not that night, but on Wednesday.

Not just that, either: how was she supposed to explain all the crazy shit that had been bubbling up in her for a while, all the stupid, big-eyed lovey-dovey crap she had been planning to tell Boyd, before that night happened. All these feelings that were still there, alive and percolating like little popcorn kernels in her chest, but now they had nowhere to go because the boy who had been her—*their*—best friend for years, the boy who had somehow become her crush, had been arrested in connection with Kit's death.

Tessa stared out the window. The yard was beginning to take shape in the morning light, fuzzy and bright. Streaks of snow still melted into the lawn. "I'm not sure."

They were silent for a moment. "What happened to Patrick Donovan?" Tessa finally asked. "I hear he's been missing since this weekend."

Lilly said nothing.

Tessa turned to face her. "Lilly, do you know?"

She shook her head, looking miserable.

"Is there any reason you'd want to protect Patrick? You can tell me the truth, you know. I'll love you no matter what."

Lilly's eyes got watery. "I've told everything I know. I just—I can't do this alone."

119

Tessa scooched closer and put her head on Lilly's shoulder, breathing in the smell of her freshly washed hair. "You're not alone, Lil."

Lilly sniffled harder. "I gotta finish getting ready for school."

Later, when she looked at her phone, Tessa realized the missed call was not from the anonymous texter. It was from the county jail. It had been Boyd trying to reach her.

VERIZON SERVICE RECORD
FEBRUARY 8, 5:45 AM

— missed call—

VERIZON SERVICE RECORD
FEBRUARY 8, 9:08 AM

Tessa Malloy's iPhone: Boyd? Is it you? They said they put me through but then—

County Jail: I—yeah, it's me. Oh, god. For a second you sounded like—her.

Tessa Malloy's iPhone: [silence] Boyd, I'm scared.

County Jail: I know. But—

Tessa Malloy's iPhone: You don't know, though. Someone knows.

County Jail: Knows what?

Tessa Malloy's iPhone: Knows we've been talking. That I want to help you. They're—they're threatening me to leave it alone. I got this text message, from an anonymous number, and it's really freaking me out.

County Jail: [sound of an inhale] That is so messed up. . . . But . . . but this could be a good thing!

Tessa Malloy's iPhone: How?

County Jail: Don't you see? That's evidence.

Tessa Malloy's iPhone: I found something else, too. Out in the woods, near where your truck was parked. Near where . . . it happened.

County Jail: [silence] What did you find?

Tessa Malloy's iPhone: A ring, Boyd. A really nice, fancy one. It looks like an engagement ring. Who would lose something like that?

County Jail: I have no idea. Someone rich?

Tessa Malloy's iPhone: And then—there's this other detail we haven't talked about. There were pills found near the truck. Did you know about that?

County Jail: Pills? No, what kind?

Tessa Malloy's iPhone: Prescription sedatives.

County Jail: Are we talking, like, roofies?

Tessa Malloy's iPhone: No. I mean, I'm not sure, but I don't think so. There wasn't anything in her bloodstream.

County Jail: [pause, breathing] Still, this is majorly fucked up. [scuffling sound] Tessa, I think—do you remember the homecoming dance? I swear, she was seeing someone in secret. We kind of had a fight about it, but I never found out who it was. Shit, I have to go, but let's try and think back to last semester, what Kit was doing, who she was hanging out with, where she would have gotten those pills. This is all—keep track, okay? This is all evidence, and—I gotta go, but, I just wanted to say one more thing.

Tessa Malloy's iPhone: Yeah?

County Jail: [clearing throat] Thank you. I did love her, you know. All of you. I—

Tessa Malloy's iPhone: Boyd? Boyd?

[dial tone]

Chapter Twelve

BEFORE

10/9

Dear Diary,

I don't know why, okay? I don't know why I didn't just tell Dar about the whole locker incident last night. I guess she's been a little distant lately and I didn't want to stir things up, especially at homecoming, which we'd all been looking forward to since the start of school. Also, those lockers aren't that easy to break into. Patrick would have had to have her combo, and he wouldn't have any reason to know that. So maybe I just saw wrong. Maybe it was a different locker—I wasn't actually close enough to definitely verify that he was standing in front of locker 172.

And by the time I'd returned to the dance, Dar looked

like she was having the time of her life, dancing with Toma. Kit and Boyd were back from wherever they'd gone, and Tessa was saying she was ready to leave. I looked around for Mel and finally spotted her—yup, you guessed it, making out with Dusty.

No one even noticed I was wearing Patrick's jacket. No one asked. I guess there are perks to being fucking invisible 90 percent of the time.

I did notice that Kit's eyes seemed a little red, though it could've just been the funky lighting in the gym. I know if she was sneaking off with Boyd, she's not going to tell me about it. Or maybe she was sneaking off with someone else, and Boyd went to find her. I'll see what I can get out of her, Diary—wish me luck. This is the same Kit who almost lost her hearing in first grade because she didn't tell anyone when she had an ear infection, admitting later that she "didn't want to bother everyone."

If she wants to keep something hidden, she will.

Anyway, I don't know what to do with Patrick's jacket, but I might keep wearing it. Is that bad? It has nothing to do with him, I swear. I just like the jacket. It looks kind of dope on me, actually. And it has this boy smell. . . .

I mean, I'm not going to wear it right now—I'm still in my pajamas and it's Sunday so I don't have to be at Lupine until one p.m. I should probably go back to sleep but all of a sudden I'm starving. I'm gonna go see if Kit's up.

Love ya, Diary. Don't do anything I wouldn't do.

Mmm, this jacket does smell good, though.
Okay, bye for now.

Lilly padded down the carpeted hall in her slippers and knocked on Kit's bedroom door. No response. She nudged it open.

"Morning," Kit said, putting her pen down on the night-stand and closing her notebook on her lap. She was sitting in bed with her knees up and her golden hair disheveled.

"Waffles?" Lilly asked/told.

Kit nodded, all business. "I'll be down in a sec. Go get everything out and put the oven to two hundred, okay?"

"Okay. Hey, Kit?"

"Yeah?"

"Did you leave the dance last night for a bit? I looked around and couldn't find you. Is everything all right?"

Kit looked flushed, and Lilly felt her chest flutter, because maybe that meant she was on to something.

"I'm fine," she said. "I just went outside because it was so stuffy in there, and then Boyd found me and we came back in. I was only gone, like, five minutes."

More like thirty, but okay.

As she turned to leave, Lilly saw Kit turn back to her note-book to jot down a couple more lines of whatever she was writing. That was Kit—always studious, even on a Sunday.

"Waffles," Lilly said loudly, giving a quick bang to Tessa's closed door as she passed it. She didn't bother to stop—Tessa always slept until the last possible second before her shift at the

Deviled Egg, the rundown diner on Main Street where she picked up a few hours on most weekends. And anyway, she always kept her door locked.

A short while later, the batter was whipped, and Lilly was busy picking through the carton of blueberries to stir in only the best ones, while Kit flipped the first waffle in the iron. After a few test waffles, she got the timing just right.

Tessa was miraculously up now, pouring maple syrup into a Pyrex measuring cup to microwave it. Lilly couldn't help but notice she was wearing an outfit that should not have been meant for public viewing—jeans that were too shapeless to be considered boyfriend style and a white thermal top that she'd almost definitely slept in.

The three worked together in a calm silence, passing ingredients in murmured tones. Everyone knew to respect the unspoken rule of Sunday mornings: no loud sounds or sudden movements until the caffeine had been distributed.

Kit flipped the waffle iron one last time and removed the batch that had already been warming in the oven, then opened the iron and popped the final waffle out onto the stack.

Lilly set down plates, forks, and knives. Their mom, who'd run out to get more coffee, returned in a burst of brisk fall air, hair staticky from her scarf, and put on a pot.

Once they were all seated around the table, passing syrup and knifing into their food, their mom took a careful survey of all their faces. "So how was the dance last night?" she asked, trying to appear innocent.

Tessa shrugged.

Kit shrugged.

Lilly shrugged.

Their mom smiled. "In other words, eventful." She took a huge bite of waffle.

"This girl Janey threw up," Lilly offered.

"Lilly," Kit said, dabbing a small pat of butter onto her plate.

Mom grimaced. "Delightful. Did any of you have a date?"

Tessa swallowed a big gulp of coffee and rolled her eyes. "Mom, people don't bring dates to the dance. This isn't the fifties."

Lilly bristled. "*Some* people go with dates."

"*You* didn't," Tessa pointed out calmly.

"Whatever." They ate in silence for a minute. "So, Kit," Lilly said, testing the water. "Tessa says Boyd's been acting weird. I noticed it last night too." Kit chewed and swallowed, staring at her plate. Lilly made her voice casual. "What do you think is his deal?"

Kit looked up. "I think he's . . . I don't know. Being overprotective. Of all of us," she added quickly. "Maybe he's feeling lonely or left out or something."

"Left out?" Tessa repeated. "How could he possibly feel left out? We see him every single day. Left out of what?"

Kit raised her eyebrows and shrugged like she had no idea. It was obvious, of course, that she did. She knew something. Lilly sensed it, and Tessa must've, too.

Well, Lilly was not one to let the subject just up and die. "Maybe he has a crush on someone. What do you guys think?"

Tessa choked on her coffee and Kit looked away. Lilly smiled, pleased.

Kit stood and started clearing their plates. "Who knows what men are thinking?" she replied—as if that was an answer.

"Since when is Boyd a *man*?" Lilly asked, but everyone was now busily moving away from the table, transitioning to clean-up mode.

"Do any of you need rides anywhere, or are you taking Boyd's truck?" their mom asked from the kitchen.

Kit called back, "We really need to get our own car, Mom."

"I like the truck," said Tessa. "I don't think I'd like driving around in some new car."

Kit headed up the stairs but turned over her shoulder to reply. "Well, you wouldn't have to. But *I* wouldn't mind my own wheels."

"Since when?" Lilly asked, finishing loading the dishwasher. But once again, no one responded.

Back in her room, Lilly threw on bright yellow jeans and a bulky cable-knit sweater that showed her midriff, then grabbed Patrick's jacket from where she'd left it on her floor. It still smelled like him, mysterious and familiar at the same time.

"No rest for the weary," Tessa groaned as Lilly hopped into the truck's cab next to her, with Kit behind the wheel. The running joke in their family was that each of their weekend jobs reflected their greatest values: Lilly's—clothes, Tessa's—coffee, and Kit's—caring for others. Regardless, none of them were particularly passionate about working on Sundays, but it was one of those things they'd just gotten used to. Sometimes it bothered Lilly a little, though; how Kit got all this credit for being such a saint, when in fact her "job" was just volunteering. That and applying to colleges. She got all the attention, while Tessa and Lilly were actually helping to support the family. Mom's single income, even as a midlevel administrator at an insurance firm two towns over, was hardly enough to keep them from worrying about bills. But if Lilly had ever admitted this, everyone would probably just say she was spoiled or something.

"Someday won't you guys miss this, though?" Kit said wistfully, staring out the window.

Tessa smirked. "See, I knew you had a soft spot for the truck."

"I don't mean the truck," Kit replied. "Just, this. Us three. Doing our ritual."

Probably, she was talking about college. It seemed so far off still, so theoretical, even though Lilly knew Kit had a stack of printouts on her desk with instructions for the Common App. Instantly, Lilly felt bad for the bitchy thoughts she'd been having. "Thanks for the ride," she said, blowing her sisters a kiss as she stepped out of the truck in front of Lupine.

She found she missed them as soon as they were gone.

Just like Kit had said.

"Good, you're here on time," announced Margaret, the store manager, right as Lilly walked in the door, as if that weren't the case 95 percent of the time. Margaret sipped from her portable university mug. She never ordered from Blue Beard's; she claimed it was overpriced, which was a tad unfair considering how overpriced Lupine was. "I want you to do the windows again," Margaret added.

"Where do I start?" Lilly tried not to sound too excited. Tall and gaunt, with pinched lips and narrow eyes like a fish, Margaret was generally the least emotive person Lilly had ever met. Being assigned windows duty was as close to a compliment as she was going to get, and she'd take it.

"New stuff's in the back."

Lilly dropped her jacket—Patrick's jacket, that is—on the cushioned bench in the employee "lounge," which was really just a tiny room located at the end of the narrow hall in the back. She spent the next twenty minutes sorting through garment bags. One item in particular caught her eye—a lacy bra-and-boy-shorts set that came in three colors: lavender, bright mint, and heather gray. The bra had a tiny silver heart pendant in between the cups that disguised a front clasp. Lilly read once in a magazine that guys loved front-clasp bras.

Once she had finished unpacking, selecting, and pairing, she began to dress the mannequins, carrying along the special pins they used to hold the clothes in place. You had to take apart their torsos and limbs in order to get the outfits on them. They reminded her of life-size Barbie dolls. She had never liked playing Barbies—probably because, since Boyd refused to join in, and though there were plenty of female Barbies to go around, her older sisters always made Lilly be Ken.

In fact, it could be a game of Barbies that first made Lilly fall in love with Boyd. He showed up in their front yard one day when they were playing on the stoop. Lilly was Ken, as usual, and none too happy about it. She'd been around five then, so Boyd must've been six. Boyd came over and kicked the Barbie playhouse over. Tessa leaped up to kick Boyd back while Kit rushed to fix the house and rescue the plastic furniture that had fallen off the side of the front steps.

While their mom put a Band-Aid on Boyd's shin, he'd whispered to Lilly that Ken was the best, because how could you know if he was really Ken or just a spy disguised as Ken?

Thinking back on this moment, Lilly realized it made no sense whatsoever. Boyd had probably just learned what a spy *was*. But still, it became their thing over the years. Like, if he asked what their mom was making for dinner, she'd say, "How do I know you're not just a spy trying to get information about what we eat for dinner?" Or on Halloween, if Lilly dressed up as the Little Mermaid (second grade), he'd say, "How do I know you're not a spy disguised as the Little Mermaid?" It was silly, but she liked it. Maybe she just liked that he was paying attention to her. Or maybe the idea of being a spy excited her, just a little—that Lilly could have some secret no one knew about.

Correction: a secret that *only he knew.*

It took a lot of convincing to get Margaret on board, but finally she agreed, and Lilly was allowed to dress the final mannequin in the bra set. She chose the lavender, then ran back to the employee lounge, tossed Patrick's coat out of the way, and grabbed the floral throw pillow that had been underneath it on the bench. She brought it back and positioned the little pillow under the mannequin's arm.

Margaret raised an eyebrow. Her eyebrows were extremely pointy and sharp looking, like the rest of her.

"It's slumber-party chic," Lilly explained.

"I don't know what slumber parties *you're* having these days."

Lilly rolled her eyes. "It's not literal. It's *fashion*."

"Actually," said Margaret, "it's oversexualizing, infantilizing, and antifeminist. But, whatever. Sex sells. I get it." She went back to reading the paper.

Lilly wondered for the millionth time why Margaret even *had* this job. Couldn't she just go work for, say, the Justice Department, or something else serious like that? Also, did Margaret even *have* sex? This too was a question that often ran through Lilly's mind. Not just about Margaret, but about all adults. It was overwhelming, and slightly disgusting, to look around on the streets at everyone older than you and think, *He's having sex; she's having sex; they're having sex. Even that person, with the hideous facial hair and sandals over socks, is probably having sex, or has at least had it at some point.*

As if on cue, Mel entered the store, with Dar following close at her heels. Lilly waved them over before Margaret could make some sort of Margaret comment.

"I'm so hung over," Dar said, in between taking tiny sips of a green juice from Blue Beard's.

"I told you to get a bagel," Mel said.

Dar shrugged. "Waste of calories."

"Whoa, love these," Mel interrupted, waving a hand toward the table where Lilly had put out a couple of necklaces, some cozy sweaters, and a few other items that all complemented the color palette. Mel fingered a price tag on one of the sweaters, then turned her attention back to Lilly. "So Dar and I were wondering where you went for so long last night."

Lilly hesitated, not numb to the irony that she'd just been quizzing Kit about the very same thing earlier this morning. "I went to look for my sister." Which was true.

"Mmm-hmmm," Mel said, eyeing a necklace now.

"What?"

"Nothing, it's just . . . Toma noticed BND was missing for a while, too."

"Did you tell Toma I like him?" Lilly said, her voice getting a little higher.

"*No*, relax! She just randomly mentioned it, I think."

"And anyway, Toma's super trustworthy," Dar added.

"Well, nothing happened," Lilly said with a sigh.

"Well, I made out with Dusty, since you didn't ask," Mel said.

"I thought you were only planning to kiss him to make Patrick jealous." Lilly blushed when she said his name.

Mel groaned. "Are you guys destined to remain virgins forever? It's so pathetic."

"*You guys?*" Dar asked, chewing on her straw.

Mel rolled her eyes. "I mean, *all* of us. Are *we* destined to sexless futures?" She tossed the necklace back onto the table, and Lilly reached over to adjust it so it was laid out pretty again.

Dar slurped loudly on her green juice. "We're only fifteen. There's still time before we, like, *die*."

"But sophomore year is almost halfway over already!"

"Mel, it's only October. Come on, let's shop." Lilly took them around to pick out a few things to try on.

While they were in the stalls, Dar's phone beeped with a text. She grinned but deleted the text before Mel or Lilly could see it.

"What the fuck, Dar? Was that from a guy?" Mel demanded.

"Chill," Dar said. "It was just Toma asking about the chem lab."

"Then why did you delete it?"

"Because I delete everything, because my mom spies on my phone, just like *some* people I know." Dar slammed her phone into her bag.

Mel ended up selecting two sweaters to buy. Dar got a bracelet that was on sale.

On their way out, Mel hugged Lilly. "Sorry I'm being such a bitch today. I just feel like I never sleep anymore, ya know?"

What? *No*, she didn't know Mel wasn't sleeping. This was something new.

Mel sighed. "I just want something to *happen* already, ya know? At least for one of us."

Lilly swallowed the guilt that had lodged in her throat.

Nothing *had* happened, at least not technically, she reasoned. But Patrick's jacket still burned in the back of her mind.

After her friends left, there was a busy period for about half an hour, and one customer ripped a tank top while trying it on. Then there was a lull, so Lilly dragged out her geometry book and tried to study equilateral triangles. It made her think of how Rohan said she danced like a parallelogram.

Margaret locked up around six p.m., and Lilly put Patrick's coat back on while she waited for her ride.

But Kit didn't come to pick her up.

And by a quarter after, she still hadn't shown. Lilly dialed her number, but it went straight to voicemail. Kit was probably still in a tutoring session. She usually kept her phone off for those.

The breeze picked up. Lilly wrapped Patrick's coat tighter around her and texted Tessa to see if for some reason Kit had picked her up first. **I got done at four and got a ride home with Bridget**, Tessa wrote back. **And Mom went to dinner at the Nestors'.** Then a third text: **just walk back if you don't feel like waiting**.

Lilly groaned. She wouldn't have worn boots with such high heels if she'd known she was going to have to walk a mile and a half! The sun had begun to set and it was getting dark. She should get a move on, but first she decided to grab a warm drink at Blue Beard's before they closed, for the walk home, hoping maybe Kit would show up while she was inside ordering.

She emerged a few minutes later and stopped in her tracks.

Directly across the street, Patrick was standing next to his motorcycle, helmet off, trying to stuff a shopping bag from Bread Basket into the carrying compartment underneath the seat. He lifted his hand, like he was going to wave, or like he was in a classroom and had the answer to a question.

She waved back, feeling awkward. Especially since she was wearing his coat. Had he noticed?

He got on the bike and circled around so he was on her side of the street.

"What are you doing here?" she asked.

"I came to get my jacket back."

"Oh." She blushed.

"I'm kidding. I mean, I do need it back. But I was just . . ." He pointed at the grocery store with his thumb.

She stared at his freckles, trying to think of a response. "Wait, aren't you guys on Kit's delivery route?"

Patrick shrugged. "She didn't come today."

That was weird.

"Not a big deal," he added. "I'm around these days, so I may as well be of use. And I just needed to grab some more, um." He paused for a minute. "Bread."

Another pause.

He raked his hand through his hair. "So what about you?"

"What *about* me?"

"What are you doing here?"

"Oh. I work here. Well, there," she said, gesturing at the now-closed Lupine.

He eyed the display windows.

"I did those," she said.

He stared at the mannequin in the bra and boy shorts like he was thinking, hard. "So how much is that set?" He asked it like he was asking the price on a carton of milk.

She blushed. "A hundred and forty dollars. We just got it in."

He turned to look at her. "Kidding again. I haven't worn a bra in ages."

She snorted, surprised.

He smiled, and she was even more startled. It was the first time she'd seen him smile—at least a real, full one like this.

She cleared her throat. "Anyway, I was just about to walk home. Do you mind if I just give this back to you at school?"

He crinkled his forehead. "Why don't I give you a ride?" A little buzz raced through her. "Then you can give it back to me when I drop you off."

She swallowed. "Okay . . . sure."

She took a big gulp of her hot tea, then tossed the rest into a nearby trash can, trying to pretend like she didn't just buy it five seconds ago for a whopping $3.75.

He propped up the bike and held it while she swung her leg over it. Then he got on in front of her and revved the engine, calling for her to hold on to him. She wanted to laugh, and as he made a sharp turn and sped down the next block, wind blowing her hair straight into her face, she did laugh. She laughed loud and free, wondering if he could hear, and whether she cared.

After directing him to her house, she got off the motorcycle and stood on her front lawn shivering, staring at him. "Um, so."

"So," he repeated.

"I mean, thank you. For the ride. And for this." She handed him his jacket and practically skipped inside. Only, she told herself, because of how cold it was without the jacket on.

It was only much later, after Kit had come home full of profuse apologies and flustered explanations about tutoring, that Lilly realized she had forgotten to notice whether Boyd was watching when she and Patrick pulled up. Forgotten to make him jealous. Forgotten about him entirely.

And then it wasn't until she'd laid out her outfit for school Monday and tucked herself into bed later that night, that she finally thought about Kit's flushed face when she came home forty-five minutes late . . . remembered that Patrick had said she'd skipped her volunteer route . . . and wondered what her sister was hiding.

Chapter Thirteen

NOW

FEBRUARY 8

COLD LIGHT STREAMED THROUGH THE school library windows, mottled and layered in dust. Tessa wondered when the glass had last been cleaned. Everything in Devil's Lake was like this—thick with the neglect that comes with not being noticed.

Around her, other students clacked away on the row of desktop computers, stood in line to check out books, ran the cranky old copying machine over printed homework assignments, or huddled over open textbooks like her. A few had their bulky backpacks on the tables in front of them, slumped onto the bags with eyes closed, using them like pillows.

These were the familiar castaways who hated lunch period as much as Tessa did, ranging from studious to antisocial. They were the shy ones, or the pariahs, or the kids whose parents simply couldn't afford the internet at home, so they had to wait for a clunky old school computer to become available in order to check their email.

She stared at the giant textbook open before her, but the words, like the day itself, had become a blur. She was supposed to be studying bio, but that only reminded her of Boyd. They always studied bio together. It was her favorite subject, and really one of the only ones Boyd had ever been any good at.

But the last time they'd studied together . . . Images of him filtered through her mind: his slightly crooked smile. His slightly too-floppy hair.

The kiss.

She couldn't keep obsessing. She could either choose to believe he was a monster and a liar, or she could choose to take his side and figure out who had really killed Kit—and why.

Tessa took a breath and grabbed a piece of scrap paper. On the back, she made a list of all the clues she had so far.

1. A sapphire ring, lost in the snow.

2. That strange new bra, the one with the charm on it, from the photos.

3. Pills, in a baggie but not in her bloodstream.

4. New tattoo—of a wolf?

5. Boyd was definitely there that night—it was his truck, and he was even wearing his signature hunting hat. Which means Boyd is at least lying about that part.

6. Then again, who sent the mysterious text: "don't make the same mistake"?

7. And where is Patrick Donovan?

All of it terrified her, and none of it added up. None of it seemed like *Kit*. But all of it made her think she didn't know her sister as well as she'd thought.

She shivered. Even though the old vents rattled out dry heat, she couldn't get warm. Hadn't been able to since that night.

She couldn't focus, either. Instead of doing research for her bio paper—the biggest part of their grade for this semester— she'd been looking up what happened to people when they froze to death. She hadn't known that sometimes people pull off their *own* clothes in the advanced stages of hypothermia—their body temperature goes so far down that they actually feel hot.

Could that be what had happened to Kit?

She shivered again and zipped her puffy coat up to her chin. She knew this paper was important—it was going to make up a huge part of her grade, which in turn would be a huge part of her GPA, which would be one of the biggest determining factors in the colleges she could get into. And that college was her ticket out of Devil's Lake.

But she couldn't bring herself to write a word of it.

Up until last weekend, and the muddy days that had followed, Tessa had been really excited by the idea of college. She'd already had in mind the schools she was going to apply to—the ones with the best programs in marine science. There were a few top geneticists she'd already looked up as well, making lists of the schools where they taught. But now all the components of biology that had once interested her—cell regeneration, early life-forms, and the implications for modern technology—just seemed like bad riddles, and the punch line was always the same: in the end we die, so what does it matter?

She closed the book. Folded the scrap paper with her clues and shoved it into her bag. The bell hadn't rung yet, but she needed to get out of this stuffy library.

She pulled mittens over her hands, careful not to snag the shiny ring she'd found in the woods. She'd been wearing it since she found it.

Now she pushed through the heavy doors.

She needed air. Needed to think.

Needed to pull a Chizhevsky.

Another thing that reminded her of Boyd.

Chizhevsky was this Russian scientific theorist known for linking things like the patterns of solar energy with historic wars and revolutions. Examining cosmic phenomena and drawing conclusions about human behavior. Sometimes, since they were both huge dorks, Tessa and Boyd would accuse each other of "pulling a Chizhevsky" when the other tried to win a debate with a totally left-field argument. They also used it to mean drawing unexpected connections.

But instead of space to think, what she got when she stepped out into the snowy courtyard in front of the school's main entrance was instantly accosted—by Melissa Knox, one of Lilly's two best friends.

"Tessa?" Mel looked like she'd seen a ghost. She was shouldering a leather hobo bag bursting with scarves, papers, and books, and held a brown paper bag lunch in her other hand; she dropped it onto the stone steps when she saw Tessa. An apple rolled out, along with a half-eaten sandwich.

She bent down to pick it up and Tessa tried to help.

"Are you okay?" Tessa asked. Which felt backward. Mel wasn't the one whose sister had just been murdered. And yet . . . she looked so shaken. "Where's Lilly? Aren't you two always glued together?"

Mel looked like she was going to cry. "Yeah. Yeah, usually we are. But." She stopped talking and just gaped at her until Tessa began to fear she had, like, a giant booger or someone had entered her into the PEN15 club in her sleep.

"Mel, what? What is it?"

Mel just shook her head. "I can't believe you're here."

Tessa sighed. "Lilly came to school today, so I felt like I had to be here too."

Mel still seemed shaken by something.

"Are you sure you're okay? Do you need to talk or anything?" Tessa didn't know why she was offering. She'd always found Mel a tiny bit annoying—maybe that was just the way you were supposed to feel about your little sister's friends. But she'd hung around their house so often, Tessa couldn't fault her for being upset about everything that had happened.

And somehow, this made it easier—it helped to focus on other people's grief. It kept her from touching her own, though she knew it was there, like a sleeping giant, beneath her feet. If she treaded too fast or too loudly, she'd wake it up. It would come after her, wouldn't rest until she'd been crushed.

Mel looked around, as if to make sure no one was listening. But of course, it was freezing out and no one else was hanging around outside except for a couple stoners coming back from the senior parking lot.

"Not here," Mel said anyway, and gestured for Tessa to follow her.

She'd always had a flare for drama.

They walked past the front offices and around the corner, toward the football field. Mel led her straight to the bleachers, and Tessa was struck by a memory.

It was last year, and she and Boyd had been in the same gym class. While the rest of the class ran the mile—four laps around the track—they would run the first half of the first lap, then duck behind the bleachers to hang out and talk for a few minutes before running the second half of the lap just as everyone else was making their fourth round. Coach never paid enough attention to notice they'd only gone one lap.

Now, under the shadow of the bleachers, Mel's eyes looked sinister.

"Okay, so what did you want to talk about?" Tessa asked softly.

Mel was breathing hard, her breath dancing and foggy in the cold air. She fidgeted with her bag. "I just . . . I wanted to say I'm sorry. About Kit . . . and everything that happened."

Sorry. Sorry? Tessa was sick of sorries. Sick of pity and apologies and inedible casseroles and haunted dreams and all the not-knowing. She didn't want sorry. She wanted answers.

"That's it? That's why we came all the way out here?" she asked.

"No, that's not the only reason. I'm . . . I'm scared, Tessa."

She did look scared. And suddenly Tessa was consumed by a wave of misgiving. What did *Mel* have to be scared of?

"Has someone threatened you?"

Mel looked away.

"Mel, do you know anything about what happened to Kit?" She thought of something. "Have you gotten any strange or creepy text messages? Any warnings or anything like that?"

"What?" Mel whipped her head back to face Tessa. "No. I—no. It's just . . . I don't believe Boyd did it. He's not a killer. I'm worried it could be someone else."

"Who, Mel?"

But she just shook her head.

"Do you know someone who wanted to hurt Kit?" Her heart felt like it was going to break out through the wall of her rib cage.

"No!" Mel said, looking more panicked than ever. "That's not what I'm saying."

"Then what *are* you saying?" Tessa was getting frustrated. It was hard to think. Hard to follow what Mel was talking about.

Mel began to tear up. "I just don't want anyone else to get hurt."

Tessa tried to calm her breathing. "I don't either."

"Just—just watch out for Lilly, okay, Tessa?"

"Lilly? Is she in danger too?" Tessa wanted to grab Mel and shake answers out of her, but the girl already looked miserable. And she was usually so bubbly and loud, it was disturbing to see her like this. Still, right now what mattered more was finding out what she knew. "Does this have to do with Patrick? I know you and Lilly were spending time with Patrick before he went missing."

"No, no, no," Mel said. "I don't think so. I think Lilly's okay. I don't know anything about Patrick disappearing. I just—I just think she needs you. That's all. It's too much for her. It's all just too much."

"Okay," Tessa said slowly. "I'll watch out for Lilly."

For some reason, this made Mel cry again, harder this time. "Thank you, Tessa," she whispered. And then, "I am so, so sorry." Then she hugged her.

Tessa felt Mel's arms around her, and for a second just stood there. Finally she hugged Mel back. The more Mel cried, the more Tessa felt the impossibility of her own tears. It was like they were locked away somewhere, behind a dam. If the dam broke, she might drown. But for now, it held.

Suddenly Mel pulled away. "Someone's coming," she said. There were two figures in the distance, making their way toward them. "I—I gotta get to class."

"Okay." Tessa watched Mel wipe away her tears, and then, while she was still standing there, pull out a compact and begin to correct her makeup. Lip gloss and a few dabs to clean up the puddled eyeliner.

Mel took a deep breath and started to walk toward the edge of the bleachers. Then she turned around. "And Tessa?"

"What?"

"Um, nothing."

"Bye, Mel," Tessa said. She stood there for a while after Mel had gone. Confused. Disturbed. Frozen. From out here, you couldn't hear the bell ring, so she was most likely missing her next class. But did it matter?

The snowy grass beneath the bleachers was damp and littered with old popcorn cartons and cigarette butts. She kicked at a Parliament carton half buried in snow. There was still an unsmoked cigarette inside it, rattling around, half soggy, forgotten. She bent down to pick it up; wondered whether it would still light, if you tried, or whether it was just a corpse now.

Maybe Kit was a secret smoker, she suddenly thought.

There were certainly plenty of other secrets surrounding her sister. She couldn't remember when it had first begun— sometime this fall. Maybe at homecoming, when she'd gone missing from the dance for a while. Or maybe it was Halloween, when she'd decided to go to Jay Kolbry's party. Or maybe, maybe, she had been changing for a long time, right in front of their eyes, and none of them had seen it happening.

Tessa crouched there long enough for the two people who had been approaching the bleachers to actually arrive, and she listened as they climbed up onto them, sitting somewhere over Tessa's head.

She looked up through the slats and could make out the fashionably jeaned legs of Olivia Khan, next to the muddy boots of her boyfriend, Jay Kolbry. For a second, she thought they were going to make out, and she started to sneak away, but she realized they were arguing about some party, it sounded like. Jay's parents were taking an anniversary trip for Valentine's Day weekend, and he was having a bunch of people over Saturday. Olivia was pissed because she thought *they* were going to have a romantic night, but now there were just going to be a bunch of sweaty heathens all around the house and they'd have no privacy. Jay made a bunch of sloppy, gross assurances that they'd still get their private time, and disgusted, Tessa finally got movement back to her muscles and snuck away, hoping they hadn't seen her eavesdropping.

Not that she really cared, because she was buzzing. She'd had a bit of a Chizhevsky, just now.

Jay Kolbry was a drug dealer; at least that's what everyone said. And he was having a party on Saturday.

This past October, Kit had gone to one of Jay's parties.

Kit had been found with drugs in her possession.

And now Tessa knew how she was going to be spending *her* Saturday.

She was going to that party.

THE FALL

BY KATHERINE MALLOY

When autumn leaves turn red, do they recall
their former green? And is it bravery

if they have always known they're going to fall?

How they come down, all thin and papery—

shaped like hearts.
The gutter's as crimson now

as stop signs, danger, bloodied hands. I'd lie
if I said I wasn't terrified by how
it must have felt the day my father died:

he lost his own to save another's life.
Sometimes Mom says she can still feel his pain,

lingering, a phantom limb. What kind of bargained strife
is love? When it's gone, what memories remain?

As winter weaves its way into the air,

leaves spread the red of warning everywhere.

Chapter Fourteen

BEFORE

10/29

Dear Diary,

Where. Do I. Even. Start.

So, tonight is the night of Allison Riley's big Halloween party. And it was a somewhat great, somewhat horrible, mostly super-confusing night. I'm so exhausted I kind of want to bury myself in the covers forever and ever, but I wanted to write this down first so that later maybe I can make sense of it.

I'll start at the beginning. I was wearing a banging costume—this slinky gold-sequined dress I ordered online. It stretches tight across my butt and legs, and has a plunging back, which makes it impossible to wear a bra. Black stilettos that killed my feet but whatever. Slicked-back hair. False eyelashes.

And the final touch: a pair of thick, black, no-prescription horn-rimmed glasses.

When I came downstairs, Boyd was already here, sitting on the couch with Tessa and Kit on either side. Tessa was lying sideways, head on the armrest and feet on Boyd's lap, with a blanket over her. Kit was reading near the lamp—she had on a fitted black skirt suit and white button-down shirt, her hair in soft pin curls.

Mom was there too, of course, her feet folded under her butt on the recliner with a bowl of popcorn. It's her tradition to watch scary movies while she waits for trick-or-treaters. It used to be my tradition with her, while Tessa and Kit made the neighborhood rounds. But that was a long time ago.

There was a huge bowl of Reese's and Kit Kats near the door which I obviously grabbed a few of.

The first thing Boyd says when he sees me is "Whoa." Which I took as a compliment ☺.

Then Tessa has to add: "Your sparkles are blinding me."

"Are you a waiter?" I asked Kit, but she got all smirky and said only: "Edna St. Vincent Millay." At the time I had literally no idea what she'd just said other than a series of names, but I looked it up on my phone just now and I guess she was a poet. Anyway, Kit looked mostly like she was about to go into an interview.

"So are we going or what?" I asked, mostly because I could barely stand in those heels but also I could not really sit in that dress.

Mom says, "Honey, don't you think you'll get cold?" And Tessa says, "Or mistaken for a street worker?" But for once Mom took my side and told Tessa to shut it.

Anyway, Boyd was ready to go and extricated himself from Tessa's legs. "Miss Cranky isn't coming," he said, mussing up Tessa's hair.

"My costume is Girl with a Fever," Tessa said. Ever the clever one.

"Okay, so Kit, get your butt up," I said, but Kit just blushes and then blurts out, "Oh, actually I'm going to Jay Kolbry's thing tonight instead."

Jay. Kolbry.

Like, what? I'm standing there basically choking on a peanut butter cup.

I know who Jay is because Mel's older brothers are friends with him. He seems nice enough honestly, but Kit is not one to hang in that kind of crowd, so my brain was having a hard time processing.

I guess I blurted out something along those lines, and Kit gets all defensive and is like "I'm meeting friends there" and "It's fine" and "I won't be out that late anyway" and blah blah.

But I have to admit, I was more excited than disappointed or shocked. I literally can't remember the last time I was alone with Boyd. I mean, not that we were going to be alone for long, since Mel and Dar were already probably at Allison's, waiting for us to show up, but still.

Once we're in the truck, Boyd turns to me and is all "I get what you are. A Bond girl."

Basically, my brain turned into a raging fire alarm of happiness until he followed up by being like "Aren't those movies sexist, though?"

I sighed. "You sound like Tessa."

"Well, she's probably the one who told me that."

"So what are you?" I finally asked. He was just wearing regular clothes—jeans and a T-shirt.

"Same thing," he says.

"A Bond girl?"

"No, a spy."

"Cop-out."

"Well, since you didn't guess it, I think that makes me pretty successful."

Much as I was enjoying our little chat, I knew we had limited time in the car together, so I asked him if Kit is mad at him about something. Maybe something that happened at homecoming . . .

He just goes, "I wouldn't rule it out." Then he said something about how I'm adorable when I'm annoyed, and I said, "Thanks, I know," and then we were there.

So, there's one semirich area outside of Devil's Lake— heavily wooded, hard to get to, where you can't see any of the houses from the next one over. Allison Riley lives out there, in one of these McMansions that I swear is built entirely of stone like a fucking fake castle.

I love it and want to move in there. (They probably wouldn't even notice an extra person living under that roof.)

Also, Allison's parties are way better than Jay Kolbry's. Hers are always sort of classy and have themes and stuff, like cheese trays with witty labels. There was a basket of masquerade masks by the door, and I forced Boyd to wear one to act like a goddamn participator. (Participant? Whatever.) He just kind of wore it high on his head like a headband, making his hair splay out all funny. Then he goes to get us drinks while I go to find Mel and Dar.

The girls are shivering out in the backyard, which is where Mel texted me they were. I finally found them on the stone patio. (It's stone everything there. There's even a stone fire pit—like, do they hunt and cook their food? Have we entered medieval times?)

Mel was a sexy nurse (short white uniform, a red cross made out of tape, a little white cap). Dar wore this pale blue slip that hung loose around her collarbones, and a bright blue wig. SUPER EGO was written in Sharpie on the front of the slip. "Do you like? It's a Freudian slip!" she says. There are goose bumps all over her arms, so I start rubbing her arms to warm her up, and Mel starts laughing and she's obviously already been pounding the punch. It was something with champagne in it. (Fancy.) Mel's lips were all red from it and Dar's like, "It's amaaaazing," which makes me think she got a head start with it, too.

"So why the wig?" I asked Dar, because I vaguely have

heard of Freud and I'm not sure he ever said anything about blue hair, but she just sways and goes, "'Cause it's Halloween so I felt like having blue hairrrr."

Okay, so yeah, definitely both of them were already tipsy.

I told them my sisters didn't come so it was just me and Boyd, and Mel is suddenly all about us finding Boyd so I can tell him he's my one true love or something, and plus it's warmer inside, so back in we go.

Boyd was in the kitchen, and when I got in there, he grabbed my hand and twirled me around and then the four of us danced in the dining room for a while—all the furniture was pushed to the side and the room was decorated like a bat cave with very lifelike bats hanging from the sealing (ceiling?) and black lights along the floor. The Rileys are hella committed to Halloween.

Greg Heiser, who I know mostly from the fact that he hangs out with Tessa and Boyd, started dancing with us. He was wearing a spice rack with a bra on it. ("Don't I have a nice rack?" Ugh. Seriously, Greg?) Dusty showed up too, and I think he was dressed as Einstein.

What. Does. Mel. See. in him.

After a while we ended up in some other room—there are too many rooms in that house, I seriously cannot keep track of what any of them are for. Jenny, Toma, Will Ferguson, Jeremy Bantolf, and a few other people were in there. I looked around for Patrick, on instinct. So I could warn Mel if he was gonna be here. But I didn't see him. (Which, why would he

be here, since he seems to have made practically no friends?)
Anyway, they were playing spin the bottle and somehow Toma
and Dar ended up kissing and Dar laughed like crazy after.
Then Dusty and Mel started going at it (I don't even think
her bottle pointed at him, but fine). Everyone got bored and
the game broke up.

Then Boyd is whispering something to me, but it was
so loud I'm screaming "What?" And he's like, "DUTY
CALLS" and holds out his hand, so I take it and he pulls
me to standing and we trip out of the room. By this point the
champagne red stuff had gone to my head, I think, because
next thing I know, we're running around Allison Riley's mansion giggling and getting lost. "We need to do some recon,"
he's saying. We end up in this room that I think must be
a library. Allison's mom is a famous professor of something.
Anyway it's a giant, gorgeous room with a skylight.

"Rumor has it Mr. Riley has a $700 bottle of scotch hid-
den in the house," Boyd tells me. "We gotta try it."

I obviously don't even like scotch, but Boyd makes the
valid point that how often do you get a chance to taste anything that's $700, to which I wittily reply, "Let's just lick this
couch, then. It probably costs way more than that."

Boyd dared me to do it, Diary. So yes, I licked Allison
Riley's mother's couch. It tasted like polyurethane.

Then we went upstairs and "slyly" tiptoed around, trying
not to laugh or fall over. Boyd made his hands into a gun shape
and approached a closed door like a cop in a movie about to

make a bust. Then he kicked the door open—but nothing was in there except a mini grand piano, facing some windows that overlook the driveway.

"Who the hell has a piano room?" Boyd asks. To which we both answer at the same time: "Allison Riley."

We have some more banter, along the lines of:

"If I were her dad I would probably keep it somewhere close to me, like my nightstand."

"Unless he's sneaky and keeps it hidden in plain sight, somewhere you'd least expect it. Like the shower or something."

"You're crazy."

"You love it."

"Let's try another room."

We "busted" a couple of closets and then a giant corner bedroom that had to be Allison's, but it looked more like a grown-up room than a teen's room. The only clue was the lineup of vampire novels, the framed, signed poster from a TV show about a family of seventeen teenagers, and a giant stuffed bear. Other than that it was all this fancy matching modern furniture, nothing like the mismatched crap we have at home. Tessa doesn't even have a bed frame, just a mattress on the floor, and her nightstand is a sideways crate. And Kit's old assemble-it-yourself bedroom set looks like it should belong to a little kid; its cheap white wood is covered in stickers and pictures.

"Damn," Boyd said as we stood there gaping. "Can you imagine what it would be like to live like this?"

I went over to the giant, beautiful white polar bear that sat on the slate-gray bedspread, flopped down, and wrapped my arms around it. "Mel would love this," I told him.

Boyd plopped down next to me. "Lemme see that thing."

"No, he's mine!" I said, and then we were sort of wrestling, which was kind of silly but also kind of extremely sexy until all of a sudden the door burst open.

It was Fred.

Yes, Diary. Fred Perovoccio.

He was wearing a pirate costume, but it did little to hide his natural state of perverted asshole. There was a drunk girl under his arm who I dimly recognized, but I don't know her name. She's definitely not in his grade, though. I think she's a freshman. She was wearing these wilted-looking fairy wings.

Boyd shot up and was like, "Oh, don't worry, we weren't busy blah blah blah blah blah run-on sentence blah."

But then Fred just goes, "Hey, man, I don't blame you," and then he eyes me like I'm the Tuesday meatball special, which makes me want to barf, though it could also be all the champagne punch. I think he said something like, "She's hot" and the Drunk Fairy hit him in the chest all like, "Heyyyy!" and then he's like, "You're hot too," and clearly he didn't even know her name and EW EW EW.

"Hey, man, don't make comments about my friend," Boyd said, getting a little bit in Fred's face. Then he turns and is like, "Come on," and we push our way out of there, but then Boyd turned around and is like, "You know what? I'm not letting you take her in there either," and guides Drunk

Fairy along the hall with us, even as Fred just stands there being like, "Dude, what the fuck!?" on repeat.

Drunk Fairy then keeps looking at Boyd like he is her hero as he gets her some water, and I looked over my shoulder to see Fred smirking at us, holding his pirate's hat in his hand.

We got her back down the stairs and spent forever trying to find her friends so she could get a ride home and felt like fucking heroes. If I've learned one thing tonight, it's that fairies and pirates and punch do not mix.

But, Diary, this is not even the most dramatic part of the night. Hang on to your pages, we're about to get there, I just need to stretch my hand. This is the most I've ever written in here!

So. Okay.

Once we got the girl's dad to come pick her up, I finally realized that Boyd was not tipsy like me but was in fact completely sober. Which was sort of a relief, but then I was a little bit embarrassed at how I was behaving. I swear I saw him with a cup of beer at one point but never actually saw him sip from it.

I guess because of his dad, you know. He doesn't really like to drink.

Which means the whole "Let's find the fancy scotch" thing was mostly just a ruse to do something silly. Or maybe. Maybe. To be alone with me? At least, you can see how THAT IS NATURALLY WHAT I WOULD HAVE THOUGHT.

But moving on.

I ended up in the bathroom line, and Boyd was right there next to me, and I finally saw Mel and Dusty again. Making out. Again. Heavily. Against a wall.

Can I simply never escape the fate of watching these two go at it?

Mel goes, "Oh, hey," and I am more in the vein of "Yo, can we talk for a sec?

"It seems like you like Dusty again," I told her as soon as we were out of the hearing range of the rest of the line. (Boyd held my spot.)

Mel was busy shrugging, and her eyes darted around in a way that kind of disturbed me, so I pushed on it a little harder. "What about Patrick?" And Mel goes, "Oh, him. Not into him anymore." Just like that.

I'm not sure why this made me so annoyed. Then I got even more pissed off when she adds, "He's just a creep and I think I just liked the idea of him—new boy, hard to get."

"He's NOT a creep." Don't ask me why I was suddenly all defensive about Patrick, it's just she doesn't even know him. I mean, not that I do either. Not really. But I guess I was just sick of the fact that Mel pushes me around, you know? First, it's all about how I have to help her get with Patrick, and now I'm just supposed to drop it after I've already embarrassed myself with him. And it's more than that—she never used to be this sex-crazed maniac. I feel like sometimes I look at her and I don't see Mel anymore, I see this person wearing a mask.

161

Not a literal mask—like I said, she was wearing a nurse costume. But you know what I mean.

And her eyes wouldn't focus. I don't know what's up with that.

The irony is, Mel then ends up being the one to calm me down, saying she just wants all of us to be happy and live it up because life is so fucked up and we should just be having fun. Once again, it felt like some fake person making a speech and not really Mel. But by that point she was grabbing my hands and trying to dance with me, right there in the hall, and act like everything was fine, and maybe it was all fine, maybe I was just being crazy, I don't know.

After a minute we both realized we had no idea where Dar was. Mel starts saying maybe Dar has a secret boyfriend and I didn't want to get annoyed with Mel all over again, but luckily we were interrupted by a bit of a commotion. This guy was banging loudly on the bathroom door and the reason the line was so long was that no one had come out of there for a while. A few people were laughing and shouting and the music was loud and Mel kept saying she was going to pee her pants. There had to be another bathroom or twelve somewhere in this vast mansion, and I was about to suggest we go find one, but...

That's when I saw it.

The blue wig.

There on the floor outside the bathroom door.

In about four seconds I was up against the door, shouting

through it, asking Dar if she was in there and if she was okay, but I couldn't hear anything because the hall was so damn loud. So I turned to the hero of the hour—Boyd. I grabbed his hand and tried to pull him out of the hall. "Dar's locked in there," I told him.

But before we could get anywhere, Fred is swaggering around in front of us. He says, "You sophomore sluts are ruining this party."

And that was when Boyd shoved him. Backward, into a wall. Then there were a bunch of people shouting, "Hey, watch it!" and "Whoa!" and stuff like that, and Fred sneers, "Just 'cause you can't get any Malloy pussy doesn't mean I can't get some."

And then Boyd reared back and punched Fred in the face.
!!!!!!!!!!!!!!!!!!!!!!!!!!!!!!!!!!

Now everyone was screaming, "Fight!" and Boyd kept apologizing and it was kind of scary because I'd never seen him so out of control before, but I yanked him out of there.

I was like, "Come on, we need to rescue Dar."

After racing outside and around the house, we finally found where the bathroom was located, and I made Boyd hoist me up. Within a second, I was able to see into the window, and after some wobbling around, I got the window open.

Dar was in there, all right. She was hunched on the floor.

I almost fell into the bushes but finally got inside. Definitely tore up the dress but oh, well. Clearly it was not designed for actual spying activities. I banged my elbow pretty hard on the counter as I fell onto the bathroom floor next to Dar. It is probably going to bruise.

Dar looked up. She seemed half awake, with dark rings of runny makeup around her eyes, her pale blue slip, well, slipping off, and her blond hair in a gross tangle from having been pinned up underneath the wig.

There was barf in the toilet.

Gagging, I flushed and helped her to sit up. I was just relieved she wasn't passed out. You can choke like that. I ran some water over a washcloth and wiped her face and hands, but she was shaking pretty hard. She seemed so cold and so brittle, like her bones could snap.

Finally I unlocked the door and got her out.

On the other side, Mel was waiting, demanding to know what happened, what happened. But Dar was just shaking her head, sniffling and crying.

Mel says the strangest thing, then. "We should have gone to Kolbry's party." As if she's friends with Jay Kolbry! As if it has literally anything to do with what's going on with Dar.

But I didn't have time to ask her why she was being so weird, because then Boyd showed up and picked Dar up like she weighed nothing, which she probably does. Mel said Dusty could drive her home, so we just focused on getting Dar into the pickup truck.

Her mom was a mess when we showed up at Dar's house—in her pajamas and all worried and shocked. I felt really bad. I mean, more bad for Dar, but also bad for her mom.

Afterward, we were too wound up to just come home, so Boyd suggested we hit the quick mart for some snacks. My stomach felt all twisted up about everything, so I wasn't sure what to do, I just went along with it. We showed up and sat in the truck in the parking lot for a while and it got really quiet.

Boyd killed the engine and turned to me and suddenly he sounded all serious. "So. Lilly. What do you want?"

It felt weird—like he wasn't just asking about the snacks.

"What do you want?" I asked, because, stalling like hell.

He rubbed his face like Mom sometimes does when she's exhausted, and I could see his right knuckles were all bruised from contact with Fred the pervy pirate's face. Finally he said, "I'm trying to decide."

The thing is, that was exactly how I felt too. Trying to decide. Do I still like him? Do I want him to kiss me? Does he maybe like me? Was that why we had so much fun running around at Allison Riley's? Or was Boyd just being Boyd? And there were still answers I didn't have, like what happened at homecoming. I think I got so nervous my fingertips went numb. I swear he leaned closer, so I did too, and then I did this super-embarrassing thing where I closed my eyes and waited.

Nothing happened.

I heard the truck door opening, and peeled open my eyes.

"Well, you can nap in here if you want," he said, "but I'm in need of a frozen burrito."

"Boyd—wait." I grabbed his hand, which was super weird just then. I dropped it. He was already halfway out of the truck. "You have to tell me something."

"*Okay.*" *He just stood there, the orange light of the parking lot morphing his face into angles and shadows like a jack-o'-lantern, except more attractive than that.*

And then I asked him. "Do you have a crush on my sister?" I needed to know. If that was why he and Kit were alone together that night. If that was why Kit had been so secretive and everything lately.

He paused, and I was worried I did something really wrong, but then he got a little red—which was hard to tell in the orange street lights—and squinted into the distance. "Yeah." He said it so quietly I almost wasn't sure. Then he turned toward me again and was like, "Promise not to tell Tessa or Kit what happened tonight." He rubbed his knuckles.

So I promised I wouldn't tell them anything.

But, Diary, I never said I wouldn't write it down.

Chapter Fifteen
BEFORE

THE HALLOWEEN PARTY AT Jay Kolbry's.

Patrick had gone hoping she'd be there. But she wasn't. She had mentioned a party. It was the only party he knew about. But either she'd lied, or changed her mind, or he'd gotten the wrong party, or maybe some combination of all three. There'd been a ton of drunk aspiring frat guys, and girls in too much glitter, fangs and wings and all that crap, a roiling sea of sweat and costumes and sticky beer-covered floors, and that constant feeling of being jostled between one person's shoulder and another's elbow, occasionally getting whipped in the face by some girl's long hair.

It's a way of being: in between. Not moving of your own accord, just letting the tides of all the oblivious assholes—no, not assholes, *people* . . . people who just don't care because they have their own shit to worry about—letting them push you along, determining your path for you.

She wasn't there.

Not that he wanted her to think he was stalking her or anything. But he'd been hoping to see her. And he needed that ring back.

At school, during the week after homecoming, he'd gone up to her about the jacket, asking if she'd happened to find anything in the pockets. She'd shaken her head and said no. He'd believed her, but became more and more distraught the more he thought about it. The ring had *definitely* been in the top right breast pocket of the jacket when he lent it to her. Had she lost it? Or discovered it and decided to keep it for herself?

So he was no closer to knowing what had happened to the ring, and on top of it, his head ached, even though he'd only drunk about a third of a beer at Kolbry's—just enough to taste it.

It was Sunday now, and Patrick raked his hand through his hair, trying to focus on the AP U.S. History book open in front of him. It would help if he was actually *taking* APUSH, but that would mean caring. That would mean college credits, and really, what was the point of college credits if you had no plan to go?

His attic room felt simultaneously drafty and too small, both confined and exposed. October wind rattled the barely insulated windowpane.

He shouldn't have had that beer at Jay's before leaving, feeling more alone than ever. He'd worn a stupid, embarrassing skeleton costume he'd paid twelve dollars for at the drugstore. Now it was lying crumpled on the floor at the end of the bed. Everything about this moment in his life was stupid and embarrassing, including that hungry, big nothingness consuming him from the inside—the vague, lurking suspicion that he existed nowhere and belonged nowhere.

The only thing he had to hold on to was his plan.

The only thing he had was escape.

He needed the goddamn ring.

If he hadn't been such a sentimental loser, he would have already gone through with it, instead of carrying the thing around in his pocket for weeks, mulling it all over.

And then, of course, there was the problem of the sister.

A bell chimed overhead, and Patrick was hit with a pungent wave of sweet, musky, flowery smells. If he'd felt a bit like a creep the time she caught him in the school halls during the dance, he felt even more out of place now, in the bright-lit doorway of Lupine, where some sort of trendy Top 40 song was playing just slightly too loudly and a couple sets of preteen girls were vigorously moving clothing around on racks like their lives depended on it.

"Can I help you?" a sharp-featured woman behind the counter asked. She looked like she was biting the inside of her mouth, like she thought his walking into this store was a strike against him.

"I'm looking for someone. Lilly?"

The woman rolled her eyes. "She's helping a customer." She nodded toward the back of the store, then went back to the book she was reading.

Head down, hands in his pockets, Patrick pushed his way determinedly past a display table and a few racks of sparkly stuff, and halted when he saw Lilly, her red hair tied in a messy bun on top of her head, talking to a younger girl about a pair of jeans.

"That's the point," she was saying, her face very serious. "The pockets are supposed to accentuate your butt. It's an optical illusion."

The comment threw him off so much, he accidentally laughed.

Lilly looked up and blushed. "Oh. Hey. Can I, um, help you . . . with something? Or something?"

Yes. No. Maybe. "Or something."

The younger girl who was trying on the jeans looked from Lilly to Patrick and then back to Lilly, before turning around and retreating to her dressing room with raised eyebrows.

Patrick briefly wondered if he'd stepped into some sort of all-female cult lair. Did they practice human sacrifice in a back room? It was possible. At the very least, goats.

Since this deeply awkward silence could in fact be the first step in preparing the victim for the altar, he cleared his throat and added, "I've just been thinking that my butt isn't getting enough attention lately. I was wondering if you could, like, help

out with that. Work some sort of optical illusion on me, perhaps." *Stop talking. Enough is enough already. Jesus Christ.*

To his slightly mortification-reducing surprise, she laughed.
"I'm sure your butt is just fine, if underrecognized by the
masses." She blushed . . . *again.* "I mean, I'm sure it's normal. I
mean, um—"

"Okay, I get it. I can live in butt obscurity for the rest of
my life."

"Ew," said the girl who had been trying on jeans and was
now standing outside her dressing room in street clothes, holding the jeans in her hands. "I still think they're too big," she
said, handing the pair to Lilly. "And you," she said, turning to
Patrick, "have a cute ass."

She walked away and Patrick nearly choked on his own
saliva. "Did I just get hit on by a twelve-year-old?"

Lilly shrugged. "Kids these days."

"I know, right?" This was stupid. What the hell was he
doing here? Why did he come? "So, um, you weren't at Jay's.
Last night. Kolbry. He had a . . . I thought maybe you . . . anyway, but you weren't." Since when had he completely lost any
capacity for the English language?

"My sister was there," she said.

"Oh. I didn't see her there."

"I went to Allison's," she said by way of explanation.

He nodded. "Is she that girl whose mom—"

"Was in a porno? Yeah. I mean, no, it's not actually true,
at least that I know of, it's just a stupid rumor. But that's her."

He nodded and shrugged at the same time, like, *All those mom-porn rumors. You know how it is.* "So was it fun? I mean the party."

Unaccountably, she blushed for the third time. "I guess so. It was weird. Actually, no, it was sort of a bad night. My friend got sick, and . . . things just . . . took a turn."

He nodded again, wondering what else people normally do with their heads, even though he didn't really know what she was talking about and in fact wasn't listening, he was just looking at her lips moving and her shoulders shifting slightly. The tiniest wisp of red hair was caught in her lip gloss, though he obviously didn't do anything about it other than stare at it. This was the most she'd said to him, since, well, ever, and he was not about to break the spell.

"Lilly, you're needed at the front," an annoyed-sounding voice called.

"Your boss?"

Lilly rolled her eyes. "Yeah, sorry, I'll be right back."

"No worries, I'll just be, um, checking out these—" He grasped for the item hanging closest to him and came away with a big billowy silky thing. "These, um . . ."

"Scarves," she said with a smile, and then she ducked behind a rack and was gone.

A moment passed, him just standing there with the scarf sagging in his hand, and then . . .

Before he had the chance to doubt himself, he was in the back room on his hands and knees.

Somehow it seemed less uncomfortable than simply asking her about the ring.

And besides, he reasoned, if she knew where it was, she'd probably have looked guilty when he asked. If it had fallen out of the jacket pocket, which maybe it had, there were only so many places it could have gone, and one of those places, he figured, was wherever the staff kept their outerwear.

Hence: the staff room.

The room was easy to find. There was a narrow hallway at the back of the shop, containing a couple of clearly marked dressing rooms, a bathroom, an unmarked door, and then, at the end of the hall, a fire exit. He made an easy guess and pushed on the unmarked door. It wasn't locked, so . . . he went right in.

Let's be honest. This wasn't his first break-in.

The room was small, like a little office, with a window overlooking a parking lot. He scanned closely, looking for signs. An L-shaped bench lined the near wall, covered in bright cushions. A coffee maker sat on a desk in one corner. Some bags had been left on the floor. No goat or human sacrificial altars to be seen.

After tossing aside several pillows from the bench, he got down to crawl beneath it.

Soon he was on the verge of giving up. This was silly.

Except there was a glint of silver in the floor vent.

He reached for it and the object—what looked like it could be a nickel, fell deeper into the vent. *Shit.* It was still visible, but barely. He got up and grabbed a paper clip off the top of the desk, then used it to gingerly scoop out the object, which took several tries, and he began to curse, but then finally it popped up and out, and in fact turned out not to be a nickel but, as he'd hoped, the sapphire-and-diamond ring.

Patrick experienced a surge of giddiness.

Once, his grandfather had given him a fishing pole and he'd lost it in a deep river near where they used to live in Illinois, within just ten minutes of getting on the boat. In early spring, the current was fierce. Still, he'd borrowed a pair of old work goggles from his uncle's shed and swum for a full hour (the goggles filling up uncomfortably with silty, mineral-laden river water), diving and surfacing, diving and surfacing, until finally, unbelievably, breathless and aching, he'd found the lost pole.

He'd never forget his desperation the moment the pole fell from the boat—the deep shame that had flooded his veins, even as a ten-year-old kid. How he'd felt he *had* to make things right, to prove that he was worth the price, worth the fishing trip, worth keeping.

Before he died, Patrick's grandfather had been the person he'd cared most about impressing. They'd had a bond—even his mom, who hardly paid attention to anything, had known it, and tried as much as possible to arrange for them to spend time together.

Once, about four years later, Patrick could swear he had seen his grandfather's ghost. It had been back in the apartment in Chicago. Their heat had gone out, and his mom had sent him down to the basement of the building to check on the boiler—was it that, or were they simply behind on their bills? In any case, in the basement, his grandfather had emerged from behind the mildewed staircase, stepping straight into the beam of Patrick's flashlight. "You're one determined son of a bitch," he'd said, exactly like he'd said it the day Patrick rescued his fishing pole from the bottom of the river, with a pleased grin stretching his wrinkled, freckled face.

He could swear his grandfather would be smiling now too, if he were alive.

Hearing the doorknob turn, Patrick stood up quickly, shoved the ring into his jeans pocket, and turned around.

"What are you doing?" Lilly asked, her arms folded across her chest.

"Investigating." He smiled.

He'd been caught. He should apologize, explain himself. But he was too happy to pretend otherwise.

She squinted at him. "What, are you interested in working here or something? Because I wouldn't have pegged you as a fashion type. No offense."

He shrugged. "Wouldn't be that bad. Working here. If *you* were working here too. Which you are." He put out his hands, palms open. "And I didn't steal anything. If that's what you're thinking. I'm not really into scarves and stuff."

"You're weird."

He shrugged. "So are you."

"Hey!"

"Sorry."

"I don't think I'm weird. I'm extremely normal."

"Is there such a thing?" he asked.

"What, normal? I don't know, yes? Anyway, you're distracting me."

"Am I?"

She nodded, a stray lock of hair slipping into her face. "From finding out what you were doing here in the staff room while I was out in the front being *normal*."

He thought quickly. "Waiting," he blurted out. "For, um, you."

She rolled her eyes.

"You know," he went on, feeling more and more like an idiot by the second. "Mood lighting." He gestured around the small space.

She studied him. "How come you said no to my friend Mel?"

"Mel? What?"

She sighed. "That first week of school. I asked you if you were interested in going out with her. You barely knew—barely know—her. Or any of us. So why did you say no?"

How could he explain he never meant to stick around—still didn't? Now that he had the ring, he could kick it out of town any day now.

How could he explain, on top of it, that he had a policy of not dating the friends of girls as pretty, and thinks-she's-normal-but-is-definitely-weird, as Lilly?

"And also," she went on, "what were you *really* doing at the homecoming dance? And why did you offer me a ride on your bike? And what are you doing here now?"

He stared at her mouth, trying to figure out what was happening, how quickly he was losing ground—if he'd even had any to begin with. "Why do you need to know?"

"Why do you only answer my questions with other questions?"

"Why do you *have* so many questions?"

"Why don't you get out of here before I tell my boss I caught you stealing?"

"Why don't you stop fighting?"

"Stop fighting what?"

"This."

He kissed her.

Oh, god, he was an idiot. Such an idiot—helplessly swimming, like he'd done that cold spring day in search of his lost fishing pole, pushing through the clouded current, holding his breath. *You're one determined son of a bitch.*

Except maybe he wasn't such an idiot. Her lips parted with a little gasp, and then their tongues met, and she gasped again, holding on to his shoulders, kissing him back, and waves of heat coursed through him, making him want very badly to press her up against the wall and keep doing this, keep diving and surfacing, diving and surfacing. It occurred to him that he had wanted this since the day he first saw her, and more every time he'd talked with her. It was unaccountable. It was like the current had caught him and dragged him and he'd lost his direction, all he could do was go with it, downriver. . . .

Suddenly she pulled back, with a look of shock.

"I—I'm sorry," he blurted out. In the moment, it seemed like the right, the *only* thing to say.

She continued to stare at him, and he couldn't tell if she was murderously angry or something else. She'd kissed him back, though, hadn't she?

"I have to get back to work," she said awkwardly. Her voice shook. She *had* kissed him back . . . but maybe she'd decided she didn't like it. Maybe she was just testing him out, and now it was clearer than ever before that he stood no chance.

"Right, right, of course," he stammered, and fled the back room, pushed open the front door to the jingle of bells, and ran out into the cold before she could realize the ring was his again.

Chapter Sixteen

NOW

FEBRUARY 10

IT HAD BEEN A COUPLE of days ago, but Tessa couldn't stop thinking about her interaction with Mel underneath the bleachers as she got home from school on Friday, the haunted look in her eyes, the way she kept saying she was sorry.

The smell of fresh pasta sauce wafted through the house when she came inside—it was, generic as it sounds, the smell she most associated with their mom. Mom was always either at work late, then coming in the door with groceries, hollering for help to unload the car, or in the kitchen with one ear on her phone and her free hand stirring sauce, adding something like basil or sautéed onion to make the jarred pasta sauce her own.

Tessa thought of going into the kitchen to hug her mother,

but she could hear her crying through the door, and it was too much. She had the sudden, uncomfortable feeling that if she stopped moving, she'd disappear.

She wandered up the stairs in a fog. Maybe she would never experience real grief, only this dizzying numbness. Her hand against the railing looked like Kit's. *Was* Kit's. For a moment, she forgot who she was.

At the end of the hall, she pushed open a door. The familiar scents of mango shampoo and vanilla perfume washed over her. She sat at her desk. She had so much work to do. She was the good girl, the one who never disappointed, the one who aced all her classes and always fell in line, but somehow, she'd lost her rhythm, and couldn't think.

This was the only bedroom that didn't face the Taylors' house. The desk sat beneath a window looking out on the back-yard, where a squirrel raced along a branch of the basswood, its tiny feet nudging clumps of snow off the branch in little spurts. Below, the yard was a patchwork of white and brown. Someone had left the sprinkler out, and its rusty frame poked up from the slush.

She could hear the squeals of three girls, now, playing in the yard. Carrot-top Lilly, her diapers sagging out the sides of her bathing suit, carrying a naked doll in both arms. Tessa and Kit, in matching suits, tackling Boyd, who held the sprinkler in his hands as if to attack. Water shooting up into their faces. Everyone laughing, screaming, slipping around in the slick grass. Lilly giggling maniacally as she ran away, only to fall face forward, bursting instantly into tears. Mom coming out with a big beach towel—the one with Goofy on it—and wrapping everyone up in it. Mom lighting the grill, and Kit running in to get hamburger buns while their old mutt, Sun, circled hungrily, nosing the air.

Tessa blinked, and realized she was in Kit's room. This happened sometimes—only when she was extra anxious or tired. She'd feel as though she was disappearing, or she'd begin to believe she was Kit. She'd even go into Kit's room instead of her own, like now. She always blamed the chimerism—their shared snippets of DNA—but now, with Kit gone, she wondered if it was something else.

She turned away from the window and caught a glimpse of herself in the mirror that hung on the back of the closet door. As she looked at her own reflection—faint rings in the pale skin below her different-colored eyes, her light hair tangled—her mouth seemed to move of its own accord, her eyes sparkling. *Please,* the reflection said.

"So, you're in here now," said a voice behind her.

Lilly had burst through the door, and now she threw herself onto Kit's bed. "It smells like her in here." She picked up one of Kit's fluffy pillows and buried her face in it, light red hair fanning out around her, like an asphyxiating mermaid.

"Do you think I'm crazy?" Tessa asked her.

Lilly rolled over and looked at her. "I was going to ask you the same thing."

Tessa shrugged. "I sometimes forget." *Who I am. Where I'm supposed to be. That Kit's not here anymore.*

"I know," Lilly said.

"Mom's downstairs crying into the tomatoes."

"I know," she said again.

"This is hard on her," Tessa replied slowly, even though she was stating the obvious. "With Kit gone . . ."

Blunt head trauma.

No foreign substances found in bloodstream.

Lilly's face looked mottled and teary. "You have to understand . . . this whole week you've been gone, too. It's like you've been somewhere else."

It was true; Tessa had barely spoken to her mom since the night it happened. She'd only been floating through the house, disconnected from everything and everyone. She just had so much on her mind, so much to keep track of. While Mom was in mourning, she was trying to puzzle things out. On her own.

For Boyd.

Or maybe just for herself.

"Hey," Lilly was saying. She'd sat up and had a funny look in her eyes. "Come here, I want to show you something."

Tessa followed Lilly into her room, which looked just like Lilly herself—cluttered yet cool. Chaotic but artful. Precious and detailed even as it was also loud and messy, as though she'd perfectly planned out which of her outfits to drape across the back of her chair or hang off the bedpost, which scarf to curl into a ball on the floor, which pile of books to leave at just the right angle by the door, stacked up to form a makeshift nightstand.

Lilly turned over her shoulder as Tessa stood in the doorway.

"Shhh," she whispered, then stuffed something into her purse. "Come on, we have to go outside."

"Now?"

"Yeah, now."

"Why?" She followed her back through the living room and out the back porch, to the Adirondack chairs partly hidden under the old pine in the far corner.

Night had started to fall, and the shadowed area beneath the tree was frigidly cold. They had to shove some old caked snow off the seats, and then Lilly rummaged through her purse.

"Dude, do you have pot or something?" Tessa asked, half laughing.

Lilly looked up with a smile.

"Oh my god, you *do* have pot."

"The weeds." It was what Lilly had called it when she was eleven and had first heard of it.

"Mom's going to find out," Tessa warned.

"Where else are we going to go?"

"Fine, but here, let's move farther back." She ushered Lilly deeper into the branches.

"Shit, I dropped it!" Lilly squealed.

"Shhh!"

She bent down into the slushy yard. "Got it." Squatting, she faced the fence that separated their backyard from the Orensons' behind them and tried to light the joint.

"Here, I'll do it." Tessa sat down on one of the chairs and easily lit the joint behind her hand.

Lilly swiveled around and sat next to her.

Tessa took a slow drag and shook her head. "Never thought I'd be smoking with you."

"I'm not a child," Lilly responded, taking the joint back and coughing a little after her inhale.

"Where did you get it?"

The burning tip arced and dipped through the darkness between them as they passed it back and forth, leaving a thin trail of smoke.

Lilly shook her head. "I'm not supposed to tell."

Tessa said nothing.

"Okay, fine, I got it from Dar, actually."

"What's *Dar* doing with weed?"

"We're not all squares and losers, Tess."

"Sure, whatever."

"Remember when Mel lost her virginity?" Lilly blurted out.

Tessa turned to her. "Yeah, I remember," she said slowly, half amused, half something else. "With that guy Dustin, right?"

Lilly nodded. "But now she broke up with him again. I just don't get it."

"Don't get what?"

Lilly's face was turned slightly toward the house, and Tessa looked at her in profile. "How I could get so left behind," she whispered.

Tessa nodded but said nothing, just took the joint and felt its tiny weight on her lips. "I haven't done it either. You're not the only virgin left in the world."

Lilly sighed and didn't look at her. "I heard Jay Kolbry's having a Valentine's Day party," she said out of nowhere.

Tessa just nodded again. "You thinking of going?"

"What? No. It's way too soon. I could barely make it through school this week. Plus, we don't hang in that crowd," Lilly said, but her voice didn't sound convinced. Obviously, they were both thinking the same thing: *Kit did.*

"I might," Tessa said.

"Why? How can you even think of partying, when . . ."

"I just . . . it's hard to explain. I feel like I have to know what it's like at one of those parties. Because *she* went, in the fall. And . . . and maybe someone saw something. I don't know."

Lilly sighed. "I think it's a terrible idea. I think you should stay here with me and Mom. We need you."

But Tessa knew she was just saying it—they didn't *need* her. No one needed Tessa. People only ever needed Kit. Kit solved problems. Kit kept her head level. Tessa only made messes and pissed people off.

They were quiet for a while. Tessa wondered what time it was; she kept missing meals, couldn't keep her hours and days straight. Only a week ago, everything had been normal. Less than a week ago, her sister's body had been found, half naked, and so, so cold.

Tessa let smoke slip through her teeth and squinted through the low tree branches, to her right, diagonally across the yard, at Boyd's darkened window next door. She still hadn't told Lilly about their kiss. What would be the point?

She pictured him moving about in his room right now, maybe trying but failing to study. Maybe lying on his bed, staring at the ceiling.

But no. She knew he wasn't home. He'd been in the local jail all week. The only light on in the house was the den light, where Boyd's dad, Innis, was probably deep into a bottle of something.

"What do you think Kit would say if she saw us right now?" Lilly mused. "She'd probably freak out."

"Hmm, yeah." Tessa's thoughts felt smoky and light. "Or maybe she would've been into it. Maybe she would've joined us."

Lilly snorted. "Right."

"You never know."

"Ha ha. Pass me that back."

"I'm serious," Tessa said, her voice going cold in her throat.

Lilly turned to her, obviously annoyed. "You are talking about the girl who told Uncle Leo when he returned from war without working fucking legs that he couldn't smoke cigarettes in our house."

"Yup."

"And who spent two New Year's Eves volunteering in a cancer ward."

"That doesn't make her a saint. Did you know she got a tattoo right before . . . before that night? On her hip. Like, right here," Tessa said, pointing to the left of her belly button.

"How do you know?" Lilly's voice was suddenly small.

"I just know. I saw it. In the reports."

The words hurt Lilly. Tessa could feel that. Lilly hated being the last to know something.

Lilly sniffled and put out the joint.

"Hey, that wasn't done," Tessa protested.

"Whatever."

"Don't get all upset," Tessa said, trying to soften her voice. "I'm just saying, she had secrets, is all."

But for some reason, this was the wrong thing to say, because Lilly exploded. "Secrets? Secrets! You don't think I realize that? All of you! All of you with your secrets! This is the year of everyone hiding things and falling away from me like fucking dominoes, and—"

"That's not how dominoes work," Tessa pointed out.

Lilly stood up. "You know what? Fuck you, Tessa. I don't need this." Then, without another word, she marched back into the house, letting the back door slam behind her.

Tessa sat out there alone in the darkness for a while, letting the cold air move through her hair, hopefully taking some of the pungent weed smell with it. Her fingers were going numb, and she shoved them into her coat pockets, noticing a bunched-up piece of paper in the right pocket.

She pulled it out, saw it was covered in scrawled words. She didn't recognize the handwriting.

This is your last warning. You're making a mistake.

Tessa stared and stared at the note, her body growing colder and colder. It wasn't just the tone of the words, the warning that echoed the one she'd received anonymously in a text. It was the fact that it had ended up inside her coat. *How?* Had the killer gotten that close to her, and she hadn't even known it? Had someone stuffed the note into her pocket earlier today, at the school library? Or sometime before that?

Now she was shivering, hard. But it wasn't all with fear. There was a rush of adrenaline moving through her too, because no matter how afraid she was, she knew what this note meant: that she *was* closer to the truth than she thought. It was spelled out somewhere right before her eyes, like the mess of mud and weeds in the yard, but hidden in a veil of snow.

The truth was right there—she just couldn't see it yet.

She stayed outside for who knew how long, wondering if she was missing dinner, if she was missing *everything*. She felt like if she moved, she might break the spell—this feeling that she was so close to understanding the truth.

She felt frozen in waiting. For something. For what? She didn't know.

Gradually, she began to imagine again that she was Kit and that she was sitting out here waiting for someone to come, some secret person who would emerge from the shadows of the pine trees and take her in his arms.

But she wasn't Kit.

And she didn't know Kit's secrets.

A Light in the Dark
BY KATHERINE MALLOY

We're kissing in the closet of night, and oh,
it comes to me in pieces, as my eyes get used

to the dark:
your hair, your hands.
The doorknob glows,
moonish and bright, like the spark I first confused

for a satellite, up there in the Milky Way.

Your thumb moves over my palm, like in some dream
where your hands are shaping me from formless clay.

I lick your lips. You taste like fresh whipped cream.

My sisters and I always fought for the cherry,
so we could try to tie its stem in a knot
using only our tongues.

I barely utter, but my body
says you are the one I'm lit for, and not

to stop.

When we touch it's as though we are just learning how.

We are breath, we are heat, we are now—now—now.

Chapter Seventeen

BEFORE

11/1

Dear Diary,

Did I like it?

OF COURSE I LIKED IT!!??!!!!

!!!!!!!!!!!!

But seriously, Diary, what is WRONG with me?

WHY did I freak out and get so awkward?

Ugh. I'm sitting here in geometry and he's sitting RIGHT. BEHIND. ME. And I just can't stop replaying the shocked look on his face, there in the staff room at Lupine. He left without another word. Fled, basically.

And I don't blame him.

And I still haven't really processed what Boyd told me after the party, either. That he likes Kit. I point-blank asked him, and he said yes. And you know what? I'm weirdly okay with it. Like, maybe I'm not as obsessed with Boyd as I thought. I mean, I thought I wanted him to be my boyfriend.

And now one single kiss—and all I can think about is . . .

Ugh.

Diary, I am sorry for the indents, but I keep slamming my forehead into you, hoping that I will eventually knock some sanity back into my brain again.

Like, I cannot concentrate on school at ALL. All day, I've just been trying to sail through the noisy, hormone-filled sea of navy-blue peacoats and bright fleece jackets in the DLHS halls (did I mention it's freezing out? Winter has officially arrived in Devil's Lake). All day, I've just been trying to make it to geometry.

Our one class together.

And now that I'm here, well . . . it hasn't gone great so far.

Allow me to recap for you:

Mrs. Gluckman comes into the classroom, and I'm pretending to stare at my phone. Patrick rolls in a minute late and sits down behind me, as always. My neck is basically burning under his gaze, but when I turn around he's like, doing math in his notebook and doesn't notice.

I swivel back quickly and pull out my diary and act like I'm furiously taking notes, like I'm a normal human being and not LOSING. MY. MIND.

Then, somewhere around the section on parabolas, I feel a TAP on my shoulder.

He's never tapped my shoulder before.

So I turn around again, and mouth "What?"

Then he handed me this note. A tiny folded thing from his notebook.

All it says is: my b.

Okaaaay. Now what? My body is basically on fire. I'm trying to figure out what the right response is . . . nbd? No, that would be untrue. Sorry I froze?

Ugh, too pathetic.

How about: I liked it.

Clearly I'm not admitting that.

Okay, here it is:

Well, it was a slow day anyway.

I just turned around and gave him the note.

Zomg. He's handing me back another one.

Okay, hang on, it says:

not for me. ☺

All right now I can't stop grinning, because that is so cute.

Uh-oh. Mrs. Gluckman is staring at me GTG!!!!!!!

"I assume if you're enjoying the lesson that much, Miss Malloy, you'll be happy to share your focus coordinates with the rest of the class." Mrs. Gluckman was eyeing her sternly over the top of her glasses.

Lilly's smile disappeared.

And when the bell rang, Patrick shot out of there.

Great.

The rest of the week continued in an awkward blur.

Kit was being mysterious and elusive and pretending not to be, Mel was obsessing over what Dusty and his friends thought of her, and Patrick passed occasional notes to Lilly in math class, all of which were basically indecipherable and noncommittal in every way.

Meanwhile, Lilly was trying really hard not to worry about Dar: the bags under her eyes seemed deeper and darker than ever, and she refused to say anything about the Halloween party or why she was crying in the bathroom.

On Wednesday, she cornered Dar alone after school. Mel was going over to Dusty's to do homework, so Lilly met Dar at her locker and waited while she opened it to exchange her books before leaving.

"Do you want to come over?" Lilly asked. "Boyd can probably give us a ride home."

"I have to meet, um . . . I have stuff to do." Dar grabbed a stapled paper from the top shelf and a little folded note came flying out after it, but she snatched the note midair and shoved it back into the locker. Then she furtively stuffed the paper into her bag like it was contraband, not looking at Lilly.

"Okaaaay. I just feel like we never hang out anymore." She stared at her friend. Dar was definitely being cagey, but why?

"We just hung out on Saturday," Dar pointed out. She finished gathering the rest of her things, and they walked toward the snack machines at the end of the hall.

"True," Lilly said, popping a dollar into the machine and clicking the button next to Diet Dr Pepper. "About that . . ." She cracked it open with a hiss and offered Dar the first sip.

To her relief, Dar took it. "Look, I'm really sorry I was such a disaster," she said, after slurping a few sips and passing it back. "I'm sure it was embarrassing. I drank too much of that punch—it was stronger than I thought, especially on an empty stomach."

"Come on. You don't have to apologize, it wasn't a big deal. I mean it was . . . I mean, I was worried, but I didn't want to *make* a big deal out of it. I don't think anyone else noticed. Especially since Boyd kind of stole all the attention."

Dar snorted, shaking her head. "I'm so glad he punched Fred, I just wish he'd punched him in something other than the face."

"Ew."

Dar rolled her eyes and Lilly experienced a bit of relief. Maybe everything *was* normal. Maybe everything was okay.

By now the hallway had cleared out and they were alone, standing with their backs against the wall and their feet jutted out slightly in front of them, not far from the art room.

"So," Lilly said, drawing up her courage. "I saw you kiss Toma. During the game." She said it quietly—almost a whisper—but still she could see Dar tense up.

"Yeah, it was just a game." Dar shrugged, not making eye contact.

195

"Is that all? I'm just asking."

Dar shrugged again. "What do you want me to say? I mean, I enjoyed it. If that's what you were wondering."

"Oh," Lilly said, trying to find the right words. "I just meant . . . did that have anything to do with why you were crying in the bathroom later?"

Dar shook her head, more to herself than for Lilly's sake. "Lilly. I kissed a girl. I'm trying to figure things out. I have no idea what Toma thought of it and I'm not sure I even care. It's not really about that. And yeah, I had too much to drink. I was crying because I was *throwing up* at stupid Allison Riley's stupid mansion. That's all."

"Okay."

Dar turned to her and gave her a quick hug. "And thanks again for getting me home. Really. I owe you."

Then she walked away.

I owe you? Since when did they talk that way to each other? Friends didn't owe each other anything. Friends just expected each other to be there. Friends just *were* there.

And they told each other everything they were feeling.

Didn't they?

Standing alone in the hallway, a crazy sensation overcame Lilly. She looked around covertly, to make sure there were no stray teachers or administrators wandering the halls.

Then she walked hurriedly back down the hall.

Back toward Dar's locker.

When she got there, she punched in the code from memory

and the door swung open with its customary squeak.

Lilly looked quickly over her shoulder again before fumbling through a few random items—a half-used pack of gum, a purple pen, lip gloss, and an old apple that was starting to get soft. She found the tiny note she was looking for.

It looked an awful lot like the notes Patrick had been passing *her* in geometry.

She unfolded it.

Next time call my cell, it said, in his now-recognizable scrawl. And there was a phone number.

Lilly stood there in shock, her hand trembling.

Patrick was leaving notes . . . for *Dar.*

And Dar had Patrick's number.

Getting all the way out to the Donovans' wasn't that hard. She told Boyd she was hanging out with Jenny Albot and Toma Ramirez, then asked Mrs. Albot for a ride into town, then took the trail through the arboretum—it was less than a mile that way.

She'd tried calling the cell number in the note a couple times, but no one answered, and she'd been too nervous to leave a message.

Still, Lilly was beginning to regret coming at all as she stood shivering on the Donovans' porch. The front of the old white clapboard house was in more disrepair than she'd realized. Dried leaves skittered across the front yard in the cold November wind like small animals scurrying for shelter.

In the time it took to get here, she'd had a chance to think long and hard about that note in Dar's locker. It could have meant anything. Dar certainly wasn't interested in Patrick—she wasn't into boys, period; she'd told Lilly that. Even though she *had* been acting strangely, that didn't prove anything specific. Or if something *was* going on between them, then it just proved Patrick didn't kiss Lilly because he wanted to—he kissed her to trick her, to distract her, maybe.

She wished he'd picked up the phone. Then again, dealing with it in person actually seemed better—maybe she'd at least be able to figure out if he was lying or telling the truth.

Now, well . . . she had come all this way.

And, after all, it wasn't like she had anywhere else to go. Mel was with Dusty. Dar was off being secretive. Tessa was studying AP Bio like her life depended on it, Kit was probably working her volunteer route again, and Boyd, well, she felt weird about spending any more time alone with Boyd, now that she knew his secret.

She rang the bell again.

No one answered.

She was just lifting her fist to knock on the front door when she heard a crackling sound, like someone approaching her from behind, through the leaves.

"Psst."

She gasped and swiveled around, her heart racing all of a sudden.

Patrick was standing there in the corner of the yard, holding a rake with the handle side touching the ground, prongs in the air. His blue eyes were shaded by his dark hair. He was wearing his army-green jacket—the same one he'd lent her at the dance. *Outside* the dance. She wondered if it was his only coat. It wasn't warm enough for this weather.

Out of nowhere, she had a rush of emotion, something like sympathy and sadness and a crazy dose of hormones, all mixed together to create this strange desire to kiss him again.

"What are you doing here?" he asked.

She swallowed. "I. Sorry. Um. I tried to call first, but . . ."

"My phone's inside," he said.

"Oh."

"So what did you need?" He shifted his weight, like he was eager to get back to whatever he'd been doing before she arrived.

"I need to, um. I need to talk. To you, that is."

He paused for a second, just looking at her. "Come on," he said at last, nodding slightly to the side.

So she followed him around the yard to the back of the house, which was much darker than the front, shaded on two sides by trees from the arboretum—their small cul-de-sac basically bottomed out at the park. Which sounded nice in theory, but it was sort of desolate.

Lilly wrapped her arms around herself and gritted her teeth. "Can we go inside? It's too cold out here."

"Sure, but we should go in the back so we don't bother my aunt and uncle."

"Are they really your aunt and uncle?"

"Great. Great-uncle. Et cetera." He held the back door open for her, then made sure it closed quietly behind her before leading her up a creaky set of stairs.

When she entered his room, she once again wondered if coming here was a mistake. First of all, she was in a guy's bedroom. And no one even knew she was here.

Anything could happen.

Second of all, it was *Patrick's* bedroom, and just standing in the doorway, smelling the cedary, citrusy boy scent of his stuff, was making her go slightly stiff and brain-dead. It struck her that she really didn't know him *at all*. Not even a little.

Not like Boyd, whose favorite everything she could list in a second: favorite ice cream, salted caramel; favorite movie, *Ghostbusters*; favorite board game, this epically long one that involved settlers and wheat and coal and stuff.

What did Patrick do for fun? For that matter, what did Patrick do *not* for fun? She simply had no idea.

Of course, other guys she'd kissed, like Rohan Reddy, never told her their favorite board game or movie either. But somehow they seemed like they'd be easy to guess.

"What's your favorite ice cream flavor?" she asked, immediately wishing she hadn't. What was this, the fifth-grade fall social?

He shrugged, taking off his jacket and throwing it over the edge of the bed. "Not really a dessert person."

Oh.

He half sat, half leaned on a windowsill—probably because

there was nowhere else to sit in here other than the bed. The room was tiny. "Is that why you came here? To find out about my culinary preferences?"

"No, that's not it." *I came here to find out about your* romantic *preferences, actually,* she wanted to say. Instead, she cleared her throat, wishing there were a chair. Standing was just making this more awkward. "I came here to find out what's going on between you and Darcy."

He folded his arms over his chest, which had the effect of making his biceps look bigger. "Honestly, I'm not trying to be a dick, but that's not really your business."

"Yes, it is!" How was it that he always had this ability to make her feel vulnerable and soft one second, then furious and annoyed the next? "She's my *friend* and something's wrong, and she won't tell me what it is, but I know you're involved some-how. Are you . . . are you, like, secretly dating or something?"

He laughed. She didn't know what to make of that. "Why would Darcy date *me*? Isn't she gay?"

Lilly's jaw dropped open. "How . . . how did you—did she tell you that?"

He shrugged. "I guess I just have good intuition." Her jaw must have been practically on the floor, because he laughed again. "Chill out, she told me."

"But she hasn't told *anyone*." Lilly felt dizzy, as if he'd just told her the world wasn't round after all, and wasn't rotating through space but falling fast—down down down—like an ele-vator whose cables had snapped.

"Look, she told me she was overwhelmed lately and that

her dad is always calling her to give her grief about her grades, which is ironic since her mom is mostly just concerned about her lack of dating life and what the neighbors think. I just put two and two together. I'm right, though, aren't I?"

"Well, that's not the point," Lilly replied, still trying to recover from her surprise. "If you're not dating, then why did you leave your cell phone number in her locker? And what were you doing in her locker on the night of homecoming—because I know now that I did see you closing *her* locker. Are you a drug dealer or something?" As she said it, she realized it had to be true—there could be no other explanation. And now Dar was caught up in some sort of horrible substance-abuse cycle about which Lilly knew nothing. Poor Dar!

But Patrick just scoffed. "I hear Jay Kolbry's your guy for that sort of thing," he said with a smirk. "Here, Lilly, sit down," he urged, standing up and drawing her by the shoulders toward the bed. The sheets were striped flannel, rumpled at the sides. "Take off your coat. Relax for a second, okay?"

She sat down.

"Do you really want to know why I left that note? I've been doing her homework. Not all of it, just writing a few papers here and there. We both figured it was easier to do drop-offs like that than risk being seen hanging out in public. I pretty much assumed she didn't want to be seen near me since I'm a social pariah at Devil's Lake, but whatever. So she gave me her locker combo. No big deal."

"Why?"

He shrugged, sitting back down on the window ledge. "Easy cash. It's what I used to do back in my old school. On the sly, of course. Wouldn't want the jocks getting wind of the fact that I have a brain or anything."

"No, I meant, why would Dar pay *you* to do her homework? It doesn't make sense."

"I can't answer that. We have gym together. She saw me writing a paper at the back of the weight room. I think she's just . . . stressed lately. That's what she told me. I figured it wasn't my business to pry."

"So you're definitely not selling her drugs." She ventured a small smile.

"Nope." He smiled back.

"And you're not . . . you don't *like* her. In that way."

He shook his head. "Are we all cleared up here?"

"Not exactly," she said slowly. "I still want to know something. I want to know . . . why you kissed me last weekend. At the store."

She could swear he was blushing, which gave her some satisfaction. "I'm really sorry about that, I swear," he said, shaking his head. "I have no idea what came over me."

"Yeah. That was weird."

"I was totally out of line. I promise you I'll never do anything like that again."

"Oh. Okay. Yeah. Um, thanks."

"I don't want you to think I don't respect you. I mean, I don't really know you very well, but I do. Respect you. So, I didn't want you to think that."

Lilly's breathing was shallow, and she felt like she was talking on autopilot. "All right. I, um, respect you, too."

"Cool."

"Cool." She shifted her weight, and his bed creaked beneath her. "I guess I should probably call for a ride home or something."

"Do you—"

"What?"

"No, nothing, never mind."

"No, what?"

"Oh, I was just going to say, do you want to stay for dinner? My aunt—my *great*-aunt—makes really good lasagna. *Great* lasagna. Sorry, bad pun."

"You're inviting me to dinner?"

"No, no, forget it." He looked over his shoulder briefly, like the trees outside might be listening.

"Wait, so now you're *disinviting* me to dinner?"

He turned back to her with an awkward laugh. "I mean, you can stay, if you want. Dinner probably won't be for another hour."

"Do *you* want me to stay?" she asked, her voice coming out thin. She cleared her throat again. The air up there must've been really dry.

"Well . . . the truth is, you might be a little bit too distracting." He gestured to a couple of textbooks that were open on the floor next to the bed. "I have a lot of work to do."

"What, like writing other people's papers for a living?"

He shrugged. "Maybe."

Lilly sighed and rolled her eyes. "You're just like my sisters. And Boyd."

"What do you mean? I'm not like that guy. I don't trust him."

Lilly raised an eyebrow at Patrick. "You don't even know him."

Patrick folded his arms. "He's sort of possessive of all of you."

"He's like a brother to us," Lilly said, feeling weird about it, as though her giddy romp through Allison Riley's house not even a full week ago must read across her face like a glaring sign.

"I don't buy that," Patrick said, moving from the window ledge to the bed and sitting down next to her. He leaned toward her slightly. "Are you in love with him or something?" Then, smug with his guess, he folded his arms and leaned back against his propped-up pillow, so that he was facing her, one knee pulled up in front of him and the other foot on the ground.

She swatted his leg. "No!"

"Hey, enough with the violence!" he protested, grabbing her hand.

She froze, letting him hold her hand in his for a moment.

Instead of letting go, he held her palm up to his, flat. "Such small hands," he stated, "yet so much force."

She could feel the heat from his palm, moving into hers.

He was looking not at their hands, still touching, but into her eyes. He had such a boyish demeanor up close and relaxed like this, in his own room—nothing like the tough vibe he gave off at school and around strangers. It was as though a wall had come down.

He cleared his throat, and she dropped her hand.

"I guess I'll stay and do some of my homework here. If I'm not going to annoy you or anything," she said.

"No, no, forget I said that. It's fine. It's all good. Stay."

They sank down next to each other on his floor, with their backs against the bed, and pulled their books out of their bags. She opened her used, dog-eared copy of *A Tale of Two Cities*, but she had a hard time concentrating.

She looked over at what Patrick was doing. He was scrawling geometry problems onto his notebook. "I haven't seen those," she said, not recognizing the assignment.

He shrugged again, sheepish all of a sudden. "I'm doing next week's. I like to get ahead when I can."

She nudged him with her shoulder. "Show-off."

He nudged her back.

She tried to go back to Dickens, but the words swam on the page and she was bored within seconds and distracted by the soft sound of Patrick's pencil against the paper. How interesting could two cities possibly be? She caught herself watching his hand. What was she doing here? Why was she staring at his hands? What did she even want from him? Did she want him to kiss her again?

Yes, she did. Of course she did.

And he'd literally *just* promised her that he'd never try to kiss her again.

But was that because he didn't want to, or he didn't think *she* wanted to?

Ugh. This had been a terrible idea, coming here.

She closed her book. "You know what? I should probably go. Sorry. I forgot I have some stuff to do at home."

She started to stand.

"Sure. Okay."

Disappointment flooded through her, but she tried not to let it show.

"Here, let me walk you out." He got up and stood there awkwardly as she put on her coat, then led her downstairs the way they'd come, and out the back door.

The cold air was a shock to her face and neck, and she wished she'd worn a scarf. It seemed to have gotten much darker in the short time she'd spent here.

"Well, I guess I'll see you at school," she said, barely turning to give him a wave as she traipsed quickly across the lawn.

Just as she was about to turn into the side yard between the garage and the house, he ran up to her.

"Lilly, wait."

She turned.

His breath formed faint clouds in the air.

He closed the distance between them with one more step. Out here, with the sun just about gone behind the thick trees of the arboretum, leaving only an inky blue stain across the sky, it was harder to read his expression. He'd gone back from the boyish Patrick of moments before to the bad boy who'd given her a ride on his motorcycle and refused to answer a single question straight—if at all. Mysterious Patrick.

He placed one hand on her shoulder, and she realized he'd come out here in only his T-shirt. When she didn't pull away, he placed his other hand on her other shoulder. Then he sighed and shook his head, "Lilly."

There was a crazy dance of nerves going on inside her chest. She let out a breath. "Patrick."

He smiled. "What am I going to do with you?"

She didn't answer. She was afraid whatever she said would cause him to stop touching her, to realize he was freezing without a coat on out here, then turn and head back into the house.

Finally she whispered, "I don't know."

He leaned forward and rested his forehead against hers. She could smell that same woodsy scent, and strange feelings rushed through her: sadness and excitement at the same time.

Why did whatever was happening between them already feel doomed?

And why, *why* did that seem so damn wonderful?

They stayed that way for a moment, and then, in tiny increments—so microscopic you'd never be able to say who was leading and who following—they tilted their heads until their lips touched. His were warm, despite the cold wind swirling leaves around the yard.

This was different from the sudden kiss at Lupine. This one was gradual, careful, as though he didn't want to scare her off. Ever so slowly, his tongue touched her lips, parting them gently, and she leaned in to him, putting her hands at his waist and pulling him closer. Waves of tingly warmth spread down her body. His torso felt strong and solid beneath his T-shirt. She grabbed the material, letting her tongue meet his, letting their lips graze, then come apart, then graze again, then press firmly. And then she really gave in, and it was not just a kiss but something more. With her eyes closed it was like she was falling forward into another world that was all touch and taste, all darkness, wet and hot and blind and . . .

"Lilly!"

She and Patrick pulled apart quickly, cold air instantly filling the space between them, but Lilly barely had time to catch her breath and register what she was seeing.

Kit, with her arms crossed, in the side yard, her green eyes blazing in the darkness.

"What are you doing here?" Lilly said, blushing with embarrassment and anger.

"*Me?* The Donovans are on my route, you know that!"

Of course. Kit's volunteer route.

"I'm gonna go check on my uncle. See you at school, Lilly," Patrick said, before darting into the house and letting the screen door slam.

"Why did you *do* that?" Lilly demanded

Kit was already walking toward Boyd's truck, which was

parked by the curb. Boyd was not in it; Kit must have borrowed it. "You shouldn't be getting involved with that kid."

Heat rose to Lilly's head. "Excuse me, what? Since when are you my *keeper*?"

Kit sighed, looking pretty and wise and much older than her seventeen years. "Let's just go home."

Lilly got into the cab and slammed the door. "I can't believe you're being like this. What do you have against Patrick?"

Kit shook her head. "The Donovans are nice people, but I'm sorry, the boy is disturbed and everyone knows about it. I'm all about giving people a second chance . . . but not when it's my little sister they're messing with."

"That's absurd. He's not *messing with* me. He's really smart. And nice. And normal. You don't even *know* him."

"I know he got in a physical fight with his stepdad and that's part of why his mom kicked him out."

Lilly stared silently at the road ahead, trying hard to swallow. "I'm sure there was a reason," she said, even though she felt anything but sure.

"*He* started it, Lilly. He hit him in the head with a glass jar. Normal, stable people don't do that."

"How do you even know this? It's probably just a rumor!"

"Diane told me! And I don't think she'd make up something like that about her own great-nephew." Kit sighed. "I mean, listen, I feel bad for him. I do. He's obviously troubled. But I don't want you sneaking around with him anymore, okay? Come on, Lils. I just want whatever's best for you."

"Kit! You're not Mom! You can't just tell me what to do!"

"I'm not *telling* you what to do, I just want—"

"You just want to butt in and ruin my life."

"You're only fifteen."

"So? You're only two years older than me! Does that make you perfect? Why do you even *care*? Are you, like, jealous or something? Maybe you don't have enough secrets of your own and you need to start prying into *my* life now."

Kit shook her head, turning the corner onto their street. "You don't know what you're talking about."

"Yes, I do! I see things. I know things, okay? I know you and Boyd disappeared during homecoming. I know he *likes* you, and now you're borrowing his truck tonight, so what's *that* about? And how come you went to Jay *Kolbry's* Halloween party? I don't know what's happening with you, but don't think I'm stupid, and don't think I'm going to go taking advice from someone who is *obviously* sneaking around and lying to all of us about it."

Kit shook her head again, and Lilly could see that her hands were trembling on the wheel as she parked. She leaned back in her seat. "Guys are . . . you can't just . . . You can't trust them, okay?" She looked weary—strained, somehow.

Maybe even a little scared.

"Not *all* guys are untrustworthy, though," Lilly argued.

Kit's eyes flashed. "Between you and your friends, none of you get it, okay? I don't want you surrounded by all these bad influences."

Lilly couldn't hide the shock or fury at this point. "*All* the bad influences? What are you even referring to?"

"Melissa, for one thing—"

"Mel is one of my best friends, Kit. What are you even saying? Mel's not a bad influence!"

Kit just shook her head. "You don't—"

"Don't even," Lilly spat, cutting her off. "Don't even bother, if you're just going to say that I don't know what I'm talking about again. If I *don't*, it's only because you're keeping secrets. At least *I* have nothing to hide. But you? Everyone thinks you're so innocent. You're just *fake*."

With that, she stormed out of the car. She was done—done trying to figure out what was going on with her sisters. Done worshiping Kit and going along with everyone else's ideas about how perfect she was. If Kit wanted to shut her out, that was just fine.

Two could play that game.

Chapter Eighteen

NOW

FEBRUARY 11

TESSA RUMMAGED THROUGH KIT'S CLOSET. She was looking for a top—a specific one Kit used to love. White, low-cut, but flowy and elegant. Sexy but demure, perfect casual party attire, with tiny strawberries lining the hem.

It was Saturday night. A full week from The Night.

And tonight was Jay Kolbry's Valentine's Day party.

Even though it seemed crazy—and it *was*—Tessa was still determined to go. Maybe it was the chimerism, maybe not, but she felt this *pull* inside her to keep going, to keep pursuing answers.

And if she was going to go to this thing, she needed something to wear. Her entire wardrobe was T-shirts and baggy jeans.

But the shirt was nowhere to be found, and Tessa wondered if maybe Kit had gotten rid of it, or had loaned it to Lilly.

Or maybe—a dark thought struck her. Maybe Kit had been wearing it the night she died.

Was that really why Tessa was in here, searching? Did she remember seeing it on Kit sometime last Saturday?

Kit, she thought. *Give me a hint.*

She remembered how Kit used to curl up on the dryer sometimes to take a nap. She liked how warm and rumbling it got when there was a load spinning inside. Sometimes Tessa would go down to the basement and find Kit like that, her flowing, flaxen hair wrapped around a face as serene as that of a lioness that had just devoured its prey. Once Tessa had found her using her push-up bra as a pillow. "Hey, that's mine," Tessa had said, startling Kit awake.

Kit sat up. "This?" she asked, dangling the bra in front of her. Kit had probably been around fourteen then—it must've been about three years ago—but she gave Tessa this wise, profound look with her pretty eyes that held just the faintest whiff of pity—if you accused her of it, she'd deny it. "I hope you know boys can tell the difference," she said simply. Then she hopped off the dryer and exited the room, leaving Tessa alone with her abandoned bra, the loud rumbling of the boxy old machine, and the familiar sense that no matter what she said or did, she was always wrong, or at least just off-center from the real issue, and missing the point.

Tessa gave up and let the dresses in Kit's closet swing back into their place, a gentle jostling of hangers, a series of pastels swaying and then settling, as if moved by a light breeze.

She turned and dumped out Kit's hamper, expecting a massive pile of dirty shirts and sweaters and underwear.

But all that was inside was one tiny piece of fabric, stowed in here as if to keep it hidden.

She reached down and picked it up. A light purple pair of underwear unfolded in her palm. Lacy boy shorts. Weirdly, it still had tags on it, like it hadn't been worn, like it was just stashed in here for safekeeping.

These were most definitely not hers.

Where had she seen this underwear before?

Holding it up, she noticed it had a tiny silver charm on it, in the shape of a heart.

Her pulse picked up. *Kit, are you here? What is it? What is it?*

Nausea threatened to overwhelm her. Where. Had. She. Seen. This.

The nausea turned to dread as the memory dawned over her.

It looked a lot like the lilac-colored bra Kit had been wearing when she died. The one from the pictures Tessa had looked at, at the precinct.

As if the two were part of a matching set.

She looked again at the tag. It was from Lupine, where Lilly used to work. *Before.*

She couldn't say why this unsettled her, but it did.

She stuffed the underwear into her bag to worry about later.

She had a party to go to.

Chapter Nineteen

BEFORE

11/21

Dear Diary,

The last three weeks. Have been . . .

There is a thing that is happening. With me and Patrick.

I don't know what to call it, but whatever is happening is . . . happening.

And oh, it is happening. Happening in secret glances in the hallways between bio and English.

It is happening when he taps my back during math with the soft part of his pencil's eraser . . . not to get my attention, just maybe to remind me he's there and thinking about me instead of quadrilaterals?

It's happening in these stolen moments after school when

no one's around to wonder where we've gone. . . .

And yes, there has been more kissing. When we can.

Like the time in the aisle of the library where I accidentally backed into an ancient microfiche screen.

It's so weird. When Mel first insisted that we take some
sort of VOW to get boyfriends this year, it was with this idea
that pairing up would actually help us boost our popularity and
rise in the ranks of the cafeteria-table hierarchy. But having
this thing, this secret . . . whatever . . . is actually WAY more
exciting than having a boyfriend? I think?

I mean, it's not scoring me invites to more parties, but who
cares? Instead I get to meet up with Patrick. In secret. Finally,
it's my turn to have one.

And besides, what else would I be doing if it weren't for
this? Mel is busy with Dusty all the time now. She even told
me she is planning to lose her virginity to him, probably before
Christmas. She bought that stupid bra set—the one I really
wanted, that I put in the window display at Lupine.

And Dar has been busy and mysterious as ever. Or maybe
not mysterious, just . . . distant. Like she's slowly shrinking
away. Maybe it's just an optical illusion, like, an effect of
winter or something, but it feels like everyone is disappearing a
little, into a fog. It feels like yesterday was a thousand years ago
and tomorrow is a million miles away and I can only be right
here, right now, wherever that happens to be.

Tessa and Kit are almost never around either—ditto,
Boyd. Everyone is "studying" or "working" or "just heading

out" whenever I approach them to ask what they're up to.

I hate this. I really do.

It's weird to say it.

I have my first . . . not boyfriend, but my first whatever.

And yet I have never felt this lonely.

Except when I'm around Patrick.

I should be happy right now.

I am happy.

But last night I couldn't sleep. I was thinking about Patrick, of course. I think about him most nights. I was thinking about how last time we kissed, his hands went up the sides of my shirt, and how I liked it, and how I really like the smell of his hair. And then for some reason I couldn't stop thinking about what Kit told me after she caught us together outside his house. Him breaking a glass jar over his stepdad's head. I haven't asked him about that.

I'm not sure what I would do with the answer.

Chapter Twenty

NOW

FEBRUARY 11

TESSA LEFT THE HOUSE THAT evening on her old bicycle—
she knew Mom wouldn't be up for driving her to a party, and
Lilly would freak. She was wearing a pair of red ankle boots
with a three-inch heel, a thin, off-the-shoulder gray sweater,
and a pair of black "vegan leather" pants—all from Lilly's room.

On her fourth finger, she wore the sapphire ring.

Now she pedaled hard through the neighborhood, passing the sassafras and tulip trees, bare branched and skinny. As
her legs cycled and the rusty bike chain whirred, facts flashed,
kaleidoscope-like, through her mind: the tattoo, the bra with
its silver charm, the sapphire ring, the keys to the truck—and,
of course, Lilly's accusations.

Where there was a lost ring, there was a halted romance.

Where there was lace, there was desire.

Where there were scratches and bruises, there'd been struggle.

On Main Street, all the stores were closed, windows dark, except for the Bread Basket, which shone like a beacon in the encroaching darkness, open until nine thirty, where frazzled-looking mothers were zipping into it for last-minute supplies. The lights along the road had flickered on hours ago, though there weren't many—Devil's Lake's roads were always in disrepair.

She pedaled past Devil's Moon, a café that served as the nicest place to go out to eat in a ten-mile radius. Tessa remembered what a big deal it had been when Mike Caprio had taken Lauren Tallerman there for a date last year. Everyone had whispered barbarically about the ways in which she may or may not have repaid him for it—but then she'd started going out with Chris Remos shortly thereafter, and the rumors quickly fizzled.

Currently, a family of four was seated by the window, squabbling over a late meal.

Tessa was about to cross Bunting, when she stopped short—an old man had rounded the corner and walked right into the middle of the road. He was facing down, scanning the ground as though looking for something he'd dropped.

"Mr. Donovan?" she called out.

He lifted his head and squinted. She hadn't seen him around in a while, and in the dim light of the nearest street lamp, he seemed older than she'd remembered, his wrinkles deeper, his eyebrows more . . . scattered.

Tessa hopped off her bike. "Do you need help with something?"

He was still squinting at her and still standing in the middle of the road. She tried to wave him over, but he shook his head and went back to whatever he was searching for.

"Mr. Donovan?" she asked, approaching slowly. It was dangerous out here on the road.

He looked at her again. "Sarah."

"It's Tessa. Let's move off the road, okay?" She tried to take his arm, but he pulled it away, staring at her hand, the one with the engagement ring.

"Don't touch me, Sarah. You're dead."

A chill shook her.

"It's Tessa Malloy," she repeated. "You know . . . knew . . . my sister, Kit. Remember?"

He stared at her. "She woke up. Talia sun and moon."

"What?"

He shook his head again. "Never mind. Just a story. She started to wake up, but—"

Thankfully, Diane Donovan popped out of the supermarket just then, pushing a cart. She didn't really glance Tessa's way, just wrapped an arm around Liam and began helping him back toward the parking lot down the road a bit, muttering to him. "Why did you get out? I asked you to wait in the car."

Tessa wanted to say something, to help, maybe, but Mrs.

Donovan looked so frazzled, her gray hair wispy and frayed around her face. She wondered what they'd been through since last weekend—since Patrick had gone missing. Were they worried about him? Had the police questioned them?

After she watched Diane tuck her husband into their car, Tessa got back on her bike and rode the rest of the way to Jay Kolbry's house, trying to shake off the mystery of Mr. Donovan's mumblings. Because that's all they were.

And yet.

She dropped the bike against a tree at the foot of Jay's long driveway and walked up the gravel path, fidgeting with her gray sweater, suddenly worried that these faux leather pants were squeaky and everyone in the party would be able to hear it. But then the strains of music and laughter reached her, and she realized how ridiculous that thought was.

No one would notice her—like usual.

For a second, she wished she could be like everyone else— could just *be*. Could come to a party and lift her arms into the air and dance for hours, and then, sweaty and happy, stumble toward a boy, alone in the dark, behind a set of stairs, against a wall, with the music still too loud—loud enough to drown out her thoughts. She wished she could have an arm around Boyd, even if he was just knuckling her head or bitching about his dad's drinking or joking about Chizhevsky. She wished she could tell him how she felt, wished she could say, *That kiss was real. I meant it. I felt it. I don't regret it. Do you?*

But that kiss had led to him, out on the road during a snowstorm, fighting with Kit. It had led to . . . *this*: Tessa, on a mission to find out why her sister had really died.

She kept walking. Because the alternative was to stop moving, and stopping might mean lying down and giving up.

Sleeping Beauty. "She woke up," Mr. Donovan had said. Tessa felt like *she* was the sleepwalker. She needed to snap out of it. She needed to wake up.

She needed to find out what Kit had been doing at Jay Kolbry's Halloween party—to retrace her sister's steps, feel what it had felt like to be her. And maybe, maybe, gain some insight into what the hell Kit had been thinking this past fall, as she spiraled further away from them and further toward that terrible night that changed everything. The night that could never, ever, be undone.

Chapter Twenty-One

BEFORE

12/10

Dear Diary,

I'm trying to write in you more because Mom says being bored means you have no inner resources or something. And also that I should spend less time online and apply myself to life instead. So, life, here's my application.

It's Saturday morning and I'm bundled in this plaid blanket scarf from last year's line at Lupine (which completely clashes with my Pink pajamas and hoodie), just sitting here at the kitchen counter, drinking swampy old coffee and staring out the window. I just saw a row of wild turkeys stalking through our side yard. They are so ugly, I swear, it's gross. All bald and wobbly. ANYWAY. I can't believe it's only two

Saturdays before Christmas. Today we had our first snowfall. Mom managed to shovel her way into the car bright and early to pick out a tree, and since my room's at the front of the house, the sound woke me up.

It is freezing out. My mom always keeps the heat way too low, complaining about the bills. I wish I'd slept over at Mel's last night—Mrs. Knox keeps the thermostat set to seventy-three all the time and you have to crack a window just to stay sane. It's so cozy there. We could spend hours online stalking everyone at school and trying on outfits and falling asleep with our latest rankings of people in our grade on crumpled notebook paper underneath our pillows.

But, no.

There haven't been any sleepovers in a while.

No offense, Diary. I like you and all, but you are no substitute for human company.

I want to text Patrick, but it's too early.

I would bother Tessa, but she's such a porcupine in the morning, so I guess I'll bother Kit, even though she hates me and judges all of my decisions.

Wish me luck.

Lilly knocked softly and, after a few seconds, lightly nudged Kit's bedroom door open. Kit was fast asleep, her poetry journal spread next to her on the bed, her arm draped over part of it. A pen with its cap off lay wedged into the binding.

Lilly started to leave, then thought again and stepped quietly into the room. She approached the bed, grabbing the pen and re-capping it.

She wasn't *trying* to spy on Kit's journal. She was just trying to protect Kit's fluffy white bedspread from a potential ink stain. That she *happened* to see some of the lines in the notebook was just a coincidence. *Even in my sleep,* it said, *it's clear that you were never mine to keep.* But the word *clear* was crossed out, with a caret inserting *plain* instead.

She leaned a little bit closer, and that was when Kit woke up with a start.

"Hey, what are you—" Reflexively, Kit grabbed the notebook and closed it, hugging it to her lap.

"I was just seeing if you were awake," Lilly said hastily, stepping back.

Kit let out a breath. "You scared me. I was trying to sleep in for once."

"You don't have volunteering?"

Kit shook her head, looking a little distressed. "Nope."

"Are you okay? Do you have a headache?"

"No. Yeah. No, I'm fine. Why are you up this early?"

Lilly shrugged. "Mom went to get a tree."

Kit sighed, and she didn't exactly smile, but her eyes softened. "All right, I'm getting up. Just give me a minute."

"Okay!" Lilly said, trying to keep the enthusiasm from her voice. She was still working on the whole eagerness thing.

She went back to her room to get dressed, weirdly excited. She'd always loved tree decorating. She liked traditions in general.

As she was slipping on a striped sweater, Tessa burst in, wearing leggings and a ripped T-shirt, her pale hair in a tangle around her face. "How come Kit's crying in the bathroom?"

"Huh?"

Tessa put her finger to her lips. "Come on, listen."

Sure enough, the bathroom door was closed, and they could hear sniffling, along with running water.

Lilly looked at Tessa with concern. She shrugged, and Tessa shook her head as if to say *I have no idea either.*

Lilly pulled Tessa into her room. "I woke her up to help decorate the tree."

"What tree?"

"Mom went out to get one. She seemed a bit . . . I don't know. Stressed-out. Kit, that is. She fell asleep writing in her poetry thingy. *Love* poems. Not that I was reading them."

When Kit emerged moments later, her eyes looked faintly red around the edges, but nothing Lilly would have otherwise noticed.

"Everything okay?" Tessa asked casually.

"Me?" Kit said. "Yeah, of course. Will one of you help me pull down the attic ladder?"

Silently, the three of them got to work unfolding the rickety trapdoor at the end of the hall, near the entrance to Kit's room, and setting up a chair so they could reach the ladder. Tessa climbed up first and handed boxes down to Kit, who passed them to Lilly, who ran them downstairs to the living room.

Even though they weren't talking much, Lilly still felt oddly happy. There was just something comfortable about going through the same motions they'd gone through every year. No matter what happened, no matter what changed, certain things were constant.

While they were unpacking the stockings, Lilly's phone buzzed. It was a text from Mel.

The outfit worked! You should've seen his face.

Lilly snorted to herself.

P.S. Sex is really not that big of a deal.

Lilly shook her head and went back to the box in front of her. She wasn't sure yet what to reply. The dismissiveness of the text made her sad, but then again . . . did she actually want more details?

"What?" asked Tessa.

"It's just Mel," Lilly said, suddenly wanting desperately to tell her sisters everything that had been going on. "She, um . . . she . . ."

"What?" Kit prodded.

"She did it. She had sex. With Dusty."

"What!" Tessa screamed. "Bratty little *Mel*? How did *that* happen?"

"Hey, Tess, just because she beat all of *us* to the punch doesn't make her a brat," Lilly said. "Anyway, she bought this sexy outfit from Lupine to seduce him, and I guess it worked."

It was Tessa's turn to snort. "Sexy outfit?"

"This bra set. It's actually really pretty. It has this tiny silver charm on the—"

"Why are *you* so quiet?" Tessa cut in, nudging Kit. "This is a big deal! It's like a rite of passage or something."

"What, that someone we know has had sex?" Lilly asked. "Lots of people have. Just because we're a house full of pathetic virgins doesn't mean the rest of the world is waiting around."

"Ow," Kit interrupted, pulling her finger out of an ornament box and sucking the tip of it. "I just pricked myself on one of these."

Lilly stared at her, thinking of the lines from her journal: *Even in my sleep, it's ~~dear~~ plain that you were never mine to keep.* Who had she written that about?

"Have either of you ever, you know . . . gotten close to doing it?" She blushed, unable to stop thinking about Patrick, how he touched her, how he kissed her. She had definitely thought about it—about sex—even though they were nowhere near that step . . . yet. But of course, how could she tell her sisters that? Not after Kit had butted in and told her to stay away from him.

Tessa and Kit were blushing also. The three of them didn't talk about sex very often, if ever. It wasn't really a dinner-table conversation topic.

Tessa shrugged. "Not me. Saving myself for the more civilized world of college."

"What about you, Kit?" Lilly asked, trying to conceal the edge to her voice.

Tessa laughed. "Come on, Lilly. Leave her alone. We all know Kit's not that kind of girl."

"Exactly what kind of girl do you mean?" Lilly demanded, folding her arms. "Why don't you let her answer for herself? Kit?"

Kit's face was the color of a roasted tomato, and she was staring hard at a toy soldier in her hand. Finally she looked up. "What? You know the answer. Everyone knows the answer."

"See?" Tessa said with a satisfied I-told-you-so sigh.

"Whatever," Lilly said, disentangling a set of clear lights.

By the time they were done unpacking all the boxes and hanging up all the stockings over the mantel on the same nails from last year, they heard the car pulling into the driveway.

Lilly pushed through the screen door and ran into the yard, through the falling snow, in her rubber-soled slippers—the ones she'd begged for *last* Christmas, just like Mel's. Tessa came outside behind her and helped hold open the door while Lilly and their mom carried the tree inside, losing a bunch of needles in the process. Kit had the tree stand ready, and they managed to secure the tree into it, even if it was leaning at a slight angle, Tower of Pisa-esque.

The next couple hours were spent wrangling lights and tinsel and ornaments onto the tree, with intermittent breaks for scrambled eggs and cinnamon buns. It was the first time in the last few weeks that Lilly hadn't had to fight the urge to stop in the middle of whatever she was doing to text Patrick.

However, in the afternoon, Tessa went upstairs to get ready for her shift at the Deviled Egg, and Kit retreated to her room to study—apparently, Mr. Green was encouraging her to enter some writing competition—and their mom announced she had to do some holiday shopping online. Lilly was left alone in the living room—the snow still fell outside the window, and a thin layer had begun to stick. She restlessly flipped channels on the TV, glad she didn't have a shift at Lupine but also feeling agitated, like she was trapped inside an itchy wool sweater, except the sweater was *life*.

She couldn't get it out of her head that Kit was upstairs working away. She'd be a famous writer one day, and what would Lilly be?

"Don't you have any passions or projects, Lil?" her mom asked through the open door. She was sitting in the kitchen with the clunky old Dell laptop. "You could use something to focus on."

Lilly sighed, trying not to snap. She was right, in a way. Kit had literature and poetry. Tessa had biology. "Mom, we can't all be like Kit, okay? Anyway, I have plans with Dar," she lied. "I should probably go get ready."

"I just think you all have the potential to do great things. . . . We all have a calling in this life, and maybe it's time you start to find yours."

"Yeah, yeah," she said, flopping off the couch and huffing up the stairs. She'd heard enough. She was the loser of the family—message received, loud and clear.

In her room, she called Dar. "Wanna hang out today?"

Dar cleared her throat. "Hey. Sure. What do you want to do?"

Relief flooded through Lilly's body. For some crazy reason she'd started to believe that Dar really didn't *want* to spend time with her anymore. "Cool! I don't know. Wanna meet at the diner? If I hurry I can catch a ride over with Tessa."

"Okay," Dar replied. "I'll be there in like twenty minutes or so."

"Awesome."

Lilly threw on her black jeans and a beaded sweater that was holiday-ugly-chic, then leaped into her boots and hollered as Tessa passed her room to head downstairs. "Wait, I'm coming with you!"

"Boyd's driving," Tessa said over her shoulder.

They piled into Boyd's truck—he was already waiting behind the wheel. "Malloy Family Chauffeur, at your service," he said, saluting them.

Lilly bit the inside of her lip as Tessa and Boyd began bantering about random school stuff. She still felt weird around Boyd, remembering the night of the Halloween party. How he'd confessed to liking Kit.

You were never mine to keep. Could Kit's poem have been about Boyd? Whatever was going on between them, it was clearly tense, and secretive, though Lilly still couldn't figure out why. And lately she'd been so caught up in the whole Patrick thing that she hadn't really taken the time to think it through. *You were never mine to keep.* Did someone else like Boyd too?

"Yeah, maybe I'll join Lilly and start the bio while you work. I could use a pancake," Boyd was saying to Tessa when

Lilly's ears perked up.

"I'm actually, um, meeting Dar," she told him. "We're supposed to talk about, ya know. Girl stuff."

Tessa snorted and informed Boyd, "Their third Musketeer just got her cherry popped."

"Tessa!" Lilly swatted her arm. "Gross."

"What? It's true. Sexist, I guess. But still true."

Boyd laughed. "All right, all right, I know when I'm not wanted." His tone made Lilly cringe inside—he sounded just a little too cheerful, like he was trying to act as though everything was normal. They'd never had to *try* around each other before. Their friendship with Boyd had always been natural and easy. But things had gotten so different since the start of this school year.

She and Tessa hopped out of the truck, and Lilly barely waved a thanks at Boyd before hurrying through the cold parking lot toward the diner entrance, its big red neon THE DEVILED EGG sign making the gathering snow on the ground pink.

"Thank god for you," Lilly said just a few minutes later when Dar rushed in from the cold, snowflakes still sticking to her scarf and her thin, staticky hair, and took a seat across from Lilly in her window-side booth.

"Me?" Dar said, unwinding her scarf. "I suck, but okay."

Lilly couldn't help but notice her collarbones making sharp lines under her V-neck sweater. "You don't suck. I'm so glad you're here. There's so much to discuss."

Hours flew by as they broke down the entire Mel and

Dusty situation—Dar posited an interesting theory, which was that Mel wasn't even that into Dusty but was using him to rebel against her mother, and also, he was popular. At least popular-*ish*. Then Lilly told her everything about the fling thing with Patrick and all about the rumors and speculations, and she even admitted that she found out Patrick had been writing some of Dar's papers for her. "But don't worry," Lilly quickly added, "I'm not going to tell anyone."

Dar nodded, saying that she wasn't sure if he was right for Lilly, but then again it wasn't her place to say. Then she told Lilly that her dad was dating someone new who was, like, half his age and how he'd tried to set up a dinner for them all to meet and it had been the most awkward event of her life, and how her mom was basically losing it and saying she wanted Dar's dad back and the divorce had been a mistake, he had to see it now.

It all sounded heavy and it started to make sense to Lilly why Dar had been so stressed and out of it lately. The thing about Dar's mom was that she was kind of delusional. She'd named her daughter Darcy because she'd been wanting a boy and had romantic notions of naming him after the hero in *Pride and Prejudice*, so even after Dar was born a girl, she apparently just couldn't let go of the fantasy. Although Lilly hadn't read it, she'd seen the movie—it was one of those stories where the normal girl gets the hot rich guy in the end. Also, the oldest sister was supposedly all perfect and kind, while the youngest sister was basically treated like a huge slut. Which was one of the reasons Lilly didn't plan on reading it.

Anyway, Dar's mom basically idolized her dad in just the same way and totally hadn't seen it coming when he'd told her he wanted a divorce, even though it had been obvious to everyone—especially the neighbors and Dar's friends—that their marriage hadn't exactly been harmonious.

And even though Dar passed on sharing a tuna melt—their usual—she did order a whole basket of fries to split, and Tessa served them a free side of cheese dip, and Lilly was pleased to see Dar put back at least her share of the fries if not more, laughing and opening up and acting like the old Dar, the normal Dar, even getting a smear of ketchup on the side of her face and wiping it off with the back of her hand. "Let's get more!" she announced, and Lilly thought that maybe things *were* going to be okay. Maybe they always had been, and she'd just lost perspective. This was the problem with keeping secrets—you ended up in your own bubble where everything you were worried about got magnified way out of proportion.

After a second basket of fries *and* a shared milkshake, Dar groaned and clutched her stomach. "I gotta get home. My mom's forcing me to watch *White Christmas* with her and she'll probably threaten to slit her wrists if I'm late, which would be funnier if I were actually exaggerating."

"Got it," Lilly said, getting up to give her a hug. Despite their giant meal, Dar still seemed breakable in her arms. "I'll pay for the food. I've been doing windows for Lupine so, basically, I'm loaded."

"Thanks, babe," Dar said.

"Is she picking you up?" Lilly asked as Dar stuffed her hands into mittens.

"Nah, I'm just gonna walk."

"In the snow?"

Dar turned to face her. "I'll be fine. Love ya, Lilly." Then she made her way toward the door and Lilly watched as she pushed out into the darkness cocooned in eerie pink light.

On Sunday, Patrick texted her. **Meet me at the corner of your block.**

"I'm going out!" she hollered cheerfully, and after touching up her concealer and lip gloss, she practically skipped down the street. It had been a good weekend. The new Christmas tree twinkled through their front window.

He was on his motorcycle wearing a ratty old hat and scarf that looked like they probably belonged to his great-uncle, his helmet under his arm. The winter air made his cheeks look pink and boyish.

"Where are we going?"

He shrugged, and she hopped on the back, taking the spare helmet and sucking in a sharp breath as he revved the engine and started off. She wrapped her arms around his body, feeling lucky, trying to take in his smell even with the cold wind stinging her face. She didn't want to let go.

They ended up at the clearing out by Devil's Lake, which lay iced and brown beneath a white-gray sky. In the snow, the woods were basically abandoned.

"What are we doing?" she asked.

He shrugged again as he parked the bike and helped her off. "What do you *want* to do?"

What she wanted to do was make out. Instead she replied, "Build an igloo?"

He laughed. "Okay."

It took awhile—there were only about four inches of snow layered on the ground—and by the time they'd built the walls, around two feet high, Lilly's hands had gone numb inside her gloves. She sat down in the narrow space between the snow walls and took off the gloves to blow hot breath onto her fingers.

Patrick grabbed her hands in his own and rubbed them to warm them up. "It still needs a roof," he pointed out, scanning their work.

"Don't be so literal," Lilly replied, pulling him toward her.

They fell back into the snow and started kissing, his lips a mix of hot and cold against hers, the snow coming down around his dark, messy hair. She pulled off his goofy hat, laughing, and they kissed some more. The back of her head was chilled against the ground, but her body was alive with heat, and as she looked up at Patrick's face for a second, she was struck by the sudden discovery that what was happening now might in fact be the very thing she'd been looking for forever without knowing it.

She didn't want to even think the words *falling in love* because if she did, somehow, maybe this would all dissolve into the snow around them, come down like a collapsed igloo and blow away.

So she said nothing, just clung to his jacket.

After a while, they were simply too cold to keep kissing. He rolled over onto his back next to her, knocking over part of one of the walls with his elbow, and sighed.

They both stared at the sky, blinking against the soft, icy flurries.

"I just—" Patrick said suddenly.

"Hmm?"

"I just wish this could, like, not end."

Lilly swallowed hard. People didn't say they wished things didn't have to end unless they thought things *did* have to end.

As heady and amazing as she'd felt just moments before, Lilly was now full of a slow, cold dread. She blinked hard. It wasn't like he was trying to break up with her. Was he? They weren't even together . . . or were they?

Finally she got her voice back enough to say, "Speaking of, I should probably get home before I die of hypothermia out here."

"Okay," he said, his voice a whisper.

He drove her home in silence, and it was all she could do to not cry as she walked back to her door, feeling like she was dragging a heavy secret behind her, a blanket of shame.

It wasn't until Monday that Lilly heard the news, from Mel. The morning bell hadn't rung yet. Mel was waiting for her on the front steps of the school, wearing a puffy parka and a hat with a pompom on top. She grabbed Lilly's arm, her eyes wide with alarm. "Did you hear?"

"Hear what? About you and Dusty? All I know is what you texted—"

"*No*, not about me and Dusty. About Dar."

Lilly's heart froze. "What about Dar? I just saw her on Saturday. We met at the diner and—"

"She's in the hospital."

"What? Why? Is she okay? What happened?"

Mel just shook her head. "She ate, like, three pizzas or something. I don't know. An old Halloween-size jumbo bag of Skittles. Her mom found her passed out on the bathroom floor covered in her own vomit."

"What? Is she sick?"

"She's not *sick*, Lilly. She's anorexic. Well, my mom says it's a mixed diagnosis. Anorexic with occasional bingeing-purging tendencies or something like that. It's horrible. The doctors say she can't even leave the hospital until she's gained twelve pounds. Did you know she was under ninety?"

"Ninety pounds? How is that even—"

"Possible? I don't know. I thought she was skinny. But she's always in those sweaters. Oh, I don't *know*, Lilly, how didn't we see it? *Did* we see it? I mean, her own *mom* didn't even realize it."

Lilly stared at Mel and shook her head. Of course Dar's mom hadn't noticed—she lived in a dream, in a snow-globe world where the normal girl gets the hot rich guy and marriages last and daughters don't fall apart, or if they do, they're rescued. "No." She cleared her throat. "I guess we didn't notice. Or if we did, it wasn't enough."

"Yeah," Mel said. Her face looked different to Lilly, then. Lilly thought how far apart they'd become in only a month or so. Mel had barely told her anything about losing her virginity. About what was going on between her and Dusty. She had a sudden chill. What else wasn't she seeing?

"Hey," Lilly said. She put her hand on Mel's arm. "Are *you* okay, though?"

Mel started to cry.

"What? What is it?" She hugged Mel, but Mel kept crying. "What happened? Are you and Dusty all right? Do you regret . . . anything?"

Mel sniffled against her shoulder. "I just . . . we should have seen. There's so much people don't know, Lilly."

"What do you mean? What else don't people know?"

Mel stood back and wiped her face. "Nothing, it's fine. It's just been a lot. Listen, sleepover soon, okay?"

Lilly nodded, and then the bell rang.

Mel headed inside for class, but Lilly remained on the stairs outside, feeling stuck, even as a flood of students pushed past her. She kept picturing Dar laughing and gossiping with her like normal at the diner. *Was* it normal, how she'd ordered that second basket of fries? Should Lilly have said something? Should she have said something before then? Weeks ago, or at the start of the school year, when she first thought Dar looked thin?

When was the right time to start worrying about someone? Could she have stopped it from getting this bad?

All this time, she'd felt pushed away, left out, like her friends didn't need her. What if they needed her more than ever and she was just too blind to see it? What if she'd been sleeping this whole time and was only just now waking up?

It had been snowing steadily since the weekend, and as the flurries floated around her face, melting against her lips and eyelids and cheeks, the lines from Kit's journal came back to her once again, like a clue, like something else she should have paid attention to—and maybe she still could, before it was too late.

Even in my sleep, it's plain that you were never mine to keep.

Chapter Twenty-Two

NOW

AS SOON AS TESSA ENTERED Jay Kolbry's house, she was overwhelmed by the noise and chaos. Adelia Naslow stumbled past her, shouting at another girl Tessa couldn't see. The house was crowded. Most of the people there were seniors she didn't recognize. She counted maybe six other juniors, and she was pretty sure most of them were cheerleaders or girlfriends of senior guys. Some of the seniors looked vaguely familiar—she'd probably seen them hovering around Jay and Olivia in the cafeteria and school halls, or at the occasional football games she'd been forced to watch from a distance while practicing throwing Milk Duds into Boyd's mouth from three bleachers away.

She nearly got corralled into a game of beer pong but managed to dodge the flying Ping-Pong balls and push her way through the crowd to the kitchen. Jay was not in there.

She moved through several rooms, unable to find him, and finally reached a sliding door. It was hot and loud and she needed air. But a guy was leaning on the glass door.

"Can I?" she asked, gesturing. As he stood aside, she slipped past him into the yard.

"It's raining out there," she heard the guy say. "But, whatever."

Outside, an old wooden swing set hung soggy and limp; the cracked plastic swing, purple on yellow rope, sparkled with rainwater. She looked around at the emptiness of the yard, swiveling the sapphire ring around her finger nervously.

The sliding door closed behind her, and she realized the guy who'd been leaning on it before had followed her outside. He stood next to her, hunched, even though the rain was hardly heavy, and took a sip from a big red cup of beer.

He cleared his throat. "Too much fun in there, huh?"

"What?" She turned to him. Realized he seemed older, like maybe nineteen or twenty.

He pointed a thumb over his shoulder. "Too much party in the party, am I right? Needed a breather?"

"Guess so."

"You friends with Olivia? I know you're not in Jay's crowd."

"Kind of. Well, no, not really. You?"

"I'm Jay's cousin."

She nodded. The yard was damp now, seeping slightly into the sides of her red boots. "Not really friends with anyone here."

The guy cocked his head. "So why come?"

She shrugged. "I guess I just wanted to, um, see for myself. What it was like . . ."

The guy nodded. "I'm Alex, by the way."

"Katherine." The name slipped out before Tessa could take it back. She wasn't sure why she'd said it, and she felt her cheeks reddening.

"So, Katherine, do you often show up at parties where you don't have any friends?" He gave her a side grin.

She couldn't really tell if he was flirting with her, and whether it mattered. She was too startled by hearing someone else refer to her by her sister's name. "No, not often," she answered finally. "My, um, sister came to one of Jay's parties last year, though. The Halloween one."

Alex nodded again. "Yeah, I was here for that. That party was killer."

Tessa looked at him, suddenly interested. "Did you see her there? Slightly taller than me, blond also, green eyes? I think she came by herself. But maybe not."

Alex shook his head. "I'm sure I'd remember another lone blonde like you."

"She was dressed as Edna St. Vincent Millay."

"Who?"

"A poet, I think. I don't know." The mist was starting to soak into the thin fabric of her sweater. "She was wearing all black. I guess I'm just wondering because I wanted to know . . . what she was acting like."

Alex shrugged. "I don't recall her, but who knows? It was probably crowded." He offered her a sip of his beer, but she declined. "Where's your sister tonight, then?"

Tessa looked around, as if the mangled shrubbery lining Jay Kolbry's yard might help her come up with an answer. "She's. She couldn't . . . she can't be here. Listen, I need to go."

"Hope to see you around, Katherine," he called after her as Tessa stumbled past and headed back into the house.

She found Olivia and Jay in the kitchen. "You guys . . ." She felt panic rising in her throat as she tugged on Olivia's sleeve. "Hey, you guys, did . . . do you remember my sister being here at the Halloween party this year?"

"Oh, girlfriend," Olivia said, a look of pure pity flashing over her. "What are you doing here, babes? And you're all wet—"

She tried to put her arm around her, but Tessa backed out of the kitchen, then swiveled and marched into the living room, where a bunch of people sat cross-legged on the floor, a messy stack of playing cards scattered between them, clearly in the midst of a raging game of Asshole.

"Hey. HEY. You guys. Do—did any of you know my sister? Kit? Katherine Malloy? Did you see her at the Halloween party here?"

"We're in the middle of a game, dude," someone said, but then looked up. "Oh, man, it's you. I'm sorry! I mean, I, uh, wow, yeah."

"Were you all at the Halloween party?" she demanded, unfazed. The music blared loud in her ears.

"I was," said another girl. "But that was, like, months ago. Are you okay?"

They were whispering now. *That's the girl. Her sister. Yeah, the one who—*

She couldn't take it anymore. All these people just going on with their lives, just partying and hanging out casually, as if the world hadn't halted in its tracks a week ago. Kit's death meant *nothing* to them, did it? It was just a thing to gossip and wonder about. It didn't *matter.* How was it possible? How could it be that something could be so devastating for some people, and not even touch others? It didn't seem the universe could accommodate it.

A bad feeling was sinking in now. She started to stumble from the room.

It was the feeling that this had all been a massive mistake— not just showing up at this party, but her assumption that Kit really *had* come to the Halloween party in the first place. What if that too had been one of Kit's secrets? What if she'd only *said* she was going to Jay Kolbry's house to throw them off the scent of her true plans?

Her throat was tight and her head was hot. This was stupid. This was wrong, all wrong. *She* was all wrong.

Tessa pushed her way out of the room and toward the front hall.

On the way she bumped shoulders with Alex.

He reached out to steady her. "Hey, Katherine, leaving so soon?"

"I'm not—let go of me. Let me go," she repeated, trying to spin away toward the door.

"Hey, hey, it's cool," someone behind her said.

Tessa swiveled, and there was . . .

"Mel?"

She felt turned around, disoriented. Mel seemed flushed, her eyes darting.

"What are you doing here?" they both said at the same time.

Mel huffed. "Come on, I can't talk to you here . . . like this."

Tessa didn't know what she meant. Why had Mel come? Did she really not care either? Even after their talk beneath the bleachers . . .

"Seriously, why are you here—alone?" Tessa asked Mel as soon as they had ducked into a quiet room. She looked around. It appeared to be a den with old video game controllers scattered across the floor. A huge, oily stain spanned the far corner of the carpet.

"Are you following me or something?" Mel asked back, fidgeting with her pockets.

"Me? Following you? Not exactly," Tessa said. "Anyway, I was here before you."

"That makes no sense," Mel said, staring into her eyes.

And that was fair. It *didn't* make sense. Tessa shouldn't be here. But neither should Mel. It wasn't either of their crowds.

"I'm here because . . . because . . . I was trying to find clues. About Kit. About what happened last fall and what she was hiding from us. Because—here's the thing, Mel." Tessa could feel her pulse racing. "I don't believe that Boyd did it, okay? I don't believe he killed Kit."

Mel let out a heavy sigh. Her eyes slid to a detached keyboard on the floor, then to a matted, sunken armchair in one corner. Anywhere but Tessa. "There's something you should probably know," she said quietly.

Tessa stood there, feeling like the rain from earlier had melted into her, and she was becoming water, becoming something not quite solid.

"There's a rumor the case is going to trial soon."

"What are you—how do you know?"

"My mom. She knows everything in this town, remember? She's a reporter."

Gossip columnist, more like. But Tessa wasn't going to correct her. "What else did she find out?"

Mel looked away. "That he plans to plead guilty."

"But there's nothing to admit to!" Panic was beginning to have a choke hold on her. It was hard to breathe. "This is wrong. This is so wrong, Mel. This is why I have to do something, I have to say something, I have to find proof—"

"Tessa!" Mel shouted. Then she clapped a hand over her own mouth and glanced at the closed door. When nothing happened, she went on more quietly. "Tessa. No. You need to stop. You need to let it lie. This isn't for you to solve."

Heat flashed through Tessa, making her hands shake. "You're wrong, Melissa. This *is* for me to solve, and only me."

Mel looked slapped. "Fine. Well, leave me out of it, at least." Without another glance at Tessa, she swung open the den door and made her way back into the throng of partiers.

Tessa slid through the main part of the house and the ruckus of the party, completely overwhelmed. What kind of proof had she really thought she could get here? This had been such a disaster. She was an amateur. A cluster of kids stood outside the front door now, and as she scooched between them and down the stoop, she felt like smoke, drifting through the party and the world, shapeless and without notice.

The rain was starting to let up, but her bike was wet and slippery.

Hurriedly, she did her best to wipe the seat with her sleeve, then hopped on and began to pedal.

The ride home was dark and wet and wavery, the rain still dripping off branches, blending with tears of frustration and confusion. Her chest rattled, like she'd been holding her breath too long.

Her ring glinted in the light of the street lamps.

Somewhere along Woodrow, a figure emerged into the road.

Tessa yelped and swerved. Her front wheel caught a puddle and she spun and flipped, landing on her side in a ditch just past the shoulder.

For a second, she lay there in shock. Her shoulder ached.

Slowly, she got up, trembling.

Mud and gravel had dug into her palms, but she was okay.

She rubbed her shoulder and looked around, trying to find the figure who'd darted past.

She spotted him, vanishing into the darkness of the road.

Before she had time to think about it, she was running. Out of breath. These stupid red boots. Her shoulder killed. It was too late. The figure in the distance had gotten too far ahead, had darted off down a side road.

A fresh gush of rain fell hard into her eyes, causing her to blink rapidly. She could taste its harsh salt on her tongue.

She felt like she was going crazy.

She could swear the person she'd just seen was Patrick Donovan.

Chapter Twenty-Three

BEFORE

1/6

Dear Diary,

She's late. Again. Kittttt!!!!!

Sigh. First, I have to work all day only two days before we go back to school (sale season). Then I don't even get my ride home, and Margaret says I have to close up. I can't believe she left the shop keys with me. She must really trust me.

So now here I am alone at Lupine, the lights off, windows edged in frost. Outside, traffic inches along Main Street. I can see windshield wipers going strong, taillights trailing dim red lines on the salted road.

There's been a total of fourteen inches of snow this winter, and it's not even the end of the first week of January—they're saying that's the heaviest snowfall in sixteen years, which I guess means the last time it was this bad, my mom was preg-nant with me.

I can't believe it's the new year already. Christmas came and went. Presents were wrapped and then immediately unwrapped. Mom got Kit a tablet with this electronic pen thingy to replace her notebook and Tessa new boots, which she immediately broke in so they'd look as distressed as her last pair. I got a couple gift cards and a new comforter I had been coveting. And we got Mom a bunch of books and the new bird feeder she wanted.

Kit also took Tessa out on the road yesterday to practice driving in Mom's car. I came along, which I deeply regret, because I was 100 percent convinced we were going to die every time she accelerated past thirty-five miles per hour. Still, it was kind of fun. It's a whole year before I even get my permit.

I'm always the one who has to wait for everything.

Anyway. Patrick came into the shop earlier today. He was glowing, I swear, full of energy like he'd just downed three Red Bulls. He told me he felt bad he didn't have a present for me on Christmas and even though it was going to be a couple weeks late at this point, he asked what I wanted. I pointed out that I hadn't gotten him anything either (P.S. Does this mean we're at gift-giving status already???), but he just grabbed my hands and pulled me down one of the clothes aisles, going, "Just tell me what you want. Anything." He grabbed a dress from a nearby hanger. "This? Or this?" He lets it go and grabs a scarf. "Or this?" By that point I was laughing, while also trying to refold everything and put it back.

It was fun. And sweet. But I guess if I'm being honest, it was also a little strange. He's not normally the bubbly, laughing type.

Then he goes, "Oh, I know . . . THAT." He was pointing to the boy shorts and bra set he'd teased me about what feels like a zillion years ago. They are no longer in the window display, but they're still full price.

Anyway, I'm sure I was blushing like crazy. "Seriously, you don't need to get me anything."

But . . . Diary. I knew what I wanted. This.

This feeling he brings out in me. That's it. That's honestly all I want.

"Since when are you so loaded?" I said. "Is there someone else you're writing papers for now that I should know about?"

"You jealous?" he asked, raising an eyebrow.

"No!"

"Good. And no, not cheating money. Just got a little cash," he says. "Just an old thing I pawned. Turned out to be worth more than I thought."

Oh, hold on—I think this is Kit. Finally!!!!!!!!

Lilly shoved her diary into her shoulder bag and hopped off the front counter where she'd been sitting as Kit finally came bursting through the door, setting off the jingly bells above and letting in a gust of snowy air.

"Where have you *been*?"

Kit's eyes were bright, her lashes wet and dark as black

spiders. "Really sorry, Lil. Hey, can I use the bathroom before we go?" It wasn't really a question—she was already halfway through the store, heading to the back.

"I mean, sure," Lilly muttered. "It's not like I have anything *better* to do than keep waiting."

When Kit emerged a couple minutes later, Lilly could swear she looked different somehow, and it wasn't just the recent haircut. She had on her backpack, her golden hair pressed down under a white wool hat and her cheeks still bright pink from the cold, but there was something else. . . .

They threw their bags into the back, then Lilly slid into the passenger seat and sighed audibly as Kit started the engine.

"Everything okay?" Kit asked, staring ahead at the road.

"With *me*? Yeah, I guess," Lilly said, even though it wasn't really true—her entire life seemed like it was whirling away from her in a spiraling storm. "The question is whether *you're* okay."

"Oh, I'm good," Kit said, still not looking at her.

Silence. Lilly felt her annoyance filling up the space between them like a taut balloon. "*Really* good, maybe," she finally muttered.

"Lilly, please."

"*What?*" she turned to her sister, who was still facing the road.

"I don't want to deal with your . . . you know." From the side, in the darkness of the car, Kit looked older than usual. More serious.

Lilly folded her arms. "My what."

"Your *comments*. Insinuations, or whatever."

Lilly huffed. "So now I'm not allowed to talk?"

"Oh, you can talk." Kit smiled. "If it's about the weather or something."

"You sound just like Tessa. I thought *she* was the bitchy one, but I guess everyone is switching roles these days."

Kit said nothing.

Snowflakes hit the windshield and melted. Lilly realized it'd been taking a long time for the car to heat up. Normally, if Kit had just returned from a volunteer route, the car would be toasty because she spent more time in it, between houses, than in any one house along the way.

Maybe she'd stopped somewhere longer than usual tonight. Maybe that was why she was late.

Stopped somewhere to meet *someone*. In secret.

Lilly sighed again, taking off her gloves and rubbing her hands together. "I just wish you'd tell me what's going on. That's all I want. I just want to *know*. What do you think I'll do—run and tell Mom? Because I won't. And I won't try and get in your way or tell you what to do—even though *you* obviously don't hesitate to tell *me* what to do. But I wouldn't, I swear." The words spilled out of her and she couldn't stop them. "Everyone's hiding from me. No one's telling me things. It's horrible and it's not fair. I didn't do *anything* to deserve that."

She knew she was pouting and probably sounded juvenile but who cared?

"You *used* to tell me things," she added, quieter.

"Well, things change, sis." Kit shrugged, but there was a slight catch in her voice.

"No—*you've* changed. And I don't like this Kit."

"Meanwhile, *you're* the same old Lilly—always spying on me and Tess, begging to be let into our rooms and our secrets instead of just living your own life."

"I *am* living my own life, and if you weren't so obsessed with your own drama these days, you would know that."

Kit turned to face her. "What do you mean? Are you still seeing that Patrick kid?"

Lilly looked at the stains on the windshield. "Not telling. If you don't, I don't."

"Fine." Kit turned back to the road.

"Fine."

They were silent most of the way home. As she parked the car, Kit looked down at her hands. "Lilly. I'm sorry."

Lilly looked at her, but Kit wouldn't meet her eyes.

"For telling you what to do," Kit added. "It's not my business. You were right. I just want you . . . I just want *us* . . . to be happy."

Then she got out of the car, leaving Lilly alone to wonder what that meant, what to feel, what had gone wrong. Because it wasn't until Kit said she wanted them to be happy that the cold truth engulfed Lilly like a tidal wave: they *weren't* happy anymore, were they?

Chapter Twenty-Four

NOW

FEBRUARY 11

PATRICK DODGED THE ONCOMING HEADLIGHTS and kept running, even as a new rush of rain slammed into his face and eyes like tiny bullets. He heard the bike swerve and the crunch of gravel behind him, sending a surge of adrenaline through him, urging him on, *almost* numbing the ache in his back and delts and neck.

He'd barely slept in about seventy-two hours. He still regretted selling the motorcycle, but at least he had been able to nod off on the bus home. It hadn't lasted long, though: there'd been a woman behind him with two screaming little kids who took turns kicking the back of his seat and wailing for most of the ride. His jaw was still tense from clenching.

It was far from the bus station to the Donovans' house, especially in the rain, but he wasn't going to try hitchhiking for fear of rousing suspicion about his return. And it wasn't like he could afford to call a cab. He was clean out of cash. Again.

Pawning the ring had gotten him pretty far—all the way to Vermont, and almost a week in. But that turned out to be a shit show. He'd found a "commune" that was more like a halfway house, most of the ratty furniture ridden with lice, the corners of the cupboards lined with trails of mouse turds, and the floors prickly with the remnants of broken bottles. The place basically reeked of piss and cigarettes and body odor, and the handful of other residents depressed him—usually they were staring glassy-eyed at a wall or causing an angry commotion in the hall. As far as he could tell, most of them didn't have jobs, so he wasn't sure how they paid for the $11-a-night rent or the booze and dirty-looking pill bottles some of them kept squirreled away.

That had lasted two nights. Then he slept in a barn one night, underneath a pile of old coats, which had been so cold and uncomfortable that he'd spent most of the night awake, shaking.

It sucked, having nowhere to go. There were a lot of things he could've tried. Maybe move to a big city to look for work. Try to get his GED, then apply for a scholarship somewhere. He'd even gone to the local library to use the internet to search for jobs, finally, but in a moment of weakness he'd started poking around on social media. That's how he learned what had really happened the night he left Devil's Lake. How the Malloy sister died—froze to death, people said, after a nasty, violent fight with a boy she'd trusted.

And that was when he knew he *did* have a place to go, as hard as it would be to come back. He had to return to Devil's Lake.

He had to explain his side.

His clothes were drenched by the time he turned down the familiar cul-de-sac and approached the house—dark except for a lamp burning in the window of Uncle Liam's study. He couldn't really see in, but there were no shadows, no signs of movement. His great-uncle had probably fallen asleep at his desk, like he sometimes did.

Patrick stood in the yard, the wet, unmown grass straggly from melted snow, as he tried to figure out what to do. It was late. He didn't want to scare Aunt Diane. He wandered to the front of the house, debating whether to knock and wake them up. Or would it be better to try the back door to see if it was unlocked?

He heard a rustle in the distance and turned. At the edge of the woods, where the street dead-ended in a cement circle, a form was moving among the trees.

Instantly all the hair on the back of his neck stood on end, and the rain suddenly seemed colder, harsher, the dark more dangerous.

He stepped away from the house and into the street, approaching slowly. "Who's there?" he called out.

No response.

More movement—not hurried or furtive, but deliberate and slow, like whoever was out there was focused on a task. Something shimmered, like wet silver or glass, as the person crouched down. Hiding?

He stepped closer still, hesitant to leave the weak halo of the single street lamp. "Who's out there?" he asked again.

A twig snapped, and Patrick heard angry mumbling.

By now he was only about ten feet from the start of the woods. Something caught the light again. A pair of glasses.

Patrick's pulse went into his throat. "Uncle Liam? Is that you?"

More mumbling.

Patrick hurried into the woods and discovered his great-uncle squatting in the rain. In his hands was a—now soaking wet—blue parka. It looked like it was a women's cut, possibly an old coat of Diane's.

He bent over his uncle and put his hand on his back. "Come on, Uncle Liam, it's time to go inside. It's raining. How long have you been out here, anyway? And let's take this in too, to dry off."

Liam looked up at him then, rain misting his glasses. "She might need it."

"Who might?"

"Sarah. She was out here alone. She was crying."

"Who's Sarah?"

Liam swallowed. "We were engaged, you know. She gave

me back the ring. Didn't want it. Beautiful sapphire ring. More than a semester's tuition, that ring. That was before." He looked down at his hands, still clutching the corner of the parka, then back up at Patrick, confusion now written on his brow. "Is that you, boy?"

"It's me. Patrick. Let me help you inside."

Liam finally put his hand in Patrick's and allowed himself to be lifted to standing. But when Patrick bent down to pick up the coat, Liam shook his head, resisting. "No. Leave it. She may need it. She was so cold. So cold. She cried herself to sleep."

"Who did?" Patrick asked, giving up on the coat. He could go back and get it later.

"Sarah."

A chill ran up his spine. "When was this?"

Liam shook his head. "Don't know. Winter. Maybe I dreamed it. Just like the fairy tale."

Patrick's chest felt like ice. "What did you see, Liam?"

What did you see, Patrick? he heard in his head. Her urgent, pleading voice. The sister.

Liam smiled now. "A princess asleep."

Patrick swallowed. "You shouldn't be out in the woods alone at night. It's not safe," he said. "For anyone."

He got his great-uncle to the front door and pushed. It was unlocked. Of course—Liam must have left it that way when he came outside, whenever that was.

Diane—her gray hair loose and wild—stood on the bottom stair in the dark, holding an unplugged lamp as though she was about to swing it like a bat. When she saw Patrick holding up her husband, she gasped, letting the lamp drop as her other hand reached up to cover her mouth. The lamp rolled onto the floor but didn't break. For some reason, Patrick was grateful. Shattered glass would have been too much.

"What are you—how did you—"

"I came back," Patrick said, keeping his voice low and steady. "I saw him outside. He was in the trees at the edge of the road. . . ."

His great-aunt seemed to snap out of her shock then. "Well, come in, come in," she said in a hurried whisper, pulling them both through the doorway, then glancing around the dark yard once before closing the door. "Help me get him to bed."

For the next thirty minutes, she was all business, ushering Patrick up the stairs with Liam still leaning on him. Handing them both towels to dry off from the rain. Fetching Liam clean, dry pajamas. Finally his great-uncle was in his own bed, snoring, and Patrick turned to his aunt in the darkened bedroom, watching her shoulders slump with exhaustion.

"You should sleep too," he said. "We can talk in the morning. I mean, if it's okay for me to . . . for me to stay."

She took his arm and led him out into the hallway, then sat on the top stair, gesturing for him to sit beside her. She put her head in her hands, and it took him a moment to realize she was crying.

Should he put a hand on her back? What do you do when an old woman cries? Was it his fault? Probably.

"He's gotten worse," she said quietly. "We have no help. There's no one. We're off the volunteer route. No one will come."

"I'm sorry," he whispered, feeling like his heart would break. "I'm so sorry I left. I know you needed me. It was . . . it was selfish," he said, suddenly recognizing how true that was. He had fucked up. Again. Maybe he was doomed to never get things right.

Diane shook her head. "I will have to tell them."

"Tell them?"

"The police." Her voice was hoarse and tired. "They said— they have to know. They've been asking. *Were* asking. They have a suspect; it's expected to go to trial, but. But they told me if I ever found out where you were—oh, Patrick, it's not safe for you here. I don't know what you've done. I don't know what to do."

Her soft words fell onto him, heavy—like damp soil collapsing in on itself, becoming a landslide.

"And I know," she went on. "I know you did something. I know you were . . . you were taking things from us." She shook her head, not looking at him.

His throat was full of lead. "We'll talk to them," he said, forcing the words out past the invisible metal choking him. "Tomorrow. *I'll* go in. I promise. I have nothing—" He paused and cleared his throat. "Nothing to hide. I'll tell them everything."

He wanted to put an arm around her, but he didn't. He just

sat there beside her, cold all over—cold and damp on the *inside*, really. In his chest an ache; his whole body a cave, hollow.

Sun poured through the streaked attic windows the next morning, and Patrick squinted, rolling over in bed, forgetting for a moment where he was. Forgetting that he was home. Then remembering.

Then remembering there *was* no home.

We fought, he recited in his head. *I knew she was distressed. Maybe it was my fault she was so upset. I didn't know what to do.*

Was there any point? Would he end up in jail like Boyd? Could it be any worse than the mental prison he'd been living in this past week? He left—he left all of them. Why had he thought they'd want him back?

He closed his eyes again and saw a girl's face, white with rage, white with the cold, her eyes blazing like hot ice, the forest closing around them, the snow coming down so hard that night. It had been like a snow globe, but a nightmare one. Everything turned upside down, unglued. How the flurries falling in his eyes had unhinged him. It wasn't just her, daring to intervene, to accuse, to cut into him, into the truth—it was her *on top of everything else.* On top of the pain in his ribs when he thought of Lilly and what *she* thought of him now. It was one more person calling him a loser, telling him there was no way out.

He knew that trick. There were two options: let yourself be buried in the snow, weighty and numbing and suffocating—or run. Run, run, run until you've burned away the pain, until the place you're running from isn't even a speck in the distance anymore, is hardly a pinprick of sadness at the very back of your mind.

So that's what he'd done. Run.

He got up now and got dressed—his hands shook as he selected a sensible-looking shirt from Liam's closet. A shirt that said, *I swear I didn't do it. I may even know who did.*

Diane had cooked Sunday breakfast, but he couldn't stomach it. She handed him toast wrapped in a napkin, and her keys; he dropped the former into the trash can out front before getting into her car, which smelled like pine and must.

He pulled out of the driveway, then drove toward the mouth of the cul-de-sac where it spilled straight out onto Route 28.

But he never made it to the police station, or even onto the main road.

Because a big red pickup truck was turning onto his street, blocking his way out.

For a minute, the sun reflected back, glaring, from the windshield, and he couldn't see who was driving. But then he did. The Taylor kid.

Boyd got out of his truck—he was even taller than Patrick remembered, and not wearing that hunting hat he basically had glued to his head all fall.

He turned off the engine as Boyd approached. Patrick got out of the car, trying to play it cool, even though his brain was screaming—*What's he doing here?* "Can I, um, help you?"

Boyd's open face contorted into what could only be called a sneer. He shook his head. "I mean, you dare to come back around here, like nothing has happened. I had to sit around in *jail* this whole time."

"How did you get out?" Bail had been posted at $25,000, from what he'd read. There was no way Innis Taylor—or anyone around here—had that kind of money lying around.

"My dad finally scraped up enough for a bail bond."

"Oh." He'd heard of that. A bond where you paid a small percentage of the bail. You could spend the rest of your life paying down the remainder. "Boyd, you should know I never—"

"Let me ask you something," Boyd said, one foot in front of the other, like he was prepared to lunge. "How do you think it *looks*? What, are you just gonna come crawling home with your tail between your legs and act like you know nothing? She's *dead*, dude." His voice got hoarser here. Patrick said nothing.

"You ran off without a word that night," he went on. "I don't know why you came back, but I'm not fucking leaving this spot until you spit out the truth."

He was only standing about five feet away, and Patrick was starting to feel claustrophobic, trapped with his back inches from Diane's car. "I don't owe you anything, and what I do or don't know about that night is none of your business. Besides, I only know Lilly. I hardly knew her sisters—"

"Oh, you knew them. You knew Kit, didn't you? A lot better than you'd like us to think," Boyd practically spat. "I know what was going on between you two. And I'm not taking the fall for you."

Patrick's head was spinning. "Nothing was going on."

He scoffed. "You *would* say that now."

"If you think I was into Kit, you're high, dude," Patrick said, feeling heat creep up the back of his neck.

"I didn't believe it at first," Boyd went on. "That she could have a thing for you. She said it was wrong. Someone with a history of being a shithead. That could mean a lot of things. Who knows, maybe if you hadn't disappeared, I never would have guessed."

"You have no idea what you're talking about, and you really need to get out of my way," Patrick said, taking a step toward Boyd. Whatever he was rambling about needed to end, and it needed to end now, before things got even more out of hand.

"It's so obvious now, though," Boyd said, ignoring him. "She was wearing that stuff from Lilly's store. The bra. Which *you* stole." As he ranted, he moved closer. Patrick could practically feel the hot anger pulsing off him. "It all makes sense now. You were two-timing with both sisters. Maybe Kit found out and wanted to tell. But you didn't want her to, did you? You fucking wanted to silence her, didn't you?" Boyd's face was red, and he was only a couple feet from Patrick now. *"Didn't you?"*

"Back off, Boyd. I didn't steal anything, and I didn't hurt Katherine Malloy, or anyone. I didn't touch her. I don't need to answer to you. If you ask me, you're the one who wants to fuck all those sisters. Maybe you should be questioning your own motives."

Boyd's eyes went wide. "Excuse me, what?"

Patrick's jaw and fists went hard. "You heard me. You have

always had a blatant hard-on for all three Malloy girls, and if anyone was messing around, it's you. You act like you own them. So step back and get into your truck. This is over."

He turned to get back into Diane's car, but Boyd grabbed his shoulder.

"Don't you *ever* talk about them that way. You're scum, you know that?"

Patrick swiveled, pushing his arm away, a little too hard. "I said back off. If I were you, I'd get in your car if you don't want to get run over."

"Are you threatening me?" Boyd's eyes were wide, his neck muscles pulsing.

"Should I be?"

"You're a fucking loser and a fucking killer, and I'm going to prove it."

"I *said* back off," Patrick said, rearing on Boyd and shoving him.

Boyd returned with a punch, his fist making contact with Patrick's jaw. Patrick felt his teeth clamp down on his tongue, tasting blood as he reeled, stumbling back against the car.

He pushed himself up to standing and lunged at Boyd, throwing himself at him without thinking. He grabbed Boyd's shoulders and butted his forehead into Boyd's face.

Blood spurted from Boyd's nose as Patrick watched him fall to the ground, catching himself on his elbow and clutching his face. "Whatthefuck," he kept saying.

Shaking, Patrick got into his car and drove off, away from Boyd, who was still lying on the pavement in the cul-de-sac.

He skirted the truck, barely missing the fender, and squealed out onto 28.

He couldn't go to the cops now. Not like this. He stared at his bloodied fist, wrapped around the steering wheel. His jaw killed, and he could see in the rearview mirror that a yellowy-purple bruise was already blooming. His hip hurt from where something—the car handle, maybe—had dug into his skin.

Returning to Devil's Lake had been a huge mistake.

He was tempted to hit the gas hard and get out of town again, keep driving and never return.

He would've done it, too, but even as Diane's old car started to sputter, he knew he had nowhere to go. Devil's Lake felt like his fate. He had to come back and face it head-on.

Chapter Twenty-Five

NOW

FEBRUARY 12

THE RAIN HAD CLEARED OVERNIGHT, and so had Tessa's mind. It *had* been Patrick she'd seen on the street, and now she had to find out why he was back. She skipped her shift at the Deviled Egg. She'd probably lose her job there for not at least calling. But she couldn't bear it—couldn't bear to act like life was normal. And she was tired of this constant feeling of *waiting* for the truth, like she was some trapped princess, locked in an icy casket. It had been a full week now. If Boyd was about to plead guilty for this thing, she needed to act, and it needed to be fast.

Patrick was outside when she arrived—his legs, in a dirty pair of jeans, sticking out from underneath an old car in the driveway. Mrs. Donovan's car. Tessa could hear clanking and watched as he reached for a wrench lying beside him on the pavement. She stood there a moment, trying to figure out what to say, when she heard him mutter to himself and then scooch out from under the car, wiping his hands on a white rag.

A dark stain was streaked across his T-shirt and forehead . . . and an ugly bruise bloomed low on his jaw.

"Oh, shit," he said when he noticed her standing there. "It's . . . you." He squinted at her, like the sun was too bright for him to be sure who he was really looking at.

He sat up, shielding his eyes with one hand. When he dropped his hand, she could see he looked . . . afraid, almost. Tired, too. Shadows laced his eyes; his dark hair looked shaggy and unkempt behind the ears.

"You came back," she said.

"For better or for worse," he said slowly, getting to his feet. He took a step back, and she noticed he was looking at her warily. As if he was afraid. Her pulse kicked up. Why would he be afraid . . . unless he had something to hide?

"Please," she said quietly. "I just need to know the truth. Did you see Kit that night? That night she . . ."

She held her breath as he opened his mouth to speak. "I did, but it wasn't just her."

"But—"

"It wasn't even Kit who made me come out that night in the first place."

Tessa stared. "Then . . . then why run away? I'm confused— you were out in the woods that night, but you saw nothing, and still you ran?"

Patrick shook his head. "She started accusing me of ruining Lilly's life. She didn't want us dating. I didn't really blame her for that, but she was a bitch about it. No offense. Said a lot of nasty stuff about how it was my fault and—"

"And what?" Tessa shook her head. Kit had never been nasty to anyone. Could he be lying to her face? "So you *did* see Kit, then?"

"You're not listening. She knew stuff about me. Just some stuff I was trying to keep on the down low."

"Like . . ."

Patrick looked at his hands, covered in grease. "Just some tests I'd taken for other kids. And . . . some things I took. A ring. She was mad about the ring."

"What ring?" Tessa's heart nearly stopped. "Was it . . . this?" She held her hand out to him, where the sapphire ring sat on her fourth finger, glimmering in the sun.

Patrick gaped. "Where did you get that?"

"I found it," she said. "In the woods. Was it . . . yours?"

Patrick shook his head. "I stole it . . ." His voice dropped low. "From them." He nodded over his shoulder toward the house. "I felt bad about it, but I needed the money. I pawned it, though. Back in December. I thought it was long gone."

Either he was a slick liar, or he was telling the truth. And if this was the truth, then who'd bought the ring, and why was it in the woods, and why had Kit known about it?

"So what happened? She was shouting about the ring, you said. Then what?"

"Then I told her some things are just broken and should stay broken. Something like that, anyway. Then I just . . . I left." Patrick hung his head. "It was the last straw. I had my own shit to deal with. I had to get out. I'd been planning to. I'd been saving up the money. All I needed to do was offload a few pills—one last burst of cash. It was all I needed. There had only been one thing holding me here, and now that was over too. So it was time. I couldn't stand to see one more person who hated me."

"Kit hated you?" she whispered.

"You're not listening," he said quietly. "It wasn't just Kit I saw that night."

He yanked the rag out of his pocket and wiped his forehead with it. Tessa wondered if he was about to cry. If *she* was about to cry. She didn't know what to make of his story.

"Who else then?"

His hand fumbled, and he dropped the rag on the ground.

Tessa bent down to pick it up, but he leaned at the same time to grab it first. And that was when something caught her eye. On the rag—which filtered through her fingers, surprisingly silky, like a torn piece of clothing.

And there was a strawberry cutout in the corner.

She knew that piece of clothing.

It was Kit's shirt. She'd loved that white blouse. It was missing from her closet. Tessa had been looking for it just yesterday.

Maybe, *maybe*, it was the shirt Kit had been wearing *that night*.

Tessa stared up at Patrick, her hands suddenly trembling. She swallowed, backing up. "Liar," she breathed, hardly able to get the words out past the fear clogging her chest. "All of it. Lies."

"No," he said, stepping toward her.

"Don't touch me." She backed up farther.

"Please, don't do this," Patrick said. He reached for her again and she turned, running.

She didn't stop, veering straight off the road and into the trees.

At first she thought she'd lost him, but then she heard footsteps. Twigs breaking in quick succession. Someone had followed her. A panicked noise wrestled from her throat and she slammed her hand in front of her mouth. But whoever it was—it *must* be him—had heard, because the footsteps came closer. She ran harder, branches lashing her face. Why hadn't she just run the other way, toward the road, and hailed someone down for help?

He had Kit's torn shirt. He'd admitted to seeing her that night. He'd lied. And Tessa had just stood there, eating up his story. She wasn't thinking straight.

He had the shirt. He must have ripped it off her.

What did he do to her? Was he going to do the same thing to Tessa now?

Tears pricked at her eyes as she pushed her way through the trees, disoriented, trying to find her way toward the bike path, hoping there would be joggers and other people about on a Sunday afternoon—the sun still hadn't set, and it sent streaks of light through the branches—but it was winter, and so cold. Still—her heart raced—surely there must be someone—

But she didn't make it that far before a strong hand grabbed her roughly, and she fell to the ground with a scream.

A Dark Form, Running through Snow
BY KATHERINE MALLOY

What's happened to me; where did it all go wrong,
and how can I undo the damage done?
You've turned into a blur, a smoking gun.

I can't stop thinking of our old dog, Sun—
we'd found her in a parking lot stranded.
We groomed and loved her, yet some kind of anguish—
some haunted past we'd never understand—
just kept on chanting run, run in a language
that only she could hear. A cry of guilt—
a wolf in the forest of falsehoods that we built.

And now, winter whispers: deny, deny,
silencing me with its little white lies.

I open my mouth and it fills with snow.
The end's a blur—I can't see where to go.

Chapter Twenty-Six

BEFORE

1/23

Dear Diary,

I cannot believe this. Cannot. BELIEVE this. It's been about two weeks since my last entry. Today was inventory day at Lupine.

Today was the day I got fired.

The call came sometime late in the afternoon. Margaret told me not to bother showing up tomorrow for my shift. I was like . . . what??? She says, "I won't press charges if you return the item."

I mean, I was in shock. Of course, my first response was "What item?"

"The bra set," she said. "The one you've had your eye

on and put on that mannequin." Her voice sounded nasally and thin over the phone, very I-knew-something-like-this-was-going-to-happen-ish. *"Never should have trusted you to lock up on Friday,"* she was saying, and that was it. She hung up. Didn't believe me, clearly, when I left her like a dozen voice messages saying I didn't do anything. I must have sat on my bed for an hour, just staring at my phone, trying to figure out what the hell was going on. I think I stared at it up until it rang and nearly jumped out of my hands.

It was Patrick calling.

I suddenly got a bad feeling. His name blinking on my screen reminded me how strange he'd been acting that time when he came to visit me at work. How he made that comment about the bra and underwear, then said he was joking. He'd said he had money to buy me something. He wouldn't have taken it. He wouldn't do that.

Would he?

For me?

I still really really like him, but I'm getting so overwhelmed and I don't know what to think anymore.

Finally the phone had rung like four times, and I answered before it went to voicemail.

"Can you get away later?" I froze for a second. *"I'm sorry about last weekend. I still need to give you your present,"* he said.

I tried to stall. *"I have to tell you something."* My palms were getting sweaty. His voice sounded so excited. But I kept *thinking about Kit's warning to stay away from him. How he broke a glass jar over his stepdad's head.*

"What?" he said, getting back to his normal, more sub-dued, sarcastic tone. Then our conversation goes something like this:

"Big sis keeping watch over you again?"

"Kit? No, it's not that. It's just—"

"Good, because it's not her business who you spend time with. Even if she's right."

"What do you mean, even if she's right?"

"Nothing, just—I want to see you. Even if I'm no good, or whatever she told you about me."

"It's not that . . ."

"Then what?"

And here's where I tried to casually be like: sodidyouumaccidentallyoronpurposemaybeliketakesomething-fromthestorewhereIworklikeasajokemaybeorsomething?

I think at that point I was pouring sweat from my ears and talking nonsense but he got the gist of it, because he went quiet and I could feel that he was upset, which is fair and makes sense but still is not an answer. Finally he goes: "You think I stole something."

And I'm like, "No no no not that," desperately trying to backtrack and all that, but I'm like, "Maybe you just thought it would be funny if—or maybe you just—or I guess I was just wondering if—"

He cuts me off at that point and says something like, "Oh, wondering if I'm the kind of loser everyone says I am. Cheating. Stealing. Lying about it. What else have you heard?"

I felt really bad then, because it sounded like his feelings were really hurt. And then I remembered that I had felt that exact same way an hour earlier when Margaret acted like it was a foregone conclusion that I was the thief in question.

It sucks to be accused of something you didn't do.

I tried to explain that I really haven't heard that much bad stuff about him, but I'm not sure if that made it better or worse, because then he's like, "Ya know what? Forget it. She's right. Everyone's right. They're all right about me."

"So are you saying you did take something . . . without paying for it?"

He didn't answer directly, just said more things like, "Everyone's right that I'm no good for you and you should just stay away from me and Kit is always right about everything, isn't she?" And I felt like a weight was crushing my chest and I was so confused because was this like supposed to be a confession or was he just pushing me away? It felt so terrible and so confusing at the same time.

And then I didn't want to be that girl but I guess I was, because I heard myself saying, "Don't be mad."

He's like, "I'm not mad. I'm just realizing something. It's time. I was going to tell you that later. It's time for me to move on."

That's when my heart really started breaking. Because this was it. Everything I dreaded and feared.

"*Move on from me?*" *I asked him, but he just said,* "*From all of this.*" *And he sounded so sad, like he really didn't want to be breaking up with me even though it sounded like that was exactly what was happening. So I was like:*

"*Wait.*"

"*Lilly?*"

"*Yeah?*"

"*Nothing, I just. I'm sorry.*"

"*Okay.*"

"*Bye.*" *And then he was gone, before I could add* "*Sorry for WHAT?*"

So, of course, I did the only thing I could possibly think to do.

I called Mel, and told her everything.

Chapter Twenty-Seven

NOW

FEBRUARY 12

TESSA'S WHOLE BODY SEIZED WITH an icy heat. Her scream seemed to ricochet off the trees, to come *from* the trees. Her elbows and knees ached from the fall, and she couldn't catch her breath. Her vision blurred as she tried to lift herself from the ground, to turn around, to face it.

He was here. He'd followed her. He'd gotten her. He—

"Tessa, Jesus Christ!"

It was Lilly.

Crouching beside her, looking worried, scared.

She grabbed Lilly's knee, coming to a seated position in the dirt, her eyes darting to the woods past Lilly's shoulder.

"Lilly, we have to get out of here. Patrick, he followed me.

He lied about Kit. He has her shirt. Lil, we have to run. We have to go. Where is he?"

"Holy shit," she said, her face stunned, staring at Tessa like she was an alien. There were tears streaking her face.

"Lilly, we gotta go," Tessa repeated, scrambling up now, ignoring the pain in her limbs. Her arms shook as she tried to pull Lilly to standing.

"Tessa. No one was following you except *me*."

"What? No. I was at Patrick's house. Come on. We have to go. I went there to ask him some questions. Did you know he was back? Let's get out of here. Then I'll tell you everything. It was her shirt, Lilly—" Tessa's voice broke into a half sob. "It was her shirt," she said again, sniffling. "The strawberry one."

She turned around in a circle, listening for the sound of his footsteps still.

"Sis," Lilly whispered, pulling her into a hug.

Even though Lilly was younger, she'd been taller than Tessa for over a year now. Tessa inhaled her little sister's perfume— not light and floral like the scents Kit wore, but muskier and grassier and smoky, the kind of stuff they sold at Lupine. She could feel Lilly's heart jackhammering, and pulled back, still dizzy and out of breath and scared.

"It's not safe here," she said.

Lilly shook her head. "It's just me, Tess." Her voice wobbled. "No one else."

Tessa began to let herself breathe normally, to see clearly. Lilly was right—there *was* no one else. Patrick hadn't come after her. No one had. "How did you get here, then? How—"

"I heard Patrick had come back, and I guess I wanted to see for myself. But instead of finding him, I found you."

Lilly looked down at her muddy Keds. "This has to stop, Tess." Her voice got quiet. "Boyd got let out on bail. Did you know that?"

Tessa went cold. She hadn't known. Why hadn't he told her? And how was that possible? The Taylors had so little.

"I—how?"

Lilly averted her eyes. "I guess his dad got a bond. They pay down a small part up front. Apparently Innis had to sell that old lawn tractor and some of his collectors' items just to get half the down payment. Who knows where the rest came from."

Tessa shook her head. She knew about those collectors' items, Boyd's dad's prized possessions, all lined up in the garage. Mostly old junk he'd collected. "He's planning to plead guilty anyway. Involuntary manslaughter. Don't you think that's messed up?"

"Yes." Lilly paused. "But whatever happened, you have to face this, Tessa: we can't undo what happened that night. As much as it hurts, we have to . . . we have to say goodbye."

"No." The word rushed out in a harsh, ragged whisper. "You sound just like Mel, you know."

"What does Mel have to do with this?"

"She was at Kolbry's party last night. Did you know that?"

Lilly looked shocked, tears drying to sticky streaks on her face. "No, I—how do *you* know that?"

Tessa sighed. "Where do you think I was last night? I went to Kolbry's to try and find out what happened to Kit at his Halloween party—to find out if she'd gotten pills from him, to find out what she was hiding. And instead, all I got was an earful of Mel saying the same thing, telling me to butt out, warning me to back off. I'm tired of everyone telling me to stop!"

"You talked to Mel, then?"

"Yeah, I did. Why?"

Lilly shook her head, but she still looked scared. "I just . . . I don't get it. Any of it. Why *she* was at Kolbry's. Was she with Dusty?"

Tessa looked at her sister. "No."

"I'm worried about her."

"About Mel?"

Lilly nodded, looking like she was going to cry again.

"You should be worried for *me*, for *us*. Someone is out there, a killer, someone who wants to finish what they started."

She stopped talking when she saw how hard Lilly was trying to keep her face from shattering into tears.

Because Lilly, of all of them, had always known how to use the waterworks to her advantage. As the baby of the family, she could constantly find ways to burst into tears at just the right moment to get Tessa in trouble for something. For years when they were little, Lilly used to have this trick of planting her Legos and dolls in Tessa's or Kit's room, then begging to be let in to collect them. Once inside, she'd hug a bedpost or desk leg and absolutely refuse to leave, like some sort of koala or desperate stalker. And if Tessa or Kit tried to kick her out, she'd scream and sob, and it was the older sisters who would end up grounded or forced to play with her as their punishment.

So seeing her like this, trying to be brave, to hold it together . . . it stopped Tessa. It woke her up.

This entire week, Tessa hadn't paused her pursuit of answers long enough to even consider what Lilly was really feeling— what her grief looked like. In fact, she realized now, she had oddly assumed that Lilly simply *wasn't* grieving. That she was doing what normal people did—coping. Moving on.

But of course, grief was a sly thing. It morphed like smoke. It hid in the cracks.

Tessa stood there gaping. A fog had lifted, and she suddenly saw the moment for what it was: two relatively normal-looking teenaged sisters standing in the arboretum on a chilly February afternoon—one with long, reddish hair, wearing skinny jeans and a trendy striped T-shirt under her winter coat; the other with stringy light hair, in a stained old plaid top and ragged black jeans—arguing and getting angry and resenting each other like sisters do . . . because you don't choose to love your family. You're stuck with them. And sisters are the hardest— they are mirrors of you; they are competition, opponents in everything from pancake servings to endless Monopoly games to who gets to ride in the front to who gets the most phone calls from boys. They're a reflection of your best and worst self, and yet strangers always on the brink of going their separate ways and leaving you, or being left *by* you—a shadow in the doorway, falling across the carpet. A hug that lasts the length it takes to snap a photo, before it turns into a shove.

They have the power to undo you. And, maybe, to save you. That's a terrifying kind of love, Tessa realized.

"Come on," she said to Lilly, feeling as overwhelmed and exhausted as her sister looked. "Let's get home."

NEVER MINE TO KEEP

BY KATHERINE MALLOY

I know her all too well: she's intact—a hard-
boiled egg—while I'm a cracked windowpane.

Her voice is the whir of a running sink: soft words
of water swirling down into the drain—

reach under; feel her falling on your hands.

I'm all adorned in black, revealing much
by way of shoulder blade, and here I stand
resting my brow against the glass—I touch

its cool but firm resistance.

If I'm the knife,
then she's your slender spoon, so take her to
your mouth, where she is home, for my shelf life
is done and now alone I must make do

with numbing dreams—though even in my sleep
it's plain that you were never mine to keep.

Chapter Twenty-Eight

NOW

FEBRUARY 13

"I FORGOT FAMILIES WERE INVITED," Tessa muttered into Lilly's ear as they made their way down the length of the indoor risers in the old DLHS gym on Monday morning. The smell of sneakers and B.O. wafted in and out of her nostrils, reminding her why she hated gym class. That, and the whole coordination, strength, and physical skill thing.

Despite everything unfolding and shattering in her world, it turned out the rest of life moved on, whether you wanted it to or not. Hence, she was back at school, filing into the gym for the winter awards ceremony.

"Hi, babes," Mel said, appearing on Lilly's other side before she could finish her sentence. She kissed Lilly's cheek and sat down on her other side. Mel leaned in toward Lilly. "You seen Boyd yet? I heard he's home."

Boyd. His dad had secured a bail bond. But from the looks of it, he hadn't come to school. Tessa ached to see him. She had so many questions. Maybe she'd skip out of school after this was over. School wasn't doing her any good these days, anyway.

Out of the corner of her eye, she saw Mel pop a pill into her mouth. The sight of it jarred something in her for a second, and she turned toward her. "Hey, where'd you—"

But now someone was shouting "Shhh!" into the micro-phone. A senior named Abigail Hart had come up to the podium in the middle of the gym floor—the very same spot where Missy Brainerd had tried to do a cheerleading stunt that landed her with a broken hip (and, as the rumors went, a broken vagina). Abigail started talking about the awards being the first step in scholarly success and becoming a master of your own fate. Some stupid senior guy shouted "Master-BATE!" and a bunch of people laughed. Abigail cleared her throat and turned over another note card, and Tessa stopped listening.

She'd wanted to go to the police last night—they should know about Kit's torn shirt in Patrick's possession. But Lilly had stopped her, claiming it was ridiculous to think Patrick would just be carrying around incriminating evidence if he'd really done anything wrong. Plus, why would he ever come back if he had? "I just want to get through tomorrow's ceremony, and Kit's award, without any drama, okay, Tess? Then you can do whatever you want," Lilly had pleaded.

She did have a point, but it still made Tessa sick to her stomach to think about that strawberry cutout shirt . . . once pure white, now stained with grease and crumpled in Patrick's hand. . . .

Lilly had insisted they sleep it off, that she was being paranoid. Maybe Lilly was right. Probably old Liam Donovan had been the one to find the scrap of shirt, out by the woods during one of his meanderings.

So instead of telling anyone what she'd seen, Tessa spent the evening rereading all her research on hypothermia.

It's a very common side effect to experience what's called "paradoxical undressing"—where the victim gets so cold she begins to feel hot . . . so hot that she panics and rips off her clothes, only to cause the hypothermia to take hold faster. By that point, there's usually no hope. Could Kit have torn off her own shirt?

Restless, Tessa had gone downstairs to try to talk to their mom. She felt like she hadn't seen her in a year—ever since the funeral, her family had splintered, like a bunch of electrons suddenly repelled by their own energy, grief causing them to unbind and disperse. She suddenly missed her mom so much, suddenly felt so cold, deep-in-her-bones cold, that she knew she'd never get comfortable in her own bed.

She wanted to hear her mom's voice, to be soothed and told it was all going to be okay even though it wasn't.

But her mom was sleeping on the couch by the time Tessa went downstairs last night—a wad of used tissues in a pile at her side. She'd been crying again.

Tessa had stood there for a minute, not wanting to wake her but not wanting to be alone either. Lilly was asleep in her room. Everyone was asleep except her. She felt like a sleepwalker, a zombie, a ghost.

She knew Lilly was right—that she'd checked out this week, had been somewhere else, on a different plane, skating over the surface of life but feeling nothing, engaging with none of it, floating, as if a breeze could blow her away. Loss had done this to her.

But what had it done to the rest of them?

Careful not to wake her mom, she lay down on the sofa beside her. It was narrow, but her mom was small, and she fit, curving around her mom's body, which felt frailer than it used to be, but also warm and comforting. She wrapped an arm around her mother, and heard her mom give one soft whimper. Eventually, the rise and fall of her breath had allowed Tessa to drift off, too.

When she'd awakened this morning, she was back in her own bed, unsure how she'd gotten there.

After Abigail finished whatever the hell she'd been going on about—futures, grades, potentials, blah blah—she stepped down from the podium, and Mr. Green, the Advanced English teacher, stepped up in her place and cleared his throat. He was wearing a freshly pressed purple button-down and jeans.

"It's my pleasure," he said, "to announce the English Department fall semester awards." He held up what looked like it could be an annoyingly long list, and began reading prize names and the students who'd won them.

"The Michigan State Award for Excellence in American Literature. Pete Semolino," Mr. Green said.

Mel whispered, "I hear he's engaged."

"Who, Pete?" Lilly asked.

"*No.* Mr. Green."

"The Michigan State Award for Excellence in Shakespeare Studies. Elizabeth Mary Jorgersen."

People clapped as Lizzie went up to take the award and shake Mr. Green's hand. "The Beatrice Howley Award. Krista Kate Smith." More scattered clapping and another handshake. "The Patricia Goddard Poetry Prize. Katherine Ann Malloy."

There it was. The reason she'd bothered to show up in the first place.

"Since she can't be here to collect the award, her sister will come claim it for her at this time," Mr. Green said, looking over to where Tessa and Lilly sat. There was probably some sort of applause, but it was white noise to Tessa.

She turned to Lilly, frozen. She did *not* want to get up in front of all these people. The debacle at the funeral had been bad enough.

But Lilly nodded subtly at her, then stood up and went to receive Kit's award, and Tessa was flooded with temporary relief. Lilly was stronger than she'd given her credit for. Lilly was going to survive this, she could suddenly see, and it set something loose that had been tight and painful in her chest for days now.

When Mr. Green finished the remainder of the list, he lingered at the podium for a minute longer. "We're very proud of our students so far this year. Now, I'd like to conclude by reading part of an interview with the novelist Vladimir Nabokov about writing and poetry, which some of my students found particularly inspiring this fall."

A few kids behind Tessa groaned, but Mr. Green pulled a folded sheet of notebook paper out of his pocket and cleared his throat. "Nabokov claims poetry started when a quote 'cave boy came running back to the cave, through the tall grass, shouting as he ran, *Wolf, wolf.*'"

Here Mr. Green paused for dramatic effect. "And you see there *was* no wolf. But poetry had been born—what Nabokov called the tall tale in the tall grass."

Tessa was only half listening. She was still wondering whether maybe she should have gone to the police after all— she still could. Even though she knew now that it had just been Lilly following her through the woods, she still couldn't shake the fear . . . the sense of footsteps cracking twigs in her wake, the conviction that at any moment someone could grab her and do whatever they'd done to Kit to *her*, too.

"Let's get out of here," Mel said as soon as the assembly was over. But as Tessa filed into the bustling hallway behind Lilly, Mr. Green somehow ended up in their way. Mel looked over her shoulder, but her face looked stricken—like maybe she felt bad for them. Whatever it was, Tessa blinked, and Mel had gone, dissolving into the crowd. Meanwhile Mr. Green was saying, "Congratulations again to your sister. I truly am . . .

proud of her." It creeped Tessa out, the way he spoke of her in the present tense, like she wasn't *gone*. It felt dirty, like an erasure of the biggest, worst thing that had ever happened to her.

"Thanks," Lilly piped up beside her. "And congratulations to you, too," she added.

He looked at her funny.

"I hear you're engaged."

Mr. Green smiled. "People do talk."

"I want to be a writer, too," Lilly said.

Tessa turned to her in shock. "You do?" she asked, at the exact same time Mr. Green said, "Well, then, I hope to see you in Advanced English when the time comes."

After he left, Tessa pulled Lilly aside, near a bank of lockers. "The bell is about to ring. I should go to class," Lilly said.

"I didn't know you wanted to be a writer too. Since when?" Tessa demanded. It wasn't that she begrudged Lilly this aspiration, she was just genuinely surprised by it.

But Lilly just shrugged. "I've been writing in my diary a little this year and it's . . . I don't know. Refreshing. I like it. I could never be a poet like Kit, but I don't know, maybe I could write blogs or articles or even books one day. Mom always says I need to have pursuits and stuff."

"Oh, okay," Tessa said. "I mean, that's great. I'm happy for you. Really."

"I gotta get to class," Lilly said again.

Tessa nodded and watched her sister move through the dwindling crowd toward her next class.

Once she was gone, Tessa headed the other way.

She felt dizzy as she pushed her way out of the school building. No, not just dizzy. Something else. She felt . . . *Kit*. Kit telling her something, inhabiting her. That damn chimerism churning in her blood again.

Or was that just Tessa, still trying to cling to the memory of her?

She thought of the anecdote Mr. Green had mentioned. The boy who cried wolf. Maybe that's all any of this had been. *He hurt me. He lied.* Maybe that was just a giant crying-wolf, a false alarm. And yet, it still felt like Kit was *here*, lingering somehow, as if for the sheer purpose of making Tessa feel—as always—like she was one step behind. But maybe she never had been one step behind. Maybe she finally needed to tell Kit's voice inside her head to shut the hell up.

Maybe it was finally time for this to end.

Chapter Twenty-Nine

BEFORE

2/4

Dear Diary,

I really needed this. It's been a week and a half since Pat-rick "broke up" with me . . . if that's even what it was. All I know is school has been supremely awkward and depressing and even though Dar is back from her dad's house, the halls feel empty and I don't know who to talk to. Mel has tried to be comforting, but to be honest, I know there's something going on with her. I saw her swallowing pills in the C hall bathroom a few days ago. She said they're anti-anxieties from her doctor, that her mom approved. Okayyy, but then I tried to ask why she was having anxiety and she was just like, "It's normal, Lilly." When I pushed her on it, she admitted that she's been really worried that Dusty will break up with her when she's least expecting it. Then I felt a little bad, like maybe me keeping my thing with Patrick a secret and then dumping on her made her freak out and get anxious about her own relationship. So maybe it's my fault. I'm honestly not sure.

But tonight I told her in no uncertain terms that we needed a slumber party. It had just been way too long and I honestly was like, "I don't care if it takes away from your weekend time with Dusty. I need you, and I think we need each other." She got a little bit teary-eyed and so I think I got through to her, and now, here we are.

So far, it has been not a terrible Saturday, either.

First, the car that her twin brothers share rolled up to pick me up. Her brother (pretty sure it was John) was driving. (I mean, I KNOW the difference . . . but they've tricked me so many times before. . . .) Anyway, his girlfriend, Alicia something, was in the passenger seat, and Mel was in the back waiting for me.

We went to the movie theater that's out just past the bowling alley in that shitty strip mall and snuck in a bunch of cheap snacks from the quick mart, hiding them in our puffy coat pockets, just like old times. The first thing Mel did when we got out of the car was hug me and say, "I really am sorry for you. Breakups suck—you're too pretty for that shit." I mean, it wasn't exactly the feminist thing to say, but I still took it as a compliment. That was Mel, trying to be sweet. Alicia Whatever got out of the car and was like, "High school guys suck," then turned to John with a smile and was like, "Sorry, but it's true."

When I'm a senior, I would like to be like Alicia. She's . . . I can't explain it, but I like her.

Anyway, it still feels weird talking about it like a breakup when no one even knows we were seeing each other and also . . . were we?

Sometimes I wonder if this is really the end. I've seen Patrick looking at me at school and his eyes seem so sad and I'm trying to use my latent psychic powers to channel over to him, "Hey, it's no big deal, let's just talk about it" or better yet, let's not even talk about it, let's just go somewhere and make out and act like nothing happened. Is that really so terrible sounding?

Mel chimed in, "I always thought he was a bit creepy," which is not really fair since she actually wanted me to ask him out for HER, but I didn't bother to point that out. At least she's been really cool about me going behind her back, which is honestly probably nicer than I would have been if it had been the other way around, because as we all know, I super-hate secrets. At least, other people's.

"I'm just glad we're hanging out tonight. I've missed you," she added, and I swear I almost started crying but was just like, "Yeah, me too."

I wanted to talk more about it—to tell her that I'm actually worried about Patrick. That maybe he's in trouble or something. I mean, whatever he may have done, I KNOW he's not a bad person. He's just not. I may be naive, but I know what I felt and I know that he is trying his best and that things are going on that we can't always see. If I've learned anything this winter, it's that.

But by then we were inside and the movie was starting.

The movie itself? Honestly, it was a dumb gross comedy and I laughed through the whole thing and almost choked on a malted milk ball. It was great. After that we went back to the Knoxes' house and played a lame game of Monopoly with Mel's mom and dad in their creepy den, and I say creepy because one entire wall is devoted to where his guns are hanging. Some pistols but mostly hunting rifles, a few of them "historical pieces" that have maybe not been used in a hundred years, but they still creep me out, especially how her dad talks about them like they're horses or daughters, like, "The walnut Remington's a beauty, isn't she?" Besides all that, though, her parents are actually kind of nice to be around, though we get tired of them after a while because they ARE parents, after all.

Then we went to Mel's room to poke around online. At one point when I tried to dig her spare phone charger out of her nightstand, I noticed the pills from before were in there. I tried to read the label, but I didn't want her to think I was snooping, and I couldn't really tell what they were—the name was super long, and the bottle was almost empty.

Anyway, we did our toenails and then fucked them up on the carpet and we spent awhile watching YouTube clips and gossiping and it was a great night and the only thing that was slightly annoying was that Mel kept checking her phone and she was clearly texting Dusty the whole time and it just made me feel *slightly* like she would rather have been spending

time with him. But I had to remember she chose me this time,
not him. Things were going to get better between us, starting
tonight.

And the only other weird thing was that she said she was
really tired around eleven and that we should go to bed. It
seemed super early but I figured maybe all that anxiety (or all
those anxiety pills) were making her tired.

So she went to bed and I turned on my phone flashlight
to write this all down, just so I don't forget that, at the end of
it all, Mel is my best friend, and she has my back and I have
hers, and everything is going to be okay.

And it is. It is going to be okay. I think.

Good night, Diary.

And the thing was, Lilly really had thought she was going
to fall asleep and stay asleep.

She really thought that that was going to be the end of the
night, and that everything really *was*, if not back to normal,
then at least headed that way.

It wasn't until about 12:36 a.m. that she woke up again, and
discovered just how wrong she'd been.

Mel was no longer in her bed. The pills from her bedside
drawer were still there, but now Lilly could see the bottle was
empty.

And, though Lilly didn't know it yet, the Mossberg Patriot
Synthetic Kryptek Highlander from her father's gun collection
was missing, too.

PART
THREE

Chapter Thirty

NOW

FEBRUARY 13

THIRD TIME'S A CHARM. That's what they say.

They're wrong.

Three strikes: you're out. That was more like it.

You're out, he kept thinking. *You're out.*

Except he wasn't. Because no one knew and maybe no one ever would—and that's what was keeping Drew Green awake late that Monday night. Not grading papers or watching reruns of his favorite historical miniseries, but the haunting vision, on repeat in his mind, of Katherine Malloy, so young and so smart and so fiercely determined, snow falling around her in the light of the street lamps, making her appear more angelic than ever, even while she was mouthing, "Three strikes: you're out."

He sat up in bed and turned on his reading lamp, shaking off the image, careful not to wake his fiancée, Claire, who had begun the gradual process of moving in with him, for which Green felt both grateful and, maybe predictably, undeserving, not least because of the sorts of alterations she had already made, not just to his home, but to his *life*, which were simply incalculable, though they included such basics as the constantly replenished stash of toilet paper in the hall and the ability to find all three television remotes at any given time. Even his shirts seemed to hang straighter than they used to in his closet.

He shivered; Claire had rolled over and taken the covers with her.

Three strikes: you're out.

He shook his head, trying to dispel the persistent phrase. Of course the real Katherine never would have uttered anything so basic as a baseball metaphor, except in the interest of irony, and that was only one of the many things he admired about her, about her poetry anyway, which was, of course, full of youth and blunder and overwrought sentimentality in its own way, as the work of any young writer ought to be, and yet it contained a grace, a fragility, an otherworldliness somehow grounded in reality, "a sort of human sadness essential to the heart of great works of literature," as he once wrote in a margin comment on one of her drafts.

In a paper about *The Scarlet Letter*, she'd written of Hester Prynne—and he'd never forget this—"What people don't seem to understand about good girls is that most of them are not good by choice—they have simply never had the opportunity to be anything other than good. Without even knowing it, they are waiting."

A deep chill had settled into Drew's bones. His bedroom, its shelves lined with texts and first editions and stacks of study guides, pamphlets, curriculum notes, syllabi, and the like, appeared smaller and shabbier at night, the wind in the trees outside the three-family house he rented the top floor of louder or at least more blatantly mournful. He was experiencing a bone-level cold that wouldn't dissipate, he knew . . . even when the weather outside warmed to spring, luring hordes of carefree students and teachers alike out to the arboretum, filling the river that passes through with fresh fishing lines and peopling its parks and pathways with bikers and picnickers, each in their own bubble of apparent immaculacy.

But would the woods in Devil's Lake really, in Green's thesis, if he were to write one on the subject, represent that early pastoral view of incorruptibility, of natural phenomena blessed by an ancient or perhaps even Edenic innocence, or instead the more puritanical connotations of a post-Hawthorne narrative in which its inherent wildness suggests a release of one's own inner passions and consequently, one's potential to wander down a bad path, to get lost, to do wrong?

Yet—*had* Drew Green done wrong, really?

He got out of bed and stood facing the window, thinking not just of Kit Malloy's eyes, but of other faces that had come before hers. All of them too young, too new, too . . .

At last a kind of heat shuddered through him, but was it the warmth of desire or guilt?

He'd hoped settling down with Claire would . . . what? Absolve him of all that—both the desire *and* the guilt.

He fingered the pale curtain that draped the edge of the window, like a diaphanous skirt, one forbidden in the school handbook. Even as a kid, he'd always been drawn to what was forbidden.

Had Drew Green done anything wrong? That was one answer he knew.

Yes, yes, of course he had.

Chapter Thirty-One

BEFORE

FEBRUARY 4

SECRETS, SECRETS. EVERYONE HAD THEM. Everyone kept them from Lilly; kept her out.

This is what comes of curiosity, the wind whispered hard and cold in her ear, swishing up into her skull. She shuddered. Snow soaked her boots.

This was the story of her life, she realized now: this winter coldness, this left-out-ness, this butt-out-and-don't-complain-or-you'll-sound-like-a-whiny-baby-ness.

But here they were: two glowing yellow headlights through the swirl of falling snow, through the blur of fading streetlights, through the dark of Route 28. Twin golden keys to the fucking *treasure.*

And she had to have it, she thought, her hands shaking—had to know the secret. The warmth of the golden orbs called to her with some kind of dark, irrepressible magic, and there was so little magic in this world. Lilly only wanted her share.

When she'd awakened after midnight to find Mel gone, and the bedroom window cracked open, she'd had to assume the obvious: Mel had snuck out. To meet up with Dusty, presumably. She'd been texting someone all night; even when Lilly had tried to ignore it, she'd noticed.

But it wasn't Dusty's car she spotted when she'd snuck outside in search of Mel. It was a red truck, pulled over at the side of the road, edging the woods. *Boyd's* red truck. A hulking metal animal heaving its breath into the cold.

Now: a male voice drifting out over the wind. The sound of a car door slamming. She was almost there, and the heat of discovery drove her on.

But it was so cold. So cold and so dark. The sparse streetlights did little to help, spinning patches of air into gold-hued snow blurs. She had to hurry.

Lilly scrunched her winter hat down lower. Still squinting, she made out a figure—no, two figures—floating from the shoulder of the road, toward the looming darkness of the woods that backed up to Devil's Lake from Route 28.

Mel and Dusty?

Mel and *Boyd*?

Voices took clearer shape in the air as she got closer, though the words themselves wove and dodged and blew away. Holding her breath, hidden by the hounding snowfall and the heavy dark, she came all the way up to the driver's side—the side facing the road—without the figures noticing. She peered through the window. The keys were still in the ignition, a faint silver clump dangling in shadow.

Shivering, she rounded the back of the truck, careful to stay hidden from view behind the glow of the taillights.

A guy and a girl, arguing.

Lilly took a step back.

Secrets. Secrets.

She watched from behind the truck as Boyd put his hand on Kit's arm, and she shook, possibly crying.

Was he grabbing her now? Had she let him?

Slowly, he pulled open her coat.

Lilly shuddered hard. Kit said something, but Lilly only caught snatches of her words: *please* and *you're making a mistake* and *I don't believe you.*

The racing of Lilly's heart became a loud ringing through her ears and head. What was happening? Kit's voice, dancing on the wind, seemed to ebb and peak and break.

She stood on the verge of calling to them when Kit got quiet, moving closer to Boyd. Then she was touching his face. And he was leaning down, and they were kissing—mist rising from where their faces met.

Hot breath in the cold night.

Oh.

So they weren't fighting.

A flash of mortification.

Everyone was coupling off, hooking up, lying to Lilly about it.

Secrets, secrets.

She backed up toward the road, the thrill of voyeurism bursting suddenly into hot shame. A car rushed past her and honked.

She gasped, swiveled—was that Dusty's car? Or someone else's?

She felt all turned around now, cold and miserable, and she needed to get inside.

She raced down the road the way she had come, back toward Mel's.

When she got there, she found Mel in the side yard, her father's rifle in her hands, crying.

"What happened?" she asked over and over again. Her head throbbed, her thoughts raced, her chest felt as hot as her fingers and toes were cold. She had to remind herself—she hadn't heard a single shot. The gun hadn't been fired. Nothing had happened. Nothing bad had happened.

Had it?

"Mel, you can tell me anything."

But all Mel told her was that she thought she'd heard an intruder, and she'd gone to get her dad's gun to scare off whoever it was. She said it was normal—claimed she often brought the gun with her to the door if it was after dark, though Lilly hadn't seen her do it before. Said her mother always told her

that's what they were for, really. Hunting, yes, but also protection. "No one messes with the Knoxes," Mel quoted with a
shaken half smile. Anyway, she said with all the anxiety she'd
been having, she no longer slept well. She heard noises. She got
scared in the dark, felt hands touching her skin, sometimes, or
eyes watching her through curtains. She just wanted to make
sure that Lilly was safe. That they were all safe.

But if there'd been an intruder, why hadn't Lilly heard anything?

"Did you see anything? Anyone?"

"I just meant to scare them off. But . . . no one was there,
Lilly. Trust me, it was no one."

And, because she wanted to believe in the things that had
kept her life together until now—sisterhood, friendship, the
snow globe of Devil's Lake that had held them their whole
lives and kept them safe—she didn't question Mel, only held
her close and dragged her quietly back into the warmth of the
house.

Even though she'd seen the blood on the butt of the gun,
just before Mel had wiped it off with her hand, wet with snow.

Even though she knew something was terribly, terribly
wrong.

Maybe she just hadn't been ready yet, for her whole world
to shatter.

Chapter Thirty-Two

NOW

FEBRUARY 13

TESSA *TRIED* TO TAKE LILLY'S advice—her own advice, too—and to let it all go. To move on. But she couldn't. Still, something snagged.

Nabokov's tall tale in the tall grass.

The boy who cried wolf.

The wolf tattoo. The ring. Who loses a beautiful engagement ring in the woods? What was she missing?

Now, in the middle of the night, she stood in the empty, ill-lit school hallway with its flickering fluorescent bulb, searching for Mr. Green's office. In her head, she told herself that she had ridden her bike to school in the middle of the night and slipped in through a half-open classroom window because she needed to read Kit's poems, the ones that had caused her to win the award. That she'd only wanted to understand, to get closure. That was all. Just some closure.

Love poems.

The answer.

She fumbled with the English Department door handle, but it was locked. She let out a breath, starting to realize how deeply insane this would look if she were caught.

She backed away, her shoes crying out softly in little gasps against linoleum. She was about to turn around and leave when she heard something.

The doorknob wiggled a tiny bit.

And then the door opened, from the inside.

"Kit? Is that you?" a man whispered.

A gasp slipped through Tessa's throat.

Mr. Green stood there in the dark doorway, staring at her as though looking at a ghost.

And she stared back, feeling somewhat the same. She thought of Kit, exclaiming how excited she was to take Advanced English this year. She thought of seeing Mr. Green outside the homecoming dance, one of the chaperones. How Kit had disappeared from the dance for a while, only to return flushed and secretive. How from then on, Kit had withdrawn more and more into herself this past fall.

The wolf tattoo.

The poem about the boy and the wolf.

The secret someone she'd been meeting up with—the reason for her lies.

Tessa's stomach was clenched so hard she didn't think she

was breathing, wondered if she'd ever breathed. She felt suffocated and at the same time, detached from her body, as if floating there, observing what was happening without really being a part of it.

How long had she suspected this?

"You're him, aren't you?" she said.

Mr. Green backed up. "It's very late. What are you doing here?" His voice was hoarse.

A laugh forced its way out of Tessa's mouth, dry and bitter and brittle. Quickly, the laugh died, replaced by a flood of anger so burning and so bright she could hardly see. "I get it now. I get it. It was *you*."

"Stop that. Stop it."

"I'm right, aren't I?" She stepped closer. "You're him."

"This isn't real." He said it with an urgency she'd hardly heard an adult use before, except that time when the toaster caught fire late one night and her mother sternly told her to get out of bed in case the house burned down.

And she followed him, like he was the light at the bottom of the well or the end of the tunnel—the sick, twisted, obvious answer to a long, sick, twisted riddle.

The ring. The tattoo. The secrets.

The kiss.

The poems.

She rounded the doorway—floated into the office, moved with no control of her limbs. Mr. Green was already sitting at his desk, his face in his hands. The overhead was off; there was only the light of his desk lamp.

He was muttering into his hands. "Threestrikesyoureout. Threestrikesyoureout."

"What?"

He shook his head, and when he looked up again, she could see he was full-on *crying*. Also something she'd never seen a grown man do before. Tear up maybe, but nothing like this. It made her want to throw up. She felt sick. Sick and furious and very, very afraid.

"What the fuck is your deal?" she burst out.

His face was a complete mess—blotchy, twitchy, red. "It's finally happening, isn't it?" He shook his head again. "Fuck, it's finally happening."

He looked bad. He looked . . . in trouble. Bad, bad trouble. She grabbed the wall, her whole body feeling wobbly like she might at any second keel over.

This *was* it. The answer.

Mr. Green was shaking, hard, wiping his face fiercely with the back of his arm, which wasn't helping his state.

"What did you do to her?" Tessa whispered. "What. Happened."

He shook his head, unable to answer. So she began to speak, and the words, too, floated out of her, a kind of chant. A kind of truth, at last.

"She was dating you. In secret." The story—the tall story in the tall grass came to her as she said it, even though the idea of it was so upsetting it sent a wave of nausea through her whole body, threatening to knock her over. "You *made* her keep it a secret. It was going on all winter. No, a lot of the fall, too, wasn't it?"

He continued to shake his head, but he didn't stop her.

"Around homecoming. Sometime around then is when it started." The facts started to slot into place. "She liked you," she said slowly, piecing it together one detail at a time. "Liked you a *lot*. She even got a *tattoo* for you!" Tessa gulped, practically choking on the dark truth pushing its way out. In the dim lamplight of his office, she could see the outline of his jaw, could understand that in some unthinkable way, he was good-looking. Appealing, even. He was as distraught as she felt, as if he too was just now learning the full story of what had happened. A strange part of her wanted to pat him and tell him it would be all right, even as a bigger part of her wanted him to suffer, to regret, to pay.

"She was out late," she spat. "So often. She said she was going to parties, or working more volunteer hours. She wasn't, was she? That's why she never went to Jay's party like I originally thought. We *knew* something was up. We thought something was wrong. Our friend Boyd—he knew. Or had an idea, anyway. They fought because he wanted her to stop, but she wouldn't. She wouldn't stop. And that night. She borrowed his truck. She was arguing with someone. Lilly saw," Tessa said, remembering the story Lilly had repeated so many times now, the story of what she *thought* she'd seen. The falling snow. The hunting hat. "She was arguing with *you*."

Mr. Green was staring at her in amazement now, but she went on.

"It was cold out. So you grabbed the plaid hat, the one

318

Boyd always kept on the dashboard or in the glove compartment. *You* wore it. You're tall like him. *You* were kissing Kit. And then she died. She was out there in the cold and she hit her head and she *died*."

She came forward and banged on his desk. "What the *fuck* did you do to my sister?"

"I did nothing!" Mr. Green screamed, finally snapping out of his shocked, frozen state. Then he dropped his voice. "I did absolutely nothing to Kit other than respect her and read her sonnets and, and, and . . ."

"Did you or did you not kiss her?"

Green looked down again at his hands.

"Was there more? How far did you go? You know what, forget it, it's so sick I don't even *want* to know."

Still looking down, and so quietly she had to lean in to hear him, Mr. Green said, "I told her it was over. That night. It had to be over. She was so . . . so young. It wasn't going to work. I tried to tell her to go live her life. It was *her*. She was the one who wanted it, who pushed for it, who pushed me for more. So full of all these ideals, all these *feelings*, and I—it just got out of hand so fast. I never meant to hurt her, or make her think I could love her. Not like that. She was just a kid. Just a girl. A brilliant, beautiful girl, but just a girl. I couldn't carry on—I couldn't—and besides, and I had to tell her, I—"

"Had to tell her what?"

Mr. Green looked up, his eyes blazing. "She knew about Claire, knew we were back together. But she wouldn't let it die.

Wouldn't believe me. I made my choice. I love Claire. I wanted to do right by her. I *am* doing right by her. I didn't want to hurt her."

At the word *hurt*, Tessa's pulse spiked again. "WHAT did you DO?"

"I tried to show her the ring.*"

The engagement ring—sitting now on Tessa's finger.

"It was proof. That I'd moved on. I didn't think she'd believe me any other way, so I agreed to meet up with her. I parked down the road. She was there, with that truck. I tried to get her to warm up. We argued and she got out, so I followed. Then she tried kissing me, tried, I don't know what. It wasn't going to work. It was a snowstorm and she's beautiful—*was* beautiful—and lovely and I told her she'd make some boy her age very happy someday, but she begged me *please* to stay and when I said no, she pushed me away."

"So you shoved her to the ground. You hit her in the head. You—"

He practically choked. "No. I wasn't the one who threatened her. I wasn't the one with a weapon, the one who screwed everything up."

But Tessa was sick of the lies. Of the cover-ups. "You've been threatening me. That anonymous text. The creepy note warning me to back off."

"No."

"Are you going to tell the cops, or am I?" she replied, an eerie calm settling over her. It was over. The whole sick truth was here. It was over.

"I'm resigning. I'm done." He reached into a drawer, and with trembling hands, pulled out a familiar-looking notebook. Kit's poetry journal.

"Yes, you *are* done. And here's your ring, by the way."

Shaking, Tessa slowly slipped the sapphire ring off her finger. She dropped it onto his desk, then lifted the journal, backing away until she was at the doorway, until she was past the brink, until she was gone.

WHAT IT LOOKS LIKE TO LET GO
BY KATHERINE MALLOY

I'm driving past the littered, torn ravine—
that icy, white-laced waterfall. It bares
its teeth, but can't cry out. The cold's so clean;
it holds everything back.

The houses stare
from the side of the road; beyond that's only road
and forest—stripped—laid down beside each other

for miles in the weak beginnings of sleet, the old
gray sky tucked down around them like a cover.

The umber grass bends east in surrender.

Sometimes we cannot know exactly what
things mean—for all the world's a great pretender:

the sleet was just a false alarm, and what
I thought was fog was not—it's hard and frozen.

But, Love: the trees still fling their arms wide open.

Chapter Thirty-Three
NOW

FEBRUARY 13

TESSA WALKED ALL THE WAY home. She walked and walked and walked, trying to feel anything other than disgusted, gross dismay. Maybe Lilly had been right all this time. Maybe she hadn't wanted to know the truth. Maybe the truth was just a set of broken pieces that didn't all quite line up. Shards of semi-truth, sharp as fangs.

When she got to their block, she sat down on the driveway between her house and Boyd's, numb. A statue.

She was still sitting there when the sun finally cracked over the horizon.

Still sitting there, shivering, sleepless, when Boyd stepped out of his house the next morning.

"Tessa? Jesus, Tess! What are you doing up this early? Out here?"

She looked up, her head heavy. Boyd was wearing boxers, flip-flops, and a T-shirt. His hair was all over the place. He must have gotten straight out of bed.

He'd been gone a little over a week, but it felt like much longer. Like he'd become a different person in the meantime. Standing on the porch for that frozen second, he wasn't her Boyd. He wasn't even Boyd at all. He was just a guy. A slightly too tall, slightly too gawky, but still oddly cute *guy*. A stranger. He'd aged in ten days, and she hadn't. This whole time, she'd been on pause.

And then he was at her side, helping her off the gravelly concrete. Her legs felt weak beneath her. The dawn was blooming behind his head.

They both stood there, facing each other. He was still holding her hands.

He cleared his throat, staring at her, expressionless, waiting. There were tears in his eyes.

"So, you're home now," she said. "And I have the proof. I know it wasn't you, I—"

"Tessa," he said softly.

She had planned to tell him everything. All about Mr. Green and the affair. The final missing puzzle piece. And she *would* tell him.

But right now, what came out of her mouth had nothing to do with any of that. It had nothing to do with Kit at all.

"Do you, um, remember that afternoon when we were in my room, studying AP Bio?"

His eyebrows seemed to soften at the edges. His lips seemed to curl up—but only a tiny bit, like he was too afraid to show either sadness or happiness, so his face paused somewhere in between.

"You know. The time, we, um . . ."

He took in a breath, and even though it was a tiny breath, she could hear it. "Kissed," he said.

She nodded.

"Yeah." He swallowed.

She didn't say anything. She was trying to say something but she wasn't sure what.

"Of course, I remember," he added. "I—"

"You said something then. About Olivia Khan. You asked if I remembered the time you guys dated in middle school. But then, we were interrupted, and, um, well, I never got to ask you why you brought it up."

He was still sort of looking at her in this way where he could be squinting or trying not to cry or trying not to burst into a huge smile.

"Yeah . . . I think maybe I remember saying that."

"So?" she asked, looking up at him, her whole body, from her toes to her chest to the top of her head filling with something she couldn't quite name. A warmth. A feeling.

"Well, this is sort of embarrassing, I guess. But you know how she sort of dumped me for being . . . well, in her words, a prude?"

Tessa couldn't help it. Maybe it was the surrealness of the whole night, her lack of sleep. She laughed.

"Well," he went on, "it was partly that. I mean, I was only thirteen and I wasn't, like, you know, ready for under-the-shirt action or whatever it was she wanted to do. But it wasn't just me chickening out."

"TMI, but okay . . ."

"See, we were kissing, and—"

"Not that I need to picture that," Tessa interjected.

He shrugged sheepishly. "Well, we *were* kissing. On the playground at school or whatever. And she pushed me away and said, 'This is dumb.' And I was like, 'Why?' and she was like, 'Because I can tell that you don't really want to be with me,' and I don't know what I said, but I was just trying to focus on figuring out what the hell she was talking about. As I'm sure you know, I've never been that good at knowing what girls want. So anyway, then she surprises me and is like, 'Come on, I know you don't like me because I know you like someone else.'"

Tessa stared at him, feeling much the way he'd just described *he* felt then—confused. Wondering what he was getting at.

He cleared his throat. He was squinting, like he did when he was struggling to get the right words out. "And the thing is, she was right. All that time ago. Three years? It was eighth grade, so a little more than three years ago. Anyway, she had it right on the nose."

"Had . . ."

"She knew that I liked you. Even then. I think it's possible everyone knew. But I didn't, until she said it. And I think I still didn't *really* know it, didn't want to commit to it in my head, that I was stupidly, dorkily obsessed with you. I'm not sure I knew what to do with the information. I didn't want to ruin everything if you found out and didn't like me back."

"You were obsessed with me in eighth grade?" Tessa asked, heat burning her cheeks, and a tiny pang slicing into her ribs—a sudden nostalgia for something she'd never get back.

Now he finally let himself smile. "No, idiot."

"Oh. Wait, what?"

"I *am* in love with you." His voice dropped to a tremor. "Always have been. That's . . . that's what I was trying, in my terrible, awkward, sucky way, to say to you. What I've *been* trying to say to you. What I should have said sooner."

The words poured over her. She should be happy—so happy. This was what she wanted to hear. But the way he was saying it, with such sadness in his voice . . .

"But why *didn't* you just say it?"

"I kept wanting to . . ."

"You did?"

He nodded, sheepishly. "Of course, but with everything that happened . . . it just seemed wrong."

She swallowed hard. "I may have found the answer. It's going to be okay, Boyd. It's all going to be okay. We know what happened now."

He let out a whimper, but tried to smile.

"Boyd," she whispered. She leaned toward him, unable to stop the gravity forcing her closer, like maybe his existence could stop her from cracking completely, from crumbling.

He nodded, swallowing hard.

"I want to kiss you again." Her voice was so thin, it almost wasn't there.

He laughed, but it was half a sob. "Me too," he whispered.

She smiled, but fear jagged through her. "I think I love you," she said.

Then he was crying. She hadn't seen him cry since seventh grade, when his dad had gone on a bender, and Boyd had thought maybe he was dead. Found him on the living room carpet, facedown.

"Don't cry," she said.

"I love you too, Tessa." He was smiling and crying at the same time. He interwove his fingers through hers.

"So do it," she said quietly. "Kiss me." She tugged him a little closer.

"Tessa," he said, touching her face. It sent shivers through her. "What if this all falls apart? What if it ruins everything?"

Tessa shrugged. "I don't know. I don't know anything. Except what I feel right now."

Boyd smiled. "You know what? Screw it," he said, and leaned down toward her, and wrapped his arms around her, surrounding her in his sleepy, cozy, early-morning smell, and kissed her.

He tasted like tears—and home.

There was more to be done. She had to see Lilly.

"Wake up," Tessa whispered, hovering over Lilly's bed.

Lilly threw back her covers and started to scream but calmed down. "We need to talk."

"Why are you . . ." Lilly sighed. "Never mind. I should be used to this kind of thing by now."

Tessa was still buzzing from her break-in at the school. Still reeling, still worried she was going to be sick. But layered through it was Boyd's kiss, lingering on her lips.

She sat down on the edge of Lilly's bed. "Lilly, I need to tell you something serious. I'm not sure you're going to be ready to hear it, but you need to know the truth."

Lilly stared at her. "Okay," she said slowly, sitting up and rubbing her eyes.

"Mr. Green. The English teacher. He and Kit were . . . a thing."

Lilly gaped at her. "Holy fuck."

Tessa swallowed. This was going to be difficult, but she had to get it out. She'd already done it once tonight, after all. "It was supposed to be a secret. Obviously. But I think—I think she threatened to tell, and he . . . he . . . He's the one who killed her. He kept saying he didn't want to hurt her, but . . . Look, we have to tell the cops. It needs to come from you. You're the one who originally said you saw Boyd out there, and they need to know he's innocent, and—"

"Wow." Lilly was looking at her with an expression both of sadness and of hope. "Kit," she said. "And Mr. Green."

"I know, it's hard to believe."

Lilly shook her head. "Not that hard, though."

For the first time, a thought occurred to Tessa. What if Kit wasn't the only one? What if Kit wasn't the first girl he went after, the first one he threatened. . . .

She pulled her list out of her pocket. The one she'd written down all the clues on, at the school library.

"What are you doing?"

"Laying out all the evidence. We're going to have to report everything."

Lilly sat up straighter, nodding. "Okay."

Next, she pulled out the creepy note she'd received the other day, the one that had mysteriously appeared in her pocket. The one that said, *This is your last warning. You're making a mistake.*

Next, she pulled out the poems—the ones she'd taken from Mr. Green's office.

Then she pulled out the boy shorts she'd found with the Lupine tags still on.

"Wait a second," Lilly stopped her. "Let me see those. Where did this come from?"

Tessa shrugged. "It was Kit's. Matches the bra she had on that night . . ."

"Holy shit," Lilly gasped. "So *she's* the one who stole them, not him."

"What?"

Lilly looked at her. "Nothing, forget it," she said. "I just— there was this night where she was late to pick me up from Lupine. She said she had to use the bathroom, but after that night, this bra set went missing. Margaret thought I had stolen it, and *I* thought it was . . . Anyway, I think I might be able to get my job back now. And my boyfriend, for that matter."

"Your . . ." Tessa looked at her. "Your what?"

Lilly blushed. "Patrick Donovan. We were hanging out a lot this fall . . . I never said anything because Kit kept telling me to stay away from him. And now . . . well, after I ran into you in the woods this weekend, after we got home, I called him. He told me the truth. That he was worried that his uncle was the one who had done something. That his uncle was the one who found Kit's shirt. But Liam's so weak, it didn't really seem possible he could have done anything that bad. Patrick told his aunt, and they are going to put Liam in a home. Patrick's been helping her out. But he . . ." Here Lilly blushed again. "I think he likes me back. I think we are going to work things out."

But Tessa was still stuck on the shirt—the strawberry cutout shirt Patrick had been holding in his hand, like a rag. "I don't know, Lilly, I—I guess I don't think he did anything wrong. Not anymore. But why was Kit so against it?"

"She thought he was a drug dealer or violent or something, but she was wrong. I *know* him. I trust him."

A drug dealer.

Tessa thought of the pills that had been mentioned in the autopsy report—the ones found at the site that night. "Are you absolutely sure, Lilly? That he wasn't carrying pills or anything?"

331

Lilly shook her head. "The only person I know carrying pills around lately is Mel."

Tessa went cold. "Mel? What do you mean? What kind of pills?"

Lilly shrugged. "To be honest, I don't really know. Do you think I should be worried?"

Tessa didn't know. She didn't know what to think. It all felt so complicated. Mr. Green had all but confessed to her. But there were still pieces that didn't add up.

She looked out the window, to the sky. She could make out a star or two, fading into the morning light. She knew how far that light had to travel to get here. It *looked* faint—hardly there at all—but in fact it was a light that was many times more powerful than the sun. It was just *far*.

Just far.

Or even if the star itself had burned out a million years ago . . . its light was real, anyway. Its light was still here. And it was still reaching her, even from out there in the cold, dark universe.

"Lilly, go back to sleep. I still have something I need to do."

And amazingly, Lilly did—after crying into Tessa's arms until they were both shaking.

Tessa tucked her back in, waited until her breathing slowed.

Lilly had mentioned a diary—*her* diary.

It was easy to find.

She kept it right underneath her bed.

Chapter Thirty-Four

BEFORE

2/13

Dear Diary,

I might be losing my mind. I've been seeing her every-where. She's haunting me.

And I know it's because this is all my fault, because I went back to Mel's and didn't call the police. By the time they got there it was too late. I've been going to school and every-one's trying to act normal around me, but nothing is normal and it will never be normal again.

Maybe I was wrong to say anything about seeing Boyd out there with Kit, fighting. But I was just trying to tell the truth. That is what I saw. Have I ruined everything?

My whole family has been put on pause. We are frozen.

We can't move on from this and I don't know if we ever will.
How am I supposed to live with that? I've cried for days, and
now I just feel . . . wilted. Wrung out.

I've tried to talk to Mel about it, but she's only gotten
more distant. I gently asked her if she remembered anything
else from Saturday night, but she basically screamed at me.
Then she told me she talked to Tessa this week—twice. Once
underneath the bleachers at school and once at Jay Kolbry's
party. I didn't even ask why she went to Kolbry's, after every-
thing that happened this week—I didn't want to set her off
again. She said Tessa has been bothering her and it's tipping
her over the edge, making her feel crazy. I was a bit shocked
that she felt it too, felt the same way as me. I feel like I'm going
crazy as well. But at least we're in it together.

I keep wondering if Mel's secrecy has anything to do with
Dusty, since she was texting him so much that night. At least
I assume that's who she was texting. But when I tried to ask
her about it, she basically broke down. Said all this crazy
stuff about how she NEEDS Dusty. I kept being like, "But
why?" and she finally said, "He makes me feel safe. Being
with him is like erasing everything that came before." I don't
know exactly what she meant by that, because she was a virgin
before Dusty, so what is she trying to erase? Who is she trying
to stay safe FROM?

Anyway. It's Monday. My first full week back since . . .
since the funeral. I was sitting in math, and Patrick walked in,
right before the bell rang.

Just sauntered into class like he hadn't been missing for the past week.

I knew he was back in town. Boyd told me. And Mel tried to as well. I had been hoping to see him yesterday but instead just had a big Tessa-related meltdown in the woods and went home to sob it out.

A few minutes into class, he tapped my back while Mrs. Gluckman was writing on the board and passed me a note. All it said was, I'm so sorry about everything. Can we talk after school?

After school we went to the art room to talk, because the door was unlocked and no one was in there.

It was weird. We kind of just wandered around the studio, looking at the papier-mâché masks the art kids are making for the spring play, and the line sketches—practices in shadow— and the nudes. I seriously did not know nudes were a thing high schoolers were allowed to draw, and I would think it would be embarrassing to be standing next to Patrick looking at nudes, but it wasn't. I feel like we're adults now, sorta. Maybe so much has happened that we've both matured into different people than we were a week ago.

Even though I wasn't looking straight at him, I was noticing every single thing. His blue soccer shirt and ripped jeans and gray sweatshirt, two-thirds unzipped. The fading bruise. The way he kept putting his hands in his hoodie pockets and then pulling them out again.

Maybe we weren't mature at all. Maybe we were just

looking at the student art so we didn't have to say anything real.

"Look at this one," he finally said, and his voice sounded rusty. He was pointing at a drawing of a girl (clothed) who was hugging her own legs.

"So where did you go?" I asked.

He let out a heavy breath. "It was stupid. I was try-ing to get to Vermont. I have a cousin out there and I just thought . . . I don't know what I thought. Basically, I spent a lot of time sleeping on busses. When I found out what was going on here, I turned around and came back. I don't really want to talk about it."

"So what do you want to talk about then?" I asked him.

I was afraid he was going to bring up something about Kit. Or Tessa. And how we have his sympathies. Which would have just felt extra shitty. Talking about it is somehow more awful than not talking about it.

But instead he said, "Quadrilaterals."

I laughed, and it wasn't much, but it was the first time I laughed since . . . before.

"I miss quadrilaterals. That's why I came back. No one teaches them quite like Mrs. Gluckman."

And maybe I was reading into it, but I think what he was really saying was something else.

"I missed quadrilaterals too," I said quietly.

Then he reached out and took my hand and I knew for sure he was not really talking about geometry but about us.

I tugged his hand a little and he turned to face me and his

face looked like such a mix of emotions then. "I'm sorry. Not just about everything. I mean yes, about everything. I guess this is just hard. Between us."

"But why? Why does it have to be hard?" I asked.

"Because I generally fuck things up," he said with a shrug.

"You're not that bad, though," I said.

And he smiled. "You think so?"

"Yeah," I said. "It's just—we're all a work in progress, right?" Maybe I said it because it sounded good, because we were surrounded by crappy student art. But it felt true in that moment.

"A work in progress. Okay. I like that."

"Come here," I said. And we hugged for a long time, and the smell of his deodorant and detergent got into my nose and made me calm, but then I started crying like an idiot. Because my life has fallen apart and I can't really deal, and no amount of starting over is ever going to feel the same as getting my sister back.

And he just stood there and held me while I cried, in the stupid art room, with winter sunlight streaming in through the high windows, and the drying watercolors dancing against the wall, and the hideous papier-mâché masks staring back at us, and tears messing up my whole face.

And then I finally got myself together and realized that I needed to go home and see my family. I needed to be home.

Chapter Thirty-Five

NOW

FEBRUARY 14

THOUGH MORNING HAD BROKEN—birds darting in and out of the trees—the outline of the woods still looked charcoal and quiet. *These woods are lovely, dark and deep.* A poem Kit had read aloud to her before. Or a poem inside her head, because she *was* Kit, and Kit was her.

Kit, the reconciler of family fights. Kit, the lighthouse in storms, the calm at the center of everything. Kit, the homework helper, the pancake perfecter. Kit, the one with a voice as pretty as their mom's; Kit of the Christmas carols. Kit, the schoolyard defender. Kit, the patient, the beautiful, the wise. Kit always knew something Tessa didn't know. It was like the future didn't exist unless Kit had lived it first, had left enough

PART THREE

of an impression in the snow to give Tessa a path to follow. Not that Tessa needed to be *like* her, just that the world was shapeless until someone had given it form and meaning, had made space for Tessa to enter into it, had left enough of a trail of bread crumbs to keep Tessa going. That's what their chimerism really was, wasn't it? A little bit of information, a set of coded clues, alluding to the sense of Kit—information that had become part of Tessa's very cells.

It was hard to explain how this felt.

Without her sister, Tessa was nothing. Potential with no form. Energy with no direction.

She thought tears would come, but still, they hadn't.

There were only a few cars on the road. Tessa hovered on the shoulder of Route 28—the site where it all had happened. The place where her sister's body had been found, half undressed in the back of Boyd's truck, like something from a cautionary tale. Little Red Riding Hood ravaged by the wolf.

Blunt head trauma.

She stared at the stand of trees, the way the branches looked like arms, thin and reaching.

She couldn't believe it had only been ten days since that night, since everything had changed. She wasn't even sure how she'd gotten out here so fast—it felt as if the night had stretched longer to keep her in it. It felt as if she'd been transported here in a dream, though she must have simply walked.

After she had put Lilly's diary away, something had slipped

339

out of its pages. A note. A note in familiar handwriting.

hey you, still up for sleeping over tomorrow night?
Excited to hang w u. love u.—Mel.

It wasn't the sentiment of the note that had startled Tessa, but the loopy scrawl. She'd stared at it for a long time, and finally understood what it reminded her of. The note she'd found in her own pocket the other day. *This is your last warning. You're making a mistake.*

It was still a while before the truth of it had sunk in.

Mel had been the one who'd threatened her.

Mel. Why would she care what Tessa did? Unless . . . unless she knew something.

Tessa thought back to Mel's frantic eyes when they spoke under the bleachers last week. And then again, the dismissive way she'd tried to get Tessa to back down at Kolbry's Valentine's Day party on Saturday.

What do you know, Mel?

She stepped off the shoulder, into the shelter of the trees.

Tessa wasn't sure anymore what she was looking for. Kit wasn't here. She was never going to be here. She wasn't going to materialize. Was she?

It was just like Lilly had said. Tessa wasn't ready to say goodbye.

So what was she thinking, coming here?

Tessa got down on her knees.

The snow was cold, soaking through her pants, but it didn't matter, she didn't feel it. The dawn had come.

Her fingers shook. She dug through snow. Near the base of this tree, then that. Pushing, crawling, twigs snapping beneath her. Was she crying?

Kit, she said aloud, or in her mind. *Kit, please. Please tell me what I am missing.*

There, in the snow. The engagement ring—or a vision of it, anyway. And that's when she knew she wasn't in her own body anymore, wasn't in time, but had fallen away somehow. She was so cold she could hardly feel the boundaries of her body anymore.

She was so tired. Hadn't slept at all tonight. Hadn't slept in—when *had* she last slept? She recalled not sleeping, only dreaming, dreaming of three sisters singing, of three sisters arguing. And nightmares—of wolves. Blunt patches of dark unconsciousness, mixed with bursts of light and waking.

She was so tired—too tired. Maybe Lilly had been right. She'd been relentless, trapped in an inability to see the whole picture, to accept the truth.

Tessa lay down in the snow.

Kit lay down in the snow.

She was herself and not, at the same time.

Kit, she called out silently.

She just wanted to help.

She just wanted for Kit not to have died.

She didn't want Kit to die.

She didn't want her big sister to be hurt.

Didn't want her to be angry, to be hurt, to be heartbroken, to be alone.

Tessa had followed her. She had followed Kit.

Hadn't she? Just now? Wasn't that why she was here? Following the inexplicable path of clues Kit had laid out for her?

The snow was a cold blanket beneath her. She shuddered against it, hot breath against the frost of broken twigs and congealed leaves.

Her eyelids were so heavy. Thoughts of Sleeping Beauty swam through her mind. She thought of old Liam Donovan and his mutterings. Princesses asleep. What had he seen?

The dream took shape, but it was not Tessa's dream, it was Kit's. Somehow Tessa knew it as she dreamed it. She was screaming at a man in the woods, the words raw in her throat, the word *please* hovering between them, pathetic and ashamed. His eyes were shadowed by the hunting hat, but she knew those eyes so well, had thought she was falling in love, but now she knew she'd just been a dumb girl, had just been one of the good ones waiting for something to come along and make her go crazy, just waiting for life to happen to her. For love to happen to her. And now it had, and she regretted it. Couldn't take it back. Had crossed an invisible line. She'd never be the Kit she'd been before. And she thought to tell him so, but his hands were on her again, and he was whispering *shhh,* and she wanted, more than anything, to not feel this broken or this hurt. She wanted, more than anything, to feel like she'd once felt before—whole. And that was why she let him kiss her one last time. It was just a kiss goodbye.

But before she could tell him that, someone else was bursting out from between the trees by the side of the road.

"Get off of her, I swear to God, leave her the fuck alone," said a girl's voice.

Kit turned and saw—Mel. Holding a rifle that looked too clunky for her frame. Her hands were shaking, and the whole gun wobbled in the snowy air, or maybe that was just a trick of the light. "Once is enough, but never again," she said, her voice low and steady. "Get off of her," she said.

Drew had already lifted his hands, but it wasn't enough. Mel was crying and shaking, and even in the swoosh and noise of the storm and the running of the truck's engine not too far away, she could still hear it when Mel cocked the gun, hand on the trigger. In that moment, Kit understood two things.

One: she hadn't been Drew Green's first mistake.

Two: whatever had happened between *her* and Drew, it hadn't been the same with Mel. Something very, very bad had happened to her.

And yet, she realized a third thing in that moment, even if it wasn't conscious—she wasn't going to let him die for it. Not like this. Not when some part of her still loved him.

She leaped at Mel, and Mel swung away, the butt of the rifle striking Kit in the temple.

Kit fell.

VERIZON SERVICE RECORD
8:23 P.M. TO 11:47 P.M., FEBRUARY 4

Hey it's me, Mel

Hello Mel

You need to say sry to Lilly, she really likes you

This isn't your business but thanks

I'm serious

You didn't like us dating anyway I thought

True but she's my best friend and she's upset so you owe it to her to talk to her

will think about it

hey

what

do you have any more of those things

You mean the meds

duh

i can check. Told you b4 im not interested in doing this

I just need a few more tho pleeeease you don't get it

You're right I don't

So can you bring me some more?

What like now?

Yeah tonight
i am almost out

no maybe tomorrow it's getting late

i have cash tho
pleeeease I can't sleep

jesus

??? so? Patrick?

Fine, where

Meet me a few doors down, you know the addy

I can be there like midnight or so

Great and don't try anything funny

What r you even talking about
I'm only doing this bc of you

I'm serious

So am i

Hey I don't see you

Around the corner.
Its freezing out hurry

Oh there you are

Chapter Thirty-Six

NOW

FEBRUARY 14

TESSA WAS STILL NOT HERSELF, but a shadow self, dreaming. Still caught in the whirlwind of snow and memory and truth. It had all unspooled in her mind—as if Kit hadn't gone entirely, her story still playing out inside Tessa, over and over, just waiting to be seen and heard. As if the truth had been in Tessa's blood, in her DNA, this whole time. Maybe it had been.

The dream, the vision, swirled on:

Somehow in the chaos, the ring had fallen into the snow, was lost somewhere in the darkness.

Drew had run off.

Mel was still standing there, shaking.

"Just go," Kit told her.

"I—I'm sorry, Kit. I hurt you. Let me help . . ."

"No. You need to go home, where it's safe. I'll just be a minute."

"What are you doing?"

"Go, Mel."

Whimpering, Mel was gone.

Alone, Kit pushed into the woods. Deeper and deeper, into the darkness, and into the cold. The farther she went, the more determined, the more desperate she became. She would not fail. She had to find the ring. She could not fail. It was her last chance *not* to fail, not to fall. She only wanted to make things right again.

But Mel's face. The gun. The guilt written all over Drew. It was too much. It changed everything. She thought it had been love, but what if it hadn't been?

She shook, retching into the snow. She was soaked through. Cold beyond belief. Teeth chattering until her jaw felt like it might break. And her head killed. She could see drops of blood falling into the snow. This was craziness, she had to stop. But how could she go home? How could she face her life, and the truth?

She crawled through snow and mud and sticks and leaves, until she couldn't crawl anymore. It was only when she finally gave up that she found it. But her hands were so numb by then she couldn't really pick it up. The ring slipped again from her fingers. She laughed, feeling delirious, and tried to call out—as if anyone would hear her—but she was shaking so hard her voice had become trapped in her throat and only a gargle came out.

Determination gave way to fear. She'd gone too far from the road. She didn't know which way the road even *was* anymore. It was too dark. It was too cold.

And no one knew she was out here.

The woods had grown thin in ragged patches, and somehow she'd made her way not to the street but to the lip of Devil's Lake itself, frozen over. Gray lace in moonlight.

It looked magical, just now.

She'd become too cold to think, but as she looked at the lake's reflective surface, she realized the cold was turning into tiredness. She couldn't feel her body, couldn't feel a thing, but she knew she was lying down, curled up, for warmth.

Minutes or hours had gone by. Kit was being carried through the woods. A deep, rumbling voice was chanting over her, but not at her, not really. Talking to itself. Himself. She was so cold—too cold. She didn't know where she was or what she'd been searching for, or waiting for. Her whole body convulsed with the cold. It was inside her, every time she breathed in, like breathing broken glass.

The arms around her were weak. In danger of dropping her, letting her fall away into darkness and nothingness and night. The wind and hail bit at her flesh like the teeth of wolves.

The old man was calling her Sarah. He was saying he was sorry. Calling her princess. "I've found you," he said.

They were stumbling toward a source of light. Before she could understand what had happened, she was—*burning*.

She was on fire. There had to be fire in the hail. There was no hail, just flame.

No, pure heat. She was at the beach—that time they went to the big lake for a full week, rented a cabin. Dad had been alive back then. It had been so hot in the cabin that at night the girls stripped down to just their underwear and covered themselves in damp towels, propping up three different fans, but none of it had helped. She could taste the cedar-scented heat of their room that summer, felt it oozing into her eyelids as she slept.

She couldn't breathe she was so hot. She tossed in the bed— no, in the arms. Next summer she'd insist they go somewhere with air-conditioning. But for now, for now. She needed to get these clothes off.

Needed to get a damp towel and find the fan.

She struggled as the man laid her down inside a coffin.

No, not a coffin. The truck. Boyd's truck. Her eyes were only half open because of the storm ravaging her. "Wait." But the man turned, startled by something in the distance.

She threw off the blanket—the exact texture and color of her winter coat—then tore at her shirt, needed to get it off her, it was stifling her. She was too hot. She'd die she was so hot. The man was gone, or had never been.

Maybe she was alone.

Maybe she always had been.

But no, that wasn't right. Where were her sisters? She'd seen them, hadn't she?

Empty bunk beds. The summer cabin on fire. That was it—the cabin was on fire.

Heat like nothing she'd ever felt before surrounded her, suffocating. If she didn't get out, she wouldn't be able to breathe.

She burst out of the cabin, but her family was nowhere to be found. She ran down to the pebbled shore, throwing herself into the lake.

She could feel her burnt flesh sizzling as she sank into the cool lake. But then . . .

Then she was shivering again. As quickly as she'd been hot, she'd gone cold again, colder than ever before.

Looking down, she saw she was damp with sweat. Or lake water. No, neither—hail and sleet and snow. She was still— where? Trees everywhere. Red taillights. Red truck. Snow everywhere. She couldn't move—too cold to move now. The wetness on her skin—*bare*—where was her shirt? Where was her coat? The wetness had hardened, turned into ice, trapping her inside like shining, invisible armor. Sealing her in. She couldn't move. The cold was a clamp, a burn, a buzz, a drill, a dread, a fact, an overwhelming truth, a god.

You can't look a god in the face.

She closed her eyes.

She was no longer lost in the woods or the lake house or the back of the truck, but slipping backward through time.

She was a child, curled in her bed. Her mother was singing

a lullaby to Lilly; through a closed door she could hear the soft voice, and even though she was two and a half years older—five to Lilly's almost three—the melody comforted her, too. Kit had always been the good one, the good girl who didn't cry at night.

She pictured the lullaby traveling through baby Lilly, like some sort of ghost song, a silver thread, then weaving through toddler Tessa, twirling itself into her hair and her mind and her arms, before making its way at last to *her*, to Kit, where she lay in her bed—until the song had united all three of them, making them one.

Finally, sleep had come.

EPILOGUE

ONE YEAR LATER

HOW MANY WOMEN DID IT take to be believed? Tessa had thought there would be power in numbers, but if you were a teen girl, that wasn't necessarily the case. The combined testimonies of her, Lilly, and Mel added up to what law enforcers could disturbingly easily write off as hysteria, a twisted friendship pact of some kind. A "witch hunt."

Which made no sense—were they supposed to be the witches or the ones hunting?

Mel had been terrified to say anything in the first place. Not only had Mr. Green been threatening her to stay quiet, but she knew her own role in it looked bad. She'd had the gun with her that night because she was afraid, just of being out alone in the dark. Plain and simple. Because of Mr. Green, she'd felt afraid *all the time*, really.

It had all first begun when Mr. Green, subbing in for a student English tutor, had begun tutoring Mel once a week. It had at first been the sum of a couple of unwelcome touches, a smile that suggested more, that had left her bewildered and unnerved, but without any concrete wrongdoing to point to.

It had escalated quickly, though, making her feel more and more uncertain. He'd talked about their special connection, and why it had to remain a secret. In her longing for a boyfriend, and status, she'd kind of thought it was flattering, even though it scared her too. It was only when it went past a certain point—asking her to do things physically she didn't want to, not knowing how to say no, how to get away, going too far—that she knew for sure it wasn't okay, that she wasn't safe. That she wanted it to end. And he wouldn't let it. Told her what everyone would say about her, they'd call her dirty, or they'd think she was a liar. What would her own mother say?

He'd been right, she realized. When she tried to talk to her mom, Mrs. Knox had slapped her, told her to shut up and stop inventing daydreams. Her mom thought she was saving herself for marriage, or at least her midtwenties. What was even the point? The path of least resistance had been to latch on to someone else, someone who made her feel safe. Dusty.

It had worked. Mr. Green seemed to have moved on. She thought—she prayed, literally—that it was all over, that the whole thing had been a wild misunderstanding, even though she knew deep down that she might never feel completely whole or safe again. She'd lost her virginity over winter break—to Dusty, by choice. Still, she'd only done it to try to write over the past. She'd cried about it for weeks, in private. She'd imagined it would be so different. But still, she wanted only to move on.

Except at night, when the memory of it all would often surface, and she grew paranoid that someone could hurt her, could violate her again, at any moment. That her body was no longer her own. That no walls would ever make her safe. *That* was why she'd gotten used to going down into her dad's den and gazing at the guns, imagining what it would feel like to hold one—to point one at Drew Green.

She just never imagined that the opportunity would come. She had only been expecting to see Patrick out there at the edge of the cul-de-sac, where they'd agreed to meet so she could buy those anti-anxieties she could no longer sleep without. The gun was gratuitous, but it made her feel better, and she figured she'd be home in five minutes and simply put it back where she'd gotten it.

Of course, that wasn't at all how it ended up happening. Not when she cut back through the woods.

The week after that night—the night Kit died—Mr. Green's attentions had turned back toward her, but unlike before, there was an open fierceness now. He made it explicitly clear that she couldn't tell anyone about that night without implicating her-self. Made it clear, too, that he thought it was all *her* fault that Kit was dead. She'd believed him.

Needless to say, it hadn't been easy for Tessa and Lilly to convince her to come forward, even after she told them all of this. "What if no one believes me anyway?" she'd sobbed. "What will my parents do with me? What will *he* do to me?"

"He can't do anything—not anymore," Tessa had said confidently, though she hadn't been entirely sure, deep down. It wasn't like any of them had any experience with this. They couldn't say how it would go. Would there be an epic trial that would take over their lives for the remainder of high school? Would they be dismissed outright? Would *Mel* be arrested for her part in Kit's death?

The possibilities seemed overwhelming and endless, but one thing held Tessa to her determination—the truth.

The truth had to matter. For Kit's sake. Even if it was worse, in a way, that she'd died knowing it.

Because they knew now that Kit had really thought she'd been in love. And Tessa couldn't blame her for wanting that. Kit had had what everyone else wanted: the reputation of being the good girl, the adored, the perfect one. But all she'd wanted was to fall, to burst the bubble, to *live*.

And what damning evidence did they *really* have, anyway? A bunch of love poems—none of them actually addressed to Drew. Fancy underwear, a coincidental tattoo—so what? They could prove Mr. Green had bought the ring from a pawn shop, but that meant nothing when it came to the actual case. The gun would only have Kit's DNA on it—and Mel had cleaned it meticulously anyway. The threatening notes had been from

Mel, in her attempt to protect Tessa from Mr. Green. Mel was afraid, too, of what would happen if Tessa thought Mel had killed Kit on purpose. And then, Tessa's visions. Her chimerism, which she still claimed had helped her make the final connection of what had happened that night, before Mel admitted it to them. But they knew trying to convince authorities that Tessa had literally dreamed it through Kit's eyes would be going too far. They'd all be laughed at.

So what *did* they have?

Nothing.

Nothing but the truth.

And so they told it—as much of it as they could.

And then they waited.

It was enough . . . at least to call in more people for questioning, including Mr. Green and his fiancée. It was enough to rerun fingerprints on the truck, which was still in custody—where they found a match to Green at last, on the glove compartment. Where, incidentally, he must have grabbed Boyd's hunting hat due to the heaviness of the snow—explaining why he looked like Boyd when Lilly saw him out there in the dark.

It was enough that they realized the keys in the ignition *had* been a spare set, the original still in Boyd's bedroom, as he'd claimed all along.

There was nothing to prove that Boyd had been there that night. Boyd was off the hook. Lilly's original claim had been debunked.

357

But that meant she wasn't a credible witness.

The whole thing was a complicated mess.

They feared it would never be resolved.

Mr. Green resigned, as he'd told Tessa he would, and they heard rumors he was moving one town over. That felt too close. It felt like a complete erasure. It seemed like maybe nothing would ever be done to resolve what had happened. That justice wouldn't be served. Tessa started to feel lost as to what would count as justice anyway. Nothing would undo what he'd done to Mel. Nothing would bring Kit back. Nothing would fix the shattering.

And then.

And then.

And then.

The rumors had gotten out.

Three more girls came forward.

One from their school, and two more from the college where he'd TA'd before he got the job in Devil's Lake.

Evidence mounted slowly, like snow.

Another winter came and went.

Eventually Mr. Green was found guilty at trial—not of murder, but of pretty much every disgusting thing he *had* done.

That night, Boyd, Tessa, Lilly, Patrick, Mel, Dusty, Dar, and Toma had all been together—they'd become a kind of pack. Oh, and Greg Heiser, too—of spice-rack Halloween costume fame. For whatever reason, he was there as well. They were at the Malloys' house, watching a movie, when Tessa and Lilly heard their mom give a little shriek from the kitchen.

They ran in, and she was crying over the phone. Somehow, Tessa had *known*, before her mom explained anything. It had finally happened.

Which meant her job chasing the truth was finally over.

A part of her melted into sadness at the thought—it was really over, and all that was left of the anger was the long stretch of grief, of missing, that would last forever.

The three of them held each other in a tight group, and eventually, the rest had come into the room to see what was going on, and the hug had turned massive.

From the center of it, Tessa felt surrounded by *life*.

Even though there were tears, and even though it still hurt—sometimes so much that it was hard to breathe—she realized that somehow, without her looking, she had begun to live again, already. Life had a sneaky way of doing that to you, of marching you forward like a bossy older sister. She'd begun to accept that while death could be random, crude, and completely unfair, *life* was something else: something wild, uncertain, and full of possibility.

And she knew, as she was warmed by all those arms, all that love, all that belief in the truth—all that knowledge of the light that reaches you even from the depths of darkness and space— that she was ready now, at least for that much.

Ready to dive into this life of hers and find out what was next.